THE EVOLVED ONES
AWAKENING
BOOK ONE

NATASHA OLIVER

AF087603

Marshall Cavendish Editions

With the support of

NATIONAL ARTS COUNCIL
SINGAPORE

© 2019 Natasha Oliver

Published by Marshall Cavendish Editions
An imprint of Marshall Cavendish International

All rights reserved

No part of this publication may be reproduced, stored in a retrieval system or transmitted, in any form or by any means, electronic, mechanical, photocopying, recording or otherwise, without the prior permission of the copyright owner. Requests for permission should be addressed to the Publisher, Marshall Cavendish International (Asia) Private Limited, 1 New Industrial Road, Singapore 536196. Tel: (65) 6213 9300. E-mail: genref@sg.marshallcavendish.com Website: www.marshallcavendish.com/genref

The publisher makes no representation or warranties with respect to the contents of this book, and specifically disclaims any implied warranties or merchantability or fitness for any particular purpose, and shall in no event be liable for any loss of profit or any other commercial damage, including but not limited to special, incidental, consequential, or other damages.

Other Marshall Cavendish Offices:
Marshall Cavendish Corporation, 99 White Plains Road, Tarrytown NY 10591-9001, USA • Marshall Cavendish International (Thailand) Co Ltd, 253 Asoke, 12th Flr, Sukhumvit 21 Road, Klongtoey Nua, Wattana, Bangkok 10110, Thailand • Marshall Cavendish (Malaysia) Sdn Bhd, Times Subang, Lot 46, Subang Hi-Tech Industrial Park, Batu Tiga, 40000 Shah Alam, Selangor Darul Ehsan, Malaysia.

Marshall Cavendish is a registered trademark of Times Publishing Limited

National Library Board, Singapore Cataloguing in Publication Data

Name: Oliver, Natasha, 1974-
Title: The evolved ones. Book one : awakening / Natasha Oliver.
Description: Singapore : Marshall Cavendish, [2019]
Identifier(s): OCN 1102660946 | ISBN 978-981-48-4144-3 (paperback)
Subject(s): LCSH: Fantasy fiction. | American fiction.
Classification: DDC 813--dc23

Printed in Singapore

Cover design by Kelley Lim

To Leya,
without whom I would have gotten a lot more sleep,
but would have missed out on the bursts of
twilight creativity that gave birth to Rox.

To Asha,
for showing me the strength in love,
the joys of motherhood, and for always
adding "more" to the end of your "I love you's".

And to Andrew,
who is 10% inspiration and 90% perspiration.
愛してる, *now and always.*

CHAPTER ONE

Hope

Her hands were at ten and two on the steering wheel as her right knee bounced to the rhythm of her thoughts. She checked the fuel gauge, but without the engine on, the dashboard was dark. Instinct told her there was enough gas to make it back to the last rest stop she passed. But then again, maybe not. And even if she made it back, then what? That was the nagging question she hadn't been able to shake. What next?

Her jaw felt like she had been using it as a nutcracker with the amount of tension she carried. She traced her finger down the shallow crevice that had formed a wrinkle in the center of her brow. The fine lines around the edges of her eyes said she should smile more, but over the years there hadn't been a lot to smile at. Fear and the need for answers kept her moving. She was surprised she hadn't developed a permanent crook in her neck given how often she looked over her shoulder. But for once, it wasn't what was behind that frightened her, it was what lay ahead.

Indecision was the mother of time wasters, and Rox had been in the car for over an hour deciding whether to get out or to drive back the way she had come. Ok, maybe just five minutes. But the problem with a retreat was that she would be traversing ground she'd already covered. A life on the run was a hard way to live. In the past eighteen months, she had stolen, lied, and deceived more people than she had in the four and a half years that her short memory was capable of stretching back. Was that really the kind of life she wanted to return to?

If Rox turned back now, her future would hold more derelict boarding houses and shelters with women who had survived the kinds of horror no human – evolved or otherwise – should have to endure. Sometimes, the grass on the other side wasn't greener.

Sometimes it was.

She pulled the photo from her backpack and slipped it into the pocket of her cargo pants. She didn't need the car's internal light to see; everything in her pack could be identified by touch: one change of clothes, an empty water bottle, a stolen hairbrush for her tight curls, and a flashlight. She had eaten all the snacks, and the little bit of money remaining from her last under-the-table job was tucked away in the bottom of her sock. Finding good hiding spaces was the third rule of living on the run.

The internal light switched on when she opened the door and she used it to tie her curls into a ponytail, making sure to tuck the ends up into a bun. She dropped the keys in the cupholder by the gear box because if things worked out in her favor, someone would return the car to its original owner. However, if things didn't, there was no chance of losing them in what lay ahead.

Rox got out and let her eyes readjust to the darkness when the door closed. She was at the road's end. Literally. The bite in the air promised snow. She inhaled deeply, hoping that somehow a deep breath would calm her nerves and stop the doubt about this plan from resurfacing. She wasn't sure what awaited her, but there was little point in thinking about that now. This felt like her last chance, and she was going to take it.

She walked carefully. It would be easy to step in the wrong place and twist an ankle. She could heal it, but why waste the energy? She used the flashlight and kept her head down. About a mile in, and a half-dozen *no trespassing* signs later, she stopped to catch her breath.

The couple back at the gas station said it was unseasonably cold, but this was Rox's first time in Connecticut. Or so she assumed. Without a lifetime of memories, it's hard to know much about yourself. And that's what had brought her to the end of a very dark road that opened upon a heavily wooded area. A very dense and obviously "privately owned" wooded area. She was in search of help, and the only people she had left to turn to were somewhere ahead of her.

It wasn't that long ago the world woke up to Darwinism in practice. There had been no rioting or violence, but people were curious. Why were some evolving and not others? Would the rest of humankind follow suit or was this a singular event? And why were most evolved human abilities passive? Like the ability to see music or taste color. There were a few whose brains could process information at the rate of a computer's central processor, but mostly everyone considered them highly intelligent and not necessarily evolved, even though they were. Rox did hear of someone who could regulate her body to withstand sub-zero temperatures while completely naked, but scientists hadn't been able to uncover how she was able to do that.

Interest in the evolved quickly waned as no one came forward with any spectacular abilities. That was good for a while, but it didn't stay that way. Rumors were that the evolved were starting to disappear; they had become the easy target of doctors and scientists looking to create a name for themselves.

Halo was an organization that helped evolved ones who were in trouble. Or that's what the "majority" of people said. Ever since Rox had decided to seek their help, her thoughts ran fantastical, dreaming that they would help her recover her memories. Perhaps even help find the family she may (or may not) have. The only key to Rox's "possible" identity was a worn photo of two kids, one of which could be her or just as easily be the model in a stock photo.

That's the problem with hope: when it was all you had, it became nigh on impossible to let it go.

Rox curled her toes into her feet to warm them. If she had the money, she would have purchased boots, but the shelter had given her a pair of used running shoes, and she didn't want to waste money on buying something she didn't technically need.

Dried wood crunched as she passed another *no trespassing* sign. A cloud reduced visibility as the first flakes of snow fell. The good news was that she doubted she could die of hypothermia. With her abilities, at best, she'd go into some kind of stasis and awake during the first thaw. Of course, during her hibernation, a wolf could find her and decide to eat her.

Could she regenerate lost tissue?

The weak energy source of small rodents darting through the underbrush was the first signs of life she sensed since turning off the interstate and following the car's navigation system to the end of the road. Natural energy was attracted to Rox, it flowed in and through her of its own accord. But artificial energy vibrated along the base of her skull like a chisel and hammer.

The wind picked up, and she flipped up the hood on her jacket. The material was thin and provided little warmth when she was outside for any length of time, but it was another "gift" from the shelter. First rule of living life on the run was that eventually everyone needed a coat; second rule was the need to protect said coat like you would the password to your bank account – second lesson she learned the hard way.

She should have been a hell of a lot more frightened than she was, but Josh had trained her. He had been there when she first woke four years ago and had nothing more than muscle memory and habit to guide her. Speech came easy even if she struggled to make sense of it half the time. But Josh was patient. He was the anchor she needed, and he trained her for the eventual fight he believed would happen between evolved humans and the non-evolved. But somewhere along the way, his help turned into manipulation, and her only choice was to run.

A breeze tore a blanket of leaves from their resting place and sent them across her path. Would it be so bad to go back? She could sleep in a warm bed, one without bugs. She could eat food for the taste instead of the hunger. The clothes she wore would fit and not carry the stench of someone else's sweat woven into the fabric. And she would belong. Tears welled at that thought. She missed belonging.

But it hadn't been real. Not authentically so. Josh had manipulated her mind to create the life *he* wanted. And she wasn't sure which was worse, living on the run or living a life where her every word was twisted to please another.

Yes, she did.

And that's why she was walking in the middle of the woods at 3:23am seeking help. Because sometime during the last year and a half, she had realized that going back to Josh or continuing a life on the run weren't her only two options. Someone somewhere had to know she existed. She was old enough to have set down roots – or at least leave footprints. She would have had a job. A family perhaps. And she had a photograph. Be it real or nothing more than the hope she refused to let go of, her only real option was moving forward.

Red carpet

Rox thought about talking to herself to combat the silence, but she was a quiet contemplator. She wasn't sure if she had always been like that or if spending a year and a half trying to go unnoticed had become a habit.

Fourth rule: never make a sound unless you have to – also learned the hard way.

A howl echoed through the trees ahead, and her flashlight swung in a wide arc to pinpoint the sound's origin. Everything froze but the snow. The animals she sensed earlier stilled in a way that marked them as prey. She was tempted to yell "hello" but thought better of it. She had no knowledge of wolves or wild dogs, and so she hoped if she continued along, they would leave her alone.

Her head looked like it belonged on a bobble given how often she looked up and down. Something caught just below the hem of her cargo pants, and Rox kicked out, thinking it was a fallen branch. But then that something slid across her ankle much too fast to be a rodent, followed almost immediately by a click.

Air flew from her lungs, and the contents of her backpack bit through the thin coat and into her back when she landed on the ground. She blinked against droplets of cold dripping onto her face, and it took her a moment to realize it was nothing more than snow. A high-pitched whine reverberated deep in her ear canal as she lay there trying to make sense of what just happened.

Rox's body pulled the kinetic energy from the blast to aid in her healing. What felt like the first sparks of fire slipped across her forehead over the cut just above her eye.

Most people underestimate the pain involved in healing.

A sane dose of fear finally gripped Rox by the time she

regained control of her lower extremities. She got to her feet and almost fell face-first into a rotting tree trunk. The bark tore through the skin of her palms as she righted herself. She had just pulled the straps of her backpack tighter when something slammed into her shoulder with such force she spun around.

The rotting trunk scraped a trio of parallel lines down the side of her face. Her forehead smacked against a root sticking up that reopened the cut on her forehead. Warm blood slid down her face as she rolled over onto her backpack. Again.

Whoever had put up the *no trespassing* signs were serious about their privacy.

Rox felt her attackers' energy drawing closer, and it was stronger and more aggressive than the rodents clambering through the leaves. She quickly sat up, but the sudden movement threw off her equilibrium, and she rolled to the side to heave into the hollow tree trunk. As much as she wanted to lie down and take a nap, the pain racing down her shoulder sobered her, and she had enough sense to keep moving.

The keys to the car were in the cupholder.

She wasn't sure if they had intentionally shot her in the shoulder or if they had been aiming for something more vital, but she didn't want to stick around to find out. She'd died a few times in the last four years, but none of them had been by gunshot to the head.

Rox kept low and started an awkward sprint back towards the car without the aid of the flashlight. She stumbled over what felt like every root and broken bough in her path as her attackers' energy rolled towards her like a wave coming to shore. The tip of a branch scratched so close to her eye she wasn't sure if it actually made contact. For a moment, she thought she heard something through the ringing in her ears and when she glanced over her shoulder, the clouds broke and a black shadow moved at a speed much too fast to be human.

"Shit!" Bad, fucking plan, Rox.

She wasn't about to die from hypothermia, but she was about to be eaten by a wolf. Its eyes glowed in the dark as it bounded past the rotting trunk she had fallen into. She picked up the pace, not caring anymore about a twisted ankle or a broken toe. The ringing in her ears and her breathing drowned out all other sounds as the wolf's energy closed in. She stumbled again and this time fell on her hands. Splinters split open the skin that had just closed on her palms, but her hand's discomfort was drowned out by the pain that gripped her shoulder. She sucked in a sharp breath, but was up and sprinting before she could fully assess the damage.

Energy from others ran alongside her, and she realized she wasn't going to make it back to the car. Her only choice was to stop and explain herself. But they didn't seem like the type to ask questions first given they had already shot her.

She was out of options, but she wasn't defenseless. Josh may have been an ass – a manipulating, deceitful, downright unforgivable ass – but he trained her, and she knew how to hold her own. She had no delusions that she could take a group this size, their energy signatures were just too many. Hell, she might not be able to take even one of them, but she was done being the victim. She'd done that for too long already. She was draining the first one who came at her.

Third option

Rox stopped, pivoted, and dropped into a defensive stance. Without thought, she shifted her weight to the balls of her feet. Snow and pain threatened to blind her as the wind picked up, but she was able to keep the wolf in sight.

The wolf slowed and started to pace about fifty yards away. It lowered its head as its lips stretched back over curved teeth. Healing from one of its bites would be painful. A growl slipped through the silence like a personal message as the others circled around her, but Rox didn't take her eyes off the wolf.

The artificial hum of a helicopter hit her moments before its blades created an updraft of wind that tossed the underbrush into the night. Its energy was almost suffocating and a dull ache gripped the base of her skull, causing the crease in her forehead to deepen. She shielded her face with her arm against the flying debris as another bullet slammed into her stomach. Pain radiated up her chest and back down to the point of impact. Rox fell forward on her palms, but her shoulder gave out and she inhaled a mouthful of wet dirt.

Frustration replaced her fear.

Someone approached. Her body felt their energy, and she was a breath away from draining them when she hesitated. There was something about it that she had never experienced before. It felt ... magnetic.

Rox spat out a mouthful of dirt and got to her feet just as the unfamiliar energy swept through her in a pulse that stole her breath. What the hell? She squinted through the darkness to get a better look at whoever had approached when a light shot down from the helicopter to cast a cone of visibility around her and her attackers.

She turned in a circle. There were six of them. Two to her right, two to her left, the man in front and the wolf just a few paces behind him. She looked down at herself and saw a thin piece of metal sticking out of her jacket, right where her bullet wound should have been.

Rox yanked it out, and a piece of polyester from her coat stuck to it. Was that a tranquilizer dart? She would have laughed if a helicopter wasn't hovering overhead and she wasn't surrounded by some kind of hostile, military types armed with tranquilizer darts.

Another pulse of energy swept through her and her knees buckled. What was that? It wasn't the tranquilizer. This felt like pure energy, and whoever had the ability to send it through her like that was powerful. That was an *active* ability.

Rox pulled out the other dart and dropped them both to the ground. The man who had approached took another step forward, but remained well outside of striking distance. He was dressed in black combat trousers and a black vest over jet-black arms that had to be his shirt because no skin tone was that dark.

Rox got to her feet, and the wolf curled back its lip as it moved to stand alongside him. The man reached down and wound his fingers in its fur, and the wolf relaxed.

He took a few steps closer and when he spoke, the sound came from a speaker on the helicopter. "This is private property."

No shit!

"Is this Halo?" Rox yelled.

Another energy pulse hit her, but this time her body absorbed it as if adapting to its frequency.

A second beam of light erupted from the helicopter as four shadows descended. Red dots tattooed her chest. The shadows were similarly dressed to the man who stood beside the wolf, but their faces were painted.

"I just want to talk," she shouted to the small group now forming a complete circle around her.

Wolf-man tapped one of the painted men on the shoulder to lower his weapon as he stepped past. He kept his hand on the gun at his waist, but remained outside of arm's reach. The wolf pushed its way through the men, its teeth once again exposed.

"Most people call first. Send a text or something."

To call this a bad idea was a colossal understatement. Rox had expected a few "guards" like the ones at the shopping mall where she had sought shelter on the days it rained. Maybe they'd put her in some small office while they figured out how best to help. She had even anticipated being turned away until morning, which would have been fair. But a small response team armed with explosives and tranquilizers, aided by a helicopter, had not factored into her list of cons for showing up unannounced.

Wolf-man reached down to calm his animal when

another pulse collided with her, and she flinched. But so did Wolf-man. She looked up at the helicopter, and the lights temporarily distracted her as someone moved at her back. She felt the presence a few seconds too late. A strong arm encircled her neck and pulled it up and to the side. Pain exploded against her jugular as a needle tore into her skin.

Rox swung her elbow back into her attacker's nose, and if she had stopped to think about it, she wouldn't have stepped back into him and flipped him over her shoulder.

Shit.

Rox pulled the needle from her neck and locked eyes with Wolf-man. His mouth hung, but then quickly closed as he drew his weapon. "Take her down."

Pain spilled across her back. Darts chipped the bones in her wrist as she raised them to protect her face. The last thing she remembered was the full weight of the wolf knocking her down and the needles snapping off underneath her skin as she crashed to the ground.

CHAPTER TWO

Rise and shine

Rox?

Hmm?

Where are you?

It was the second time he had asked her that. Obviously, she was right there, with him. But when she opened her eyes, a chill raced down her spine.

Stay with me, babe. Where are you?

Rox tried to sit up, but restraints held her down.

Babe, look around. Show me what you see.

Memories burst into her consciousness. She'd come in search of Halo, and instead trespassed onto some secret military base or something.

Halo? You mean you're at the Halo?

Josh was inside her head, and she needed to get him out. There was a time when she would have lowered her defenses to let him in, but finding out that the love she had for him was nothing more than thoughts he had created inside her mind meant he was just as dangerous as the people holding her captive.

Rox slammed her eyes shut as she struggled to gain

control of her mind. *A is for apple. B is for banana. My favorite color is blue,* she thought.

Stop that!

Sally sells seashells on the ... Random thoughts confused Josh and made it harder for him to influence a person's mind.

Babe, you're hurt and you're scaring me.

Scare. How many words can I think of that begin with "s"? Sunshine. Sa ... saturate. Silly. Sharp. Shore. Seashells! Why didn't I think of that first? Seashells. Sally! Seashells.

Rox, open your eyes, dammit!

She moved on to the letter "x". Five words. She couldn't stick with letters for long because that was forming a pattern, and patterns were just as easy to latch on to. She started thinking of animals. And weird places to find them. Fish in a tornado. Turtles creeping along in a snow storm. *Can turtles live in cold weather?*

An energy shifted behind her, and physical awareness flooded her consciousness. The temptation to open her eyes broke her train of thought, and she felt Josh gain mental ground.

A door slid open, and cold air swept in the room at her feet. Rox lifted her head to see who had entered, but the bright light overhead formed white spots in front of her. She blinked until a woman's figure came into focus.

The woman was thin with brown hair that was half contained in a bun somewhere at the back of her head. She was dressed in pajama bottoms and fur-lined house slippers that resembled moccasins.

"She's up," the person pacing behind Rox said. His voice was heavy, just like his energy.

The woman stared at Rox as if she were having trouble trusting her vision. "This is extraordinary."

Rox flinched when the woman pressed her cold hand against her neck to feel for a pulse.

"I'm Dr Bethany Grace." She smiled. "It's okay. I'm just going to check you over. We weren't expecting you up this soon."

"Why am I tied down?" Rox pulled against the restraints without looking at them.

The man behind her snorted, and Rox felt the derision in his tone.

"I've asked myself the same question," Dr Grace said, but looked at her partner.

The man behind her moved into Rox's field of vision, and Rox swallowed at the sight of him. He stood beside the doctor with his legs apart and arms crossed over muscles that were too big to be anything but weapons. He wore black combat pants and a shirt that fit so tight it could've been painted on. There was no way she could take him. She'd have to drain his energy first.

Rox turned her attention back to the doctor. She looked like an easy takedown. She was too thin to put any weight behind an attack and her pink, floral-printed pajamas couldn't be more of a contrast to the man beside her.

"That right there is why you ain't getting outta that chair." The man pointed his finger at Rox. It was as if he read her thoughts, and if she could have moved, she would have taken a step away from him.

Dr Grace pulled something from her lab coat's pocket and held it against Rox's head. It gave a soft beep, and a frown formed on the doctor's forehead a few moments before it reached her mouth. She reached over and took Rox's temperature again, but the crease in her brow remained. She turned the thermometer upside down and opened its back to check the batteries. Rox waited for the beep a third time.

"Let me see?" the man said.

The doctor showed him.

"What's your ability?" he asked Rox.

The length of Rox's memories spanned no farther than that of a child's, but it was Josh's training and her instincts that had kept her alive thus far. She couldn't explain how she knew certain things or why she felt one way or the other most of the time, but she'd learned to listen to herself. Josh had wanted her because she was a healer. And she had no reason to think that wasn't why he still chased her. So, if a man she loved and who had supposedly loved her in return would twist her thoughts so that she would never leave his side, what would complete strangers do if they knew of her ability?

"Curtis, you know we don't ask that."

Curtis' eyes bore into Rox, and she knew if it were just the two of them, the same conversation would be had quite differently.

The doctor looked back at Rox. "I'm told you put up quite the fight up there?"

So they were "down" somewhere. Basement, perhaps. "I just wanted to talk."

"Got a helluva way of communicating."

Rox had run into men like Curtis many times in the last eighteen months. They didn't hesitate to use their size to intimidate. A part of her wanted not to be afraid of him, but she was tied down, and she doubted the doctor would be any help to her if Curtis wanted things to become more physical.

"Signs all over the place that say 'no trespassing'," Curtis continued. "And even if you can't read, a fuckwit knows a skull and crossbones means 'stay the fuck out'."

"That's enough, Curtis. Ever thought that she might just need our help?"

"Not when she put four of our guys down."

"I didn't attack anyone," Rox said, finding her voice.

Curtis stepped around Bethany and leaned down close enough that Rox could smell his breath. That's when she noticed the mud on his shirt and the dried blood in his nostrils. "I was there and if we hadn't pumped you full of tranqs, God only knows what you would've done. So I ask again, what's your ability?"

He must have been the one who attacked her from behind before all hell broke loose and everything went black. Her mind tried to piece together the events, but the only time she used her ability to take energy from someone was when she was seriously injured. When that happened, her body would take what it needed from the closest source to heal. And she must have been hurt pretty badly to take down four of them without knowing it.

Rox closed her eyes and sent her energy circulating up and down her body.

Strong fingers squeezed her jaw, and her eyes flew open. "I asked you a question."

"Curtis!" Dr Grace tried to pull him away, but Rox could tell from the strength in his hand the doctor didn't have a hope.

And that's when she felt it. Her left shoulder. She couldn't see it because her face was paralyzed in Curtis' grip, but a dull ache radiated up from her shoulder to the base of her neck.

The wolf.

It must have attacked her. The familiar pain of healing started its march across her wounds, announcing each one with a clarity that stole Rox's attention.

Panic made her suck in oxygen much faster than she could process. What the hell had she been thinking?

Rox's breathing grew shallow. If Curtis had his way, she was going to die. And she had died a few times, and each time was unpleasant. A gunshot was like having lava poured into a single part of her body with its heat pulsating out in perpetual waves around the wound. Being stabbed to death was a pain so acute and precise that her brain struggled to register it. Poison was painful in a way her body couldn't isolate and she couldn't quite remember.

Rox fought to sit up, but Curtis pressed her left shoulder back against the chair. Sweet agony exploded down the side of her body, and she had no choice but to obey. He continued to put pressure on her shoulder, and where panic had gathered in Rox, anger now took its place.

Her right knee curled up and slammed into Curtis' side. He cried out and released his grip on her shoulder.

"What are you doing?" Dr Grace asked Curtis, her voice filled with worry. "She's had enough, Curtis! Stop."

Rox looked up behind her as Curtis came back into view. He was batting away Dr Grace's hands as he advanced on her. She thought he was carrying a scalpel, but then a needle pierced her skin mere millimeters from her windpipe, and the cool liquid slipped into her blood stream.

It wasn't nearly enough to incapacitate her.

He leaned into her face as if he was about to say something, and that's when Rox did the only thing she could do. She reached out as far as the restraints allowed and grabbed the front of his trousers. It wasn't a good grip, but she didn't need a lifetime of memories to know a man's weak spot. He jumped and attempted to break her hold, but she didn't let go.

When their eyes locked, Rox yanked, not with her hand, but with her ability. His energy slid off him like water gliding over an oiled surface. It crashed into her as he went flaccid, falling face-first across her.

Rox squirmed in her seat like an animal in the desperate throes of escape. Adrenaline overdosed her as she yanked against the restraints. That was the drawback of taking someone's energy. It needed to be used and if she couldn't find a way to expend Curtis' energy soon, it would pass on, and the only other person it could go to was Dr Grace. And Rox didn't think pumping her with his energy was going to help her cause.

"I just wanted to talk, I promise." Rox bucked, and Curtis slid down off her abdomen, making it a little easier to breathe.

"What did you do to him?"

Rox wasn't prepared to answer that.

"Is he ... is he ... "

"I swear I didn't hurt him." And she didn't. He would wake with a headache and low blood sugar, but he would be fine. "Please, help me."

"You should be unconscious." Dr Grace looked at her in confusion. "You're definitely evolved. But—"

"I just want to go home." Real tears stung Rox's eyes as her right knee started to bounce. She held the doctor's stare as if she could somehow express her sincerity in a single gaze. And the fear she saw in the doctor just moments ago melted into ... curiosity?

"There's no way your kidneys can process that amount of sedatives so quickly. No living mammal could." The doctor's right hand curled into a small fist and her forefinger began to pick at the cuticle of her thumb. "Do you have to go to the lady's room?"

That caught Rox off guard. "Like you wouldn't believe," Rox said with a small laugh.

Dr Grace smiled. A genuine one that said despite the fact that Rox had somehow knocked Curtis unconscious, she may have gained an ally.

"I need your word that you won't hurt me – or anyone else," Bethany quickly added.

"I promise you I just came here to talk. But they attacked first."

She tsked as she unbuckled one of the restraints. "The signs clearly say 'no trespassing'. And I can tell you can read by how you speak."

"Bethany!" A voice cut through a speaker in the wall at the back of the room.

Rox ignored the interruption and used her free hand to unbuckle her other one.

"What's your ability?" Dr Grace said as she gripped the waistband of Curtis' trousers to slowly lower him to the ground and feel for a pulse. "I mean, under normal circumstances I wouldn't ask, but let's face it, we've surpassed normal."

The voice cracked through the speaker again and instructed Dr Grace not to allow Rox to leave the room, but they both ignored it.

"When they first brought you in, you had deep lacerations across your stomach and chest. I pulled no less than fifteen tranq darts from your body. Your shoulder was ripped to shreds ... " She reached into the pocket of her lab coat and stepped closer with a curiosity that frightened Rox. She clicked a button and the tip of her pen lit. "Hot to the touch, dilated pupils ... "

Rox did need to go to the bathroom. And do about a hundred sit-ups. Curtis' energy was pushing at her barriers and she wasn't going to be able to contain it much longer. She got up off the chair with a little too much excitement and stumbled over Curtis' body.

Would Bethany still consider her non-threatening if she just did fifty jumping jacks really quick? "Bathroom?" Rox did need to go.

You don't have a lot of time. You can go to the bathroom later. Get her to open that door. They'll be sending others.

Renewed terror swept through Rox. How could she

have forgotten about Josh? Had he been there the entire time listening to her thoughts?

Dr Grace stepped back. "You promised you wouldn't hurt me. Or anyone else."

The fear in her eyes reflected in Rox's. It wasn't that simple anymore. *Please. Just let me go, Josh.*

"Are you in pain?" Bethany asked.

You can explain everything to me later. But babe, please let me help. I'm sorry. So –

Rox squeezed her eyes shut against Josh's voice inside her head and did a quick sprint in place. There was no question that it looked like she had lost her mind, but she needed to expend some of Curtis' energy. People amped up on adrenaline usually made poor decisions – another lesson learned the hard way.

The speakers barked alive again with instructions, but Rox couldn't make out what was said because her mind was divided between blocking out Josh and attempting to regain control of herself.

Cool fingers pressed against Rox's forehead and her eyes flew open.

"You're dangerously hot," said Dr Grace. "And why are you exercising?"

Had she just been doing squats?

The first tear fell. "I can't get him out." Rox's voice was just a whisper, and the look on the doctor's face softened and hardened at the same time.

"I need ice," Bethany screeched at the camera mounted to the ceiling in the corner of the room. "Sam! Ice!" Then she turned back to Rox. "Who? You can't get who out? Is someone trapped?"

Josh pushed through her barrier and slammed inside her head. His thoughts invaded her personal space and sent her consciousness to the corners of her mind.

Rox! His voice echoed throughout her thoughts, and she stilled. More tears slipped down her cheeks because she knew that he was close to having the upper hand.

She wanted to tell Dr Grace to run, but Josh stopped her.

"Where am I?" Rox said, but it was Josh who was in control now.

"Halo," Dr Grace said. "You're here for help, aren't you?"

"Open the door."

Bethany hesitated. "Are you okay?"

Rox knew right then and there she liked the doctor. Bethany knew something was wrong, and Rox wanted to smile at her, but before her lips could pull up, Josh slammed them down.

Rox couldn't move her head, but her eyes slid close and she pushed with every ounce of willpower. She turned to face Josh in her mind, and she saw the absolute fear that he had lived with ever since she had gone missing, and the beacon of hope he held on to now that he'd found her.

"Run!"

Rox's eyes were still closed, but she felt Bethany's energy move away from her. Josh's grip slipped, and Rox renewed her efforts to push him out. She hummed a horrible tune as loudly as she could. It was something she was making up on the fly. Then she screamed.

A single focused point of pain slid into Rox's arm. Her eyes opened, and she watched as Bethany stuck her with a second needle. She was pumping Rox full of sedatives. Three syringes. That wouldn't be nearly enough.

Rox grabbed Bethany's arm because Josh made her.

The door slid open, and the same energy pulse from the woods swept through Rox.

"Beth, I told you to get out of here!"

It was Wolf-Man. More energy poured into the room. He hadn't come alone.

"Sam, we've never encountered an EO like this," Bethany said. Her arm was still in Rox's grip and it was obviously hurting her by the way she flinched, but still she smiled when she looked at Rox. "It's okay. He's going to help you. It's what we do. What's your name?"

"You will not give them your name."

Rox hadn't wanted to say that aloud, but she wasn't sure who had control anymore. Nothing this violent, this evasive had ever occurred between her and Josh, but then again, there had never been a need for it. When they were together, he just had to touch her, plant a simple suggestion, and she ate it up like it was the truth.

I love you. And I know what I did –

Rox hadn't realized she was on the ground until Bethany knelt beside her. Another pulse of energy swept through her, and for a moment she wasn't able to inhale. She teetered on the edges of unconsciousness, and only Josh kept her lucid.

Another pinch at the side of her neck, and Rox looked up at Wolf-Man. The syringe dropped to the floor and soon another pinch, and another.

Time seemed to stop and then continue again at a slower pace. Strong arms circled her waist and pulled her back so she was leaning on something. Someone. Wolf-Man. His touch stopped the energy pulses and erased all presence of Josh. It was like a switch had been flipped and the only thoughts left in her head were hers.

"No, wait!" Bethany's voice lifted Rox's eyelids.

"We don't have any other choice, Beth," said Wolf-Man.

From the corner of her eyes, Rox caught the handle of a weapon. Probably a gun. He was going to kill her. She chuckled and it caused her body to convulse, but his arms only tightened.

The muzzle pressed against her shoulder. A head shot would be cleaner, and his aim was too high for her heart. He needed to lower it by a good inch or two.

"Brace yourself." It was barely a whisper, and she wasn't even sure she heard him correctly. But then she convulsed once, twice, three times before everything went black.

CHAPTER THREE

Wolf-Man

Sam poured himself a glass of whisky and swirled it simply because that's what his father did. He leaned against the edge of the desk and swallowed it in one mouthful. It went down hard, burning his throat, and the fumes singed the hairs in his nose. He coughed, and Shaira lifted her head from the carpet to snort as if she found him amusing.

Sam grabbed the end of the towel from around his shoulder and ran it over his face. What the hell had just happened down there? The energy that woman put out was seismic, and it pulled at him like an industrial strength magnet. He meant to ask if any of the others had felt it, but everything happened so fast. Back in the woods, she flipped Curtis over like he wasn't six-foot-five and weighed an easy two-twenty. And how many tranquilizers had they given her?

He'd never met another human – evolved or otherwise – whose heart could keep beating after such a high dose of sedatives. They had to hastily attach restraints to her chair because no one who posed a threat had ever set foot into Halo. This was their classified location – supposedly secure

– and she had hiked up to their perimeter like she had been given a map. For her to come alone, in the middle of the night, signaled she meant business. She would have to have an active ability because no way someone would take a midnight stroll through the woods – past countless *no trespassing* signs – with a passive ability like eidetic memory or a hyperactive olfactory sense.

She could also just need their help. This *was* Halo, and his parents had started this organization to help evolved ones.

But why show up in the middle of the night?

Perhaps someone was chasing her.

But she hadn't said anything about being followed.

Well, shooting someone with a tranq dart wasn't the best way to strike up a conversation.

Sam lifted the glass to his lips before he remembered it was empty. An intruder was the last thing they needed. For the past eight months, they had directed all of Halo's resources toward searching for his sister, and he couldn't deny that a small part of him had grown hopeful when the announcement came that there was a woman trespassing. Maybe his sister had found her way back home. Maybe she was confused and that was why she was walking through the woods. Maybe she was purposefully setting off the alarms because she was being followed and needed help.

He was disappointed when he discovered it wasn't Val. His sister was still missing, and the only hope they had of finding her was a scrap of information his father had blackmailed out of a former military acquaintance who had a lot to lose should some of his past discretions become known.

Sam scratched his jaw where the beginnings of a beard irritated his skin. Flakes of dried mud drifted to the floor while the woman's blood stained the back of his hands like dried henna. He had planning to do, but instead he was trying to figure out if he just killed a woman who might have only been seeking help – help like Val probably needed.

The door slid open.

"She dead?" Walter asked as he entered. He smelled of cold and sweat. It was still snowing outside, but he was dressed in black running tights and a gray long-sleeved exercise shirt. His skull cap was slid to the side, exposing the top of his right ear in a style that made him look much younger.

"Too soon to tell. Find anything?" Sam asked.

"Car. About three clicks from our perimeter."

"That's a hell of a hike in the middle of the night."

"And the snow," Walter added. "Probably stolen."

The woman had brass. Or she was desperate. "Find anything else?"

Walter drank until his water bottle was empty, then put it on the desk beside Sam's glass. "A doe. Not sure who scared who more. Any idea what her story could be?"

Sam had no clue what her story was, but he intended to find out. She was definitely evolved. It was like every minute, a pure wave of her energy gripped his insides, rode up his spine and tightened in his chest. He had to fight the urge to go to her, but then when he touched her, it was like everything settled and a calmness washed over him.

"How you doing?" Walter asked.

"Tired."

"You know what I mean."

And he knew what his father meant. Sam was restless, and ever since his forced retirement, he had been trying to find different ways to adjust to his "new" lifestyle.

Sam held out his hand in front of Walter for a long two seconds to show that he was okay.

Walter nodded back to the empty glass on the desk. "How many?"

"Just three."

"Doubles?"

Sam gave him a look that said he wasn't in the mood to be fussed over. He'd agreed to slow down his drinking, and he had. "I'm fine."

"Needed something to take the edge off?"

"I said I'm fine."

Walter nodded, and for a moment, Sam thought that was the end of it. "Just the way you came thundering down those stairs when the call came in that we had an intruder shook the entire house. I was already dressed and even you beat me."

"You're like twice my age," Sam said.

"Can still beat the shit out of you."

And he probably could. Walter was in his early sixties, but he was obsessed with fitness and adhered to a strict diet so bland it had to reverse aging. Walter was two inches shorter than Sam's six-three and had about a quarter less body mass. Both had piercing blue eyes and a smile that was crooked on the same side. Sam's ginger locks were fading to a pale blonde while Walter sported a bald look because he refused to admit that his hair was thinning.

But the two still looked more like brothers than father and son.

"So I'm told you let Curtis in there."

Sam sighed. Curtis had … issues. There was no point denying it. He wasn't polite. He rarely cared about anyone's feelings, but that's what made him effective.

"I checked with the men and none of them said you gave Curtis the green light to tranq her," Walter said.

"She shows up on our doorstep, takes down four of our men, and what? You want us to offer her a back rub or something?"

Walter shrugged like it could have been a good idea. "Just saying. Bethany thinks she's a healer."

That would explain why she was up so soon after being attacked by a ninety-pound wolf.

"Think she can heal other people?" Walter continued.

That would be a truly spectacular ability. Healing oneself was miraculous, but to heal others? Sam pushed off the edge of the desk. If she could heal others, did that mean she could also *unheal* them? That must be how she incapacitated Curtis, twice.

"Did Bethany say anything else?" Sam asked.

"Just that she was certain she needs our help and that we had to play nice with her."

Shaira's head popped up when Sam started to pace.

"You must be thinking what I'm thinking," Walter said.

She was a woman in need. To take advantage of her would be against every moral principle that he and his father believed in and which, not to mention, also contradicted the very nature of Halo.

But Val was missing. He and his father had used all their favors to get as much information as they could about her possible whereabouts. In the end it wasn't a lot, but it did point to a very dangerous place. A healer would be a huge advantage if things went sideways trying to get Val out. Especially if that healer could heal others. And *unheal* them.

"We'll offer her help," Walter said. "We're just going to ask her for a little something in return first."

Sam wasn't sure they could describe what they were thinking about as "little". It wasn't that he disagreed with the idea. Before Sam was forced into retirement, he followed in his father's footsteps and worked for a small cyber team that was tasked with gathering information to aid in the economic advancement of North American business interests. Technically, they weren't part of the US military or the intelligence community. They existed as a budget line item under "tech support", which granted them anonymity, and senior officials deniability.

Between Sam and his father, they had blackmailed, coerced, outright threatened and ruined more than their fair share of lives in the name of country and democracy. But this was different. They'd never harmed anyone in need of help. Halo was supposed to be the good guys.

But Val was his baby sister.

"What if she doesn't agree to it?" Sam asked.

"She will."

"What makes you so sure?"

"Anyone who marches through the woods in the middle of the night, armed with a flashlight and a hairbrush is either bat-shit crazy or desperate. And we can use a little of both right now."

~

Josh

Josh slid his finger across the screen and pressed the second name on his contact list.

"Mr Mendez." She answered on the second ring, her voice heavy with sleep.

"I made contact," Josh said.

"With?"

"Who the hell do you think with?"

Silence. And then, "Are you with her now?"

"No." He heard the rustling of bedsheets and then the sound of her laptop opening.

"How can I help?"

"I need you to narrow down a list of probable locations." Based on what? The fact that it was night time? Rox was cold and in the woods somewhere? Hell, that could be an entire country.

"Mr Mendez?"

"Yeah, I'm still here. It's ... She was ... "

"Relax. Just talk to me. It doesn't have to make sense," Meita instructed

"She's hurt. Bad. But she healed herself." He was silent for a few moments. "They're tranq'ing her."

"What did she see? Did she tell you where she's being held?"

"Nothing. And no, I mean, she ... " How to explain that

she wouldn't open her eyes? That she preferred captivity to him. "It's cold where she is. Snowing, I think."

The sound of her fingers flying across the keyboard echoed through the phone. "Day or night?"

"Night. Definitely night, but after midnight."

"Like pre-dawn?"

He thought about that for a moment. "I think so. Maybe."

"Were there a lot of people nearby? Like a city?"

"No, she was in the woods. Like, private property, I think." He was trying to piece together her scattered thoughts. "Shit ... " How'd he forget that?

"What?"

"She found Halo."

There was a thud followed by a rustling sound. "Meita?"

"Yeah, dropped my phone." She switched him to speaker. "Halo? You sure?"

Josh nodded even though she couldn't see him.

"And Halo was attacking her?"

Yeah, he wasn't sure what to make of that either. He hated to think that Halo weren't the do-gooders that EOs needed them to be, but he had been inside of Rox's head. They had hurt her. And that was all he needed to know.

"I *just* ... " he took a deep breath before he continued. "I just need you to narrow her possible locations down to something I can manage. I need to find her."

There was a moment of silence while he listened to her fingers tap against her laptop. "I doubt you could connect with her if she was on another continent." Meita was talking to herself now, something Josh realized she did when she was organizing her thoughts. "It's cold here. Cold on the entire northern hemisphere. Woods and snow." Meita sighed. "Ok, so let's just assume she's still here and not somewhere in Siberia or Kazakhstan, that just narrows it down to a few hundred locations." Her fingers were at the keys again. "It snowed in seven large cities last night."

"And the surrounding areas?" He knew it was a long shot.

"And the surrounding areas. I simply need more to go on."

He didn't have more to give her. "Wolf! She was attacked by a wolf. So maybe a—"

"Nature reserve." More typing. "No chance you can narrow it down to the type of wolf that attacked her?"

"For fuck's sake, Meita—"

"That was a good question, actually. But fair enough if you don't have the answer. Ok, I need time to set up search parameters. How long ago did you make contact?"

"We connected around five-fifty-five, and I was able to stay with her for about fifteen minutes. Maybe more." Maybe less.

"Ok. I'll call you back in an hour with an update."

He didn't want to hang up with Meita because he wasn't sure Rox had that long. Eighteen months and this was the first time he'd had a meaningful connection with her since he came home to find her gone.

"One more thing," Josh said. "Look for a military base or some kind of ... I don't know, government facility if you can."

"You think Halo's government?"

He didn't know what he thought. "I don't know. Call me back."

Their connection ended and the silence threatened to consume him. He looked around the room they used to share, unsure of what to do with himself. Normally, when he was this amped up, he'd do something with Rox. They'd make love or go for a run. But they hadn't done either in over a year. An uncomfortable mixture of hope and frustration wound its way through him.

Josh threw open his closet doors and rummaged through his drawers until he found his favorite pair of running pants. Dawn had brightened the sky, but it was still too early for anyone but the serious runners to be in the park. It was cold, but the snow from the north hadn't impacted Manhattan yet.

After he was dressed, he crept down the hallway, not wanting to wake his son. Jay had school in a few hours and would want to sleep until the last minute. Josh slipped into his running shoes and took the elevator down to the lobby. Connecting with Rox had shaken him, and his control on his ability was slipping. If he didn't find a way to calm his mind soon, he'd be inundated with the thoughts of every person he passed. And the more minds he connected with, the harder it was to maintain his own barrier.

Josh caught a glimpse of himself in the elevator's mirror and turned away from the dark circles under his eyes. A lack of sleep and the fear of not finding her had left their marks. His dark brown hair began to curl at the ends from neglect, and if he allowed himself to look hard enough, he'd notice the other signs of living with regret.

The thoughts of the security guard formed in Josh's mind as the doors chimed open. He was surprised to see Josh so early, but then understood when he took in Josh's attire. "Enjoy your run, Mr Mendez."

Josh placed his gratitude in the guard's mind and breathed in the cold air as he stepped outside. A chill chased its way down into his stomach as he took off at a controlled pace.

The red man glowed confident and strong, but Josh looked left and right before he ran across the empty street and down the sidewalk, past two carts brewing their special blend of coffee for morning commuters. His running shoes splashed in a puddle and last night's rain dripped down his calves.

The skyscrapers stunted the earliest onslaught of morning, but enough light slipped around the corners and reflected its presence off office windows to create the ambience of a new day. Steam rose from the grates down the street's center as the sound of his footsteps cut through the silence of dawn.

Josh slowed and pressed the heels of his palms into his brow and blinked back the tears that threatened to fall. She had been wet, cold, and hurt. So why wouldn't she open her eyes? She had to know he was there to help her. Why the mind games to keep him out? Why wouldn't she let him apologize?

Meita had been running Rox's image through the daily archives of every major city's surveillance cameras that she could tap into – and that was all of them – and had come up with nothing. Then out of the blue, just like that, he found Rox in his dreams.

Josh sent a quiet thought into the universe. He had no reason to believe that Rox would receive it, but he sent it anyway.

Hold on.

CHAPTER FOUR

Journey

Death, for Rox, was anticlimactic. There was no light to walk toward or away from. No voices. No visitors from the past to act as a guide. It was nothing more than the simple cessation of life.

But the same could not be said for the return journey. It was itchy.

Energy gathered at the base of her skull until there was enough to fire off the first synapse. It sent an electro-chemical message along its network, causing her atria to relax. Blood flowed into her heart, and with each constriction, more blood hurtled through her veins.

She laid there, passing through some single-cell stage of conscious evolution, where the ability to acknowledge self was still beyond her. There was only instinct, and the physical obedience to it.

The itch rose hard and fast. An assault of pins and needles unlocked her sense of touch and without the benefit of memory, her nails raked across her face like sandpaper across a smooth surface. Suddenly, Rox was aware that she existed in some type of compact space, separate from that around her. It wasn't an intellectual awareness, just an understanding that at some point her physical presence ended.

She cried out, but the sound was weak, foreign to her virgin ears. Cause and effect took root, and her fingers stopped their digging. Riding on the back of the itch was an intense cold. Her brain sent tiny electric impulses to her muscles, telling them to contract and expand.

The muscles in her jaw complied first, and her teeth started to clash. It was her attempt to make sense of that sound that kickstarted her brain into a higher level of reasoning.

And that was when her sense of smell overrode all other thought. She took in a breath that raised her back up and off the bed. Her eyes opened on their third attempt, and she turned her head to the side much faster than her vision could track. Her ability to relate to time had not yet resurfaced, and she had no idea how long it took for her sight to narrow, clear, and focus.

There, just to the side of her bed, was the source of that smell. She couldn't see it because its origin was hidden beneath some type of shiny cover, but she knew what it promised with an illogical certainty reminiscent of a newborn rooting for its mother's milk.

Unchallenged tears slipped down her face as she reached for the shiny dome. Two objects rattled and slid to one side, but stopped just short of tumbling to the floor as she pulled the tray closer.

Thought fragments and clips of images circled on the periphery of her mind. There was a familiarity to them that abated her fear and so she tore the silver dome free and bit into the first thing her fingers circled.

Chicken. And with its identity, the memories closest to her death began to reform.

Rox swallowed as an image of his face became the catalyst for further recollections. The pull of his energy. The quiet of his embrace. When he touched her, the voices and the confusion evaporated. Common sense said she should fear him – he did, after all, kill her – but there was something in his eyes that made her think he hadn't wanted to.

She chewed another piece of cold chicken and just after swallowing, an involuntary burp escaped. It was loud and startled another memory to the surface.

The memory swirled around her head like water fighting against the pull of a drain. A hum rose along the base of her spine as the hairs on her arms lifted. Goosepimples broke out along her skin and she pushed the tray away from her. She got up to her knees as the hum turned into a throb. She cried out as a sharp pain shot behind her right eye, and she pressed the heel of her hand against it.

The balloon encapsulating her memories burst, and the last four years came back in a flood. Rox was a healer, and death was an old acquaintance who never lingered. Her stomach churned at the thought of what that meant, and she looked up at the ceiling to stop from losing the sustenance she had just gained.

The past four years resettled in her mind with perfect clarity. She had found Halo. They were not what she expected, but at least she wasn't restrained to a chair anymore. Maybe they realized she wasn't a threat and only needed help. They could also just as easily think her dead and were discussing what to do with her body.

But why the food?

Rox pulled the tray closer and tasted something that looked like rice, but reminded her of cardboard. At least it wasn't out of the trash, or stolen.

When her plate was empty, fatigue settled in. Her body needed to heal, and no one healed faster than when they slept. She drifted off quickly to the sounds of her stomach digesting its first meal.

When she woke, it was with a sense of urgency. She wanted to get up but instinct kept her still. No sudden movements. Check your surroundings. Play dead.

The room reminded her of a halfway house she had stayed in a few months back. Its central theme was a kind of "survival chic": nothing matched and most everything smelled of a rubbish heap doused with Mr Clean. But this room was well cared for.

Rox sat up and her muscles ached at being forced into action. She lowered to the floor, and the rug fibers felt like heated bristles against her skin. She sat still, taking in the fact that she was once again alive.

She inhaled deeply and coughed. Death had a distinctive odor that was designed to repulse the living, and she was wearing it like a designer fragrance. A hot shower was exactly what she needed. There was only one other door in the room and common sense told her it led to the bathroom. It squeaked open, and Rox smiled at the memory of warm water cascading down her body, but that smile slipped when she looked in the mirror.

For a moment, all she could do was stare. The image reflected to her was something she couldn't quite comprehend. Tears blurred her vision and her head lowered in shame. That woman was ... broken. Her complexion was gray and lacked vitality. Her eyes were sunken and her skin looked stretched over facial bones in a manner that was too sharp to be attractive. The lines that decorated her forehead were dark, like they had been drawn on with a marker of a different shade. Her hair was naturally curly, but now it looked like fried wires held together by something she'd rather not identify.

Rox closed her eyes. It was one thing to know that she had died, to know that her heart had stopped beating and, for a moment in time, she was simply no more. It was quite another for her to see it.

She hiccuped and a mournful sob slipped out. She had forgotten about this part – *seeing* herself. Josh was usually nearby. He would wrap her in his arms and whisper just how beautiful and special he thought she was. Now, she knew the truth for what it was – that he had *made* her feel better because coming back from death was never beautiful.

Her legs gave out, and Rox sunk to the floor. What had she been thinking? She had made absolutely zero progress since leaving Josh. In fact, she had gone backwards. She had been living on the streets, and by all legal definitions, she was a thief and a low-rate con artist. And for what? How much closer had she gotten to uncovering anything about herself?

Rox rested her head on the cabinet beneath the sink and cried, her reflection in the glass shower door crying with her. There was nowhere to go from here.

She used that reflection to knock down a box of tissues from the counter. It bounced off the toilet seat and landed just in front of her feet. She yanked a tissue from the box and wiped her face. She reached for another to blow her nose, but the box was empty, and for some reason that made her laugh.

For a while, she simply alternated between sobs and bursts of laughter at the absurdity of her predicament and the choices that led to it. When she recovered, she realized that sitting on the bathroom floor was achieving nothing. It wasn't freeing her from Halo. It wasn't helping her find her identity. It was just eating up her energy and making her feel sorry for herself.

She used the counter to pull herself to standing and didn't try to hold back the fresh wave of tears when she looked in the mirror again. "You just died," she whispered to herself. "The beauty is that you're not still dead."

Not all beauty can be seen. And not all strength is physical. Funny that it was Josh's words that brought her comfort.

Rox stepped into the flow of water and immediately began to feel better. On instinct, she ran her hands over her body to check for injuries, but there were never any. She looked down at the lump of scar tissue that ran along her right knee. She had gotten that more than four years ago. In fact, every scar or imperfection had come from before, when she had been normal. The truth was, she had no idea if she had ever been "normal". Perhaps she had been born like this. Maybe every decade or so she lost her memories and simply had to start over again. Or maybe she had died a terrible death and not all her memories could come with her when she woke up. Who knows how many moments she lost with each death.

Rox thought back to the photo. Halo would have taken it. She would ask for it back, but she wouldn't be surprised if they wouldn't give it to her. For whatever reason, Josh had kept it hidden too. She had stared at that photo for hours, sometimes creating memories to go with the two girls. Their faces felt familiar and she wasn't sure if that was because she had made them so. Hell, one of them looked so much like her that she wondered if it were an image of her younger self.

Rox had no idea how old she was. She looked like a woman in her thirties, and not the early part. Movement didn't come easy enough for her to be young. Josh had her training with women in their twenties and they had an agility she could only envy. No matter how many sit-ups, star jumps or whatever other method of torture they put her through, she was never quite as fluid as they were.

Rox plaited her hair into a thick braid down her back and twirled the end around her finger in the direction of the curl. "Right. Clothes."

She searched the closet, but it was empty except for a pair of running shoes and two stacks of car magazines pushed to the back. She found boxer shorts and t-shirts in the dresser near the door. She lifted a pair and sniffed – clean, but old.

Rox looked in the dresser's mirror and ran through her list of options. Once again, none of them were what she wanted. But at least she wasn't restrained. Her eyes settled on the doorknob. A knock sounded, and she froze, not sure if it were real or her imagination.

The door eased open and a man's head peered through the crack. "Shit!" He jumped. "You're up."

Rox nodded.

He stepped in and looked around as if there could be others in the room. For a moment, she wondered the same thing and looked as well.

"Name's Walter."

For a moment they simply stared at one another, both unsure of how to break the awkward silence. Then Walter pulled his shoulders back a little and settled into a stance with his arms tucked behind his back.

"I've got a proposition for you," he said.

She wasn't sure she understood him, but as the silence stretched, reality sat in, and a slow smile spread across her face. No matter how manipulative Josh had been, he was right. Everyone wanted something, which meant everything had its price. Food and security cost money. But help? Well, help was the most expensive service of them all.

"So what's my freedom going to cost me?"

"Oh no," Walter said. "You are free to go now."

Rox hadn't anticipated that. "What's the catch?"

"No catch. More like a trade. You help us and we help you." When she didn't respond, he continued. "I mean, you obviously need our help because why else show up in the middle of the night, right?"

Rox took a step back to put some space between them. "And if I say no?"

"You don't want to help us, you're free to go. Back to wherever you came from. Stolen car. Presumably running from someone very powerful. Someone who knows you're some kind of a healer."

What had ever made her think that Halo would just help her without asking for anything in return? She cleared her throat. "What is it that you need help with?"

"'Fraid I can't tell you that until you've agreed to help us."

"That hardly seems fair," she said.

"Guessing you've already found out that life's hardly fair. Else you wouldn't be here."

~

Check-in

There were a series of clicks before the person on the other end spoke. "It's secure. What do you have?"

"Josh made contact with her using his ability," Meita said.

There was a moment of silence. "Then he's more powerful than we assumed. Are you recommending a new threat level for him?"

It was Meita's turn to be silent. Every EO they discovered was to be assessed and assigned a numerical threat level between one to five. One meant the ability was innocuous, while a three fell into the category of "continued monitoring, but no immediate action required".

"He remains a three," Meita said.

"A three?" Katherine repeated. Her tone indicated that

she knew Meita was feeding her a line of shit. The silence meant she was trying to figure out why. "And can you confirm she's an actual healer like he says?"

"No, but ... "

"Do you have her location?"

"I'm working on that, ma'am, but something's come up."

"What?"

"There's been an unauthorized system access to server WD-11," Meita said.

"Damage?"

"Assessing," Meita replied.

"Do we have complete access to that server yet?"

"No, ma'am. We're about a day or two away." More like three or four.

Katherine swore. WD-11 stood for Watership Down, one of the many undisclosed facilities running illegal and unethical experiments on evolved ones, and they were using her funds to do it. Katherine was head of the Global Frontiers Organization (GFO), a non-profit research group that – theoretically – didn't exist. They provided objective advice to independent Senate subcommittees about the economic and security risks posed by the discovery of evolved humans.

"Do we at least know who accessed the system and what they were looking for?" Katherine asked.

Meita took a deep breath. "It was Harry, ma'am."

Harry was the former head of GFO and had a much more relaxed approach to research. Under his leadership, GFO had quietly funded the creation of at least thirteen different facilities spread across the globe, all with the aim of demystifying human evolution before any other nation did.

"Did you put a trace on him?"

"Yes."

"And?"

"He accessed the location blueprints—"

"You mean we have a physical location?"

"Yes, ma'am, I believe so," Meita said. They've been working on decrypting the files on the WD-11 server ever since they discovered it existed a little over a year ago. This was as close as they'd come to finding anything tangible.

"Great work. Let's put Richardson and his team on this," Katherine said.

"Actually, I'd like to run point—"

"You can't run point on two active cases, Meita. Look, I know this Josh case feels like a damn love story, but if you're right and he can connect with minds hundreds of miles away, and if he's right and she's a healer, I need my best on this. Love saga or not."

"I believe the two cases are connected."

Katherine was silent and Meita took that moment to explain.

"Before Harry accessed the server, he received a call from a retired First Lieutenant Walter Watts. I don't know what that call was about, but shortly afterwards, Harry accesses the WD-11 server. He copies nothing. Deletes nothing, only accesses the location folder, and then makes two calls. One back to the First Lieutenant—"

"And the other?"

"Dr Clifford Tusk, but it was fifteen minutes after he hung up with Watts. It could be unrelated—"

"Please tell me you got the trace protocols up and running."

Meita tried not to sound offended. "Yes. That's how I know who he called and what files were accessed. I think he shared the location and blueprint details with Watts and Dr Tusk."

"Send me everything you can find on this retired lieutenant and this doctor."

"Already done, ma'am," Meita said. "But here's the thing, I think Watts might be linked to Halo."

Finding Halo would be a serious win for them. Most people didn't know whether Halo was a group of evolved ones doing good for their kind or a group of radicalized ordinary humans hunting them down.

"Explain."

Meita told her about Josh's connection with Rox, and how he believed she had found Halo. "Josh met with a sketch artist for one of the faces he saw while connected with Rox. I ran it through facial recognition and got a hit. Bethany Grace Loven."

"And she is?"

"Our retired First Lieutenant Walter Watt's niece, by marriage – his first one. And this same niece's digital footprint disappeared at the same time her uncle stopped collecting his pension. It's just sitting in an account piling up."

If Rox *had* found Halo and saw Bethany there, and Bethany was with Walter, then Walter and Bethany must be Halo. But if Halo was contacting Harry for information, that cast serious doubt on the organization's benevolence. Harry ran GFO for seven years, and in that time he had allowed experiments, abductions, and received illegal funding from countries with a lot less to lose than gain. Katherine and Meita were still trying to uncover all the operations he had running.

Could Halo be a part of it? Josh said that Halo had hurt Rox, had killed her, but everything Meita had uncovered about Halo said they were trying to do some good for EOs. To kill Rox just seemed contrary to the information she had gathered about them.

"Have you been able to ascertain why Harry accessed the WD-11 location file? What does that facility have to do with any of this?"

That was what Meita was hoping to find out. "Let's assume that Halo is helping EOs, then it makes sense that Rox would go to them ... "

"But how did she find them when *we* have not been able to locate them?"

"I don't know. Maybe she got lucky. Maybe she knew someone who knew someone. Hell, maybe they found her and needed her healing ability. But I want to use Josh's connection to her to follow up on Halo."

"This is good, Meita."

Meita couldn't hold back her smile. Katherine was far from an easy boss; the reputation she had gained was anything but kind, but Meita liked her. More importantly, Meita trusted her.

"I was able to get a lock on Walter's location," Meita

continued. "One of my resource assets is en route. They're only tasked with data retrieval."

"And the doctor?"

"That's proving a lot more difficult."

There was a moment of silence before Katherine spoke. "You've got forty-eight hours to find me something solid that links Rox with Halo and Halo with this First Lieutenant and then WD-11."

Meita gave a swift nod. "Understood." She had a few scripts to write before she could set the next phase of her plan in motion.

Meita

He'd never met her before, and so when she requested a meeting at his office after business hours, he had to admit he was surprised. Almost everyone who used her services did so anonymously, and so he hadn't given much thought to her appearance, but the opportunity to know the face when so many only knew the name was one he didn't want to forfeit.

She was dressed in winter-white, wool trousers and a simple black sweater designed for the weather. Hell, he even noticed her boots, and Josh wasn't overly into fashion. Her skin was the color of coffee with just a dash of cream, and it made the charcoal color of her nail polish pop.

"Mr Mendez," she said as she extended her hand. "Pleasure to meet you."

"Likewise, Meita." Her grip was strong, but not posturing-ly so. "Do you have a surname?"

She offered him a smile that was meant to convey neither joy nor sadness. "Meita will be fine."

She was not what Josh had envisioned in the hours before their meeting. For the hacker type, she definitely broke the mold. Meita looked ... well, she looked important. Her clothes were stylish and obviously tailored. Her accessories were tasteful accentuations as opposed to status symbols. Her hair was chocolate brown, not a single highlight, and was styled short and lacked that salon-finish so many women coveted.

This was *the* Meita. She was older than he'd imagined.

"I've narrowed it down to three possible locations," she said.

Right to business. He liked that. "And the most probable?"

"Connecticut."

Connecticut? Halo was located in Connecticut. That was less than two hours by private plane. Had she been this close the entire time?

"What makes that the most probable?" Josh asked.

"Two things. The weather information matches your description, with a remote possibility of wildlife. And there's a perpetual lack of satellite coverage around a specific target location there."

While Josh had been hoping for just this kind of information, it still took him by surprise. Had he truly finally located her?

"May we sit?" Meita asked.

"Of course," Josh said, slightly embarrassed by his lack of etiquette.

After she had taken her seat, Josh reached out with his mind to listen in on her thoughts. It would be faster to get the information he needed that way, and of course, more accurate. But he slammed into a solid wall when he tried to penetrate her mind.

"Are you all right?" Meita leaned forward as if she were about to rise.

It felt like a splinter had wedged itself in his brain. He had never met a mind he couldn't eavesdrop on. He leaned away from her and stared. A hacker wasn't this beautiful. Was she EO? Was this some kind of set-up?

"Who are you?"

Meita inhaled and let her breath out slowly. "I'm sorry that my appearance confuses you, but just like not all Latin men are mechanics living in the inner city, not all hackers dye their hair green and wear entirely too much eyeliner."

His father was of Spanish descent, but he took her point nonetheless. She had found Rox. Something he had failed to do for over a year now. He had promised his son, Jay, that he would bring her back. It was a foolish promise, something a parent would make to buy themselves more time.

And time was something he felt he was running out of. Who cared what Meita looked like. She could dress herself like a fairy tale princess if it took her fancy. Right now his priority was Rox.

"You said there was a *lack* of coverage?"

Meita nodded. "Government satellites passing over these coordinates ... " She reached into a black leather bag no larger or thicker than a ten-page notebook and pulled out a clear, plastic folder sealed on two sides. Inside the folder was a single sheet of paper with bolded GPS coordinates in the middle of the first paragraph of text. " ... repeatedly capture no image at all. That wouldn't be interesting if it were a base or some type of military or top secret facility, but these coordinates are listed as 'private property'."

Holy hell, Rox *had* found Halo. Government agencies were looking for them. Hell, he had been looking for them himself. He had gotten close a couple of times, but none of his leads ever turned up anything. At first he wanted to work with them, see if there was a way they could partner to help EOs together. Now, he just wanted to discover who they were so he could find Rox.

"And there's no satellite footage over that area?" he asked.

Meita tilted her head like the answer to that question wasn't a simple yes or no. "While there is no *government* satellite footage, there is an organization that I know of that stores images in their cloud for a short period of time. I believe that they have footage of that area."

This was good. "So hack into their system and let's get confirmation that Rox is there."

Meita smiled at him for a moment and then leaned back on the sofa. "Josh, this isn't some TV show."

"I thought you said you were the best," he snapped.

She leaned forward with her arms resting on her thighs. "I am the best. But hacking into anything takes time. And getting in and *out* without being discovered requires even more time. A lot more. Aside from the time it would take to securely breach their systems to get a copy of those images, it's just not something I'm willing to do when I'm quite confident that this is the most probable location."

Josh stared at her. Logical, but ... He tried to penetrate her thoughts once more and once more he struck a wall. He was so close to finding Rox that perhaps he simply couldn't think straight. She had just died. She would be disoriented when she woke up. Hungry. And probably afraid and horribly insecure. Death did that, he learned. It shook your understanding of everything to the core. It's why when you died, you were meant to stay dead.

"And you think she's here?" Josh pointed to the GPS coordinates on the piece of paper. "And this is Halo."

Meita looked at her watch, which didn't illuminate until she lifted her wrist. "Yes. For about another hour and twenty minutes."

"What?"

"Hacking into most organizations undetected takes a bit of time, but this location, Halo, is private property. I have to admit, I was impressed with their firewalls, but still, easy enough if you know what you're doing, and what you're looking for."

"So, you got through?"

"Of course. That's how I've come to the conclusion she will no longer be there in just over an hour. Instead, my guess is that she'll be aboard an unscheduled flight to this location." Gray nails slid down the page to a second set of GPS coordinates in the second paragraph.

"Joder!" Josh shot to his feet. "Why there?" He waved his hands in frustration at the piece of paper. "Where is … there?"

Meita sat back abruptly, but he sensed no fear from her. It was more like she was waiting for him to regain composure. He wasn't sure if that made him like her a little more or a little less.

She didn't continue until he was seated. "I'm not sure of the why, but the where is a place called Watership Down."

"Watership Down?" It was a whisper on his lips. He'd heard that name before. But when? It reminded him of another place. A place that scared the hell out of him. He sucked in a deep breath and his head fell forward as he exhaled. If Watership Down was what he thought it was, then Rox was headed towards something far worse than death. Places like that shouldn't exist. He had been inside one once and had barely escaped with his life. It's why he trained. And why he trained everyone else he cared about.

If he got caught in a place like that, his money wouldn't save him. His connections might get him out. Eventually. Ultimately, a facility like that would break him. He knew it because he had seen the broken people. Oh sure, it was all too easy to think you're invincible. Watch a movie or read a book, and suddenly you think you could do what the hero does. But books aren't written about those who failed. Broken people don't get to share their stories. And there were a hell of a lot more broken people than heroes.

He brought his hand to his face and was surprised how it shook. He met Meita's gaze and cleared his throat. "Do you have anything else?"

"From my search?" she asked. "No. But you should know that Watership Down is ... it's not a nice place. It will be heavily guarded with protocols that need to be set in motion well before you arrive if you wish to bypass. You will not be able to just talk yourself into that kind of place."

Josh's laugh was anything but pleasant. "Oh, I know."

And for the first time since meeting her, he saw a look of surprise on her face, but she quickly hid it beneath a smile. "Good. It will take another three hours for my package to upload into their system. And then from there, we'll have to rely on luck that it'll be manually transferred to the right places by the time we arrive."

Josh froze. "We?"

"You haven't found her yet. And while I'm over ninety percent confident of my findings, the final fee isn't payable until physical sighting." She left the folder enclosing the GPS coordinates on the coffee table and closed her bag before she stood. "It's probably best that I join you for this next part."

Josh hesitated. "You said yourself that this isn't a nice place – and that's putting it lightly. I've been inside one of these facilities before. I'll be lucky to make it out myself."

"I appreciate your concern, but I'm afraid that this is non-negotiable. Besides, I can take care of myself."

It was the way that she said it that gave Josh cause for concern. "What the hell does that mean?"

"It means I'm not stupid," she said, her tone professional.

"I will go in as your assistant. My bags are packed and I am ready."

"And if I say no?"

"Then I stop my upload."

So she had her own angle in this. It wasn't just about fulfilling their contract. How much did she help her clients versus her clients inadvertently helping her? "Why do you want to go?"

"Let's just say I have a personal interest in places like Watership Down."

Personal interest? In a place like that? "You know what I am? What I *can* do?" Except, just not to her.

She nodded.

"Are you ... evolved?"

Meita tilted her head like the answer to that question wasn't a simple yes or no.

∼

Fear

The blades of the Lockheed AH Night Air Drift sliced through the darkness in silence. Rain and the wind made it a tough flight pattern to follow as lightning flashed across the sky like randomly cast spells.

Sam checked his seatbelt again and glanced at Rox as another pulse of her energy slipped through him. She was staring nervously out the other side of the helicopter. He didn't blame her. Flying through a storm was ill-advised, so flying through lightning was just plain insane. But their window for saving Val was closing. According to the information that his father had received, she was at a place called Watership Down, but they couldn't be certain for how much longer. Apparently, whatever they had wanted from her, they had obtained and the likelihood of her being sold was high.

Sam swore under his breath.

His baby sister was used and then sold like merchandise. He was twelve when she and her twin brother were born. She came out screaming, and she hadn't quite shut up since. She was a talker, not a fighter, and when she wasn't talking, she was reading.

He ran his hands down his face and turned back to the window. Rescue missions were a downright risky business. The captors always knew you were coming. Sam had been on a couple, and they were never simple and always took more time than anyone preferred. First you had to locate the one you were trying to save. Then you had to gather intel. Scope out the location. Make judgment calls based on the type of extraction to deploy. And that was when he had access to satellite coverage, a team of trained personnel on the ground, and a budget that had at least five to six zeros attached to it.

His stomach lurched, and he put his head down between his legs to stop himself from throwing up. They would have raped her. He hated himself for thinking it, but it was the most effective way of disarming a woman and reducing her threat for a time. In eight months, they would have had enough time to systematically deconstruct her. They could have harvested her organs, implanted things in her … hell, she would have been at the mercy of scientists whose main purpose was to unlock the understanding to evolved DNA. They would be smart enough to know that just because she wasn't one didn't make her useless. Instead she'd be a test subject. A lab rat they could experiment on.

And if she fought back?

He snorted at the idea. Of course she fought back, but if he had to subdue someone without killing them, he would just keep them sedated. There were sedatives that could keep someone lucid, but leave them immobile. She would be aware of everything that was happening to her and powerless to do anything about it.

Sam looked at Rox again. Her hands were balled in her lap and her right foot tapped to a tempo that had to be driven by nerves. What if Rox had escaped from somewhere just like that? He hadn't even stopped to ask her. No, Sam and his team had just pumped her full of tranquilizers and then painted her into a corner where helping them was her only way out.

What would he do if Val had escaped only to run into the same set of options they had presented to Rox?

Sam was torturing himself with what-ifs and memories, but there was a certain connection made when you watched a younger sibling grow that was different from the connection you had when you grew up *alongside* one.

Sam hadn't realized he was still staring at Rox until another energy pulse went through him. She flinched and then wiped a tear from her face. A healthy dose of shame struck him. They had never bargained with anyone who needed Halo's help. That wasn't how they operated. But they *needed* her. Who knew what state Val would be in when they found her. Besides, their escape relied on way too much luck as it was. With no time to prepare a proper extraction, a lot was left to chance, and a healer was an advantage they couldn't afford not to exploit.

And if she died? he asked himself.

It wouldn't come to that.

Why?

The truth was that places like Watership Down didn't exist on military maps or satellite imagery. The intel about them was gathered through hearsay and everyone knew better than to ask questions. It was the type of place where governments allowed certain corporations to run experiments. Sometimes it was on equipment, like the next generation of weaponry, and sometimes it was on humans, like the next generation of evolved ones.

The helicopter dipped as it broke through the storm, and the rain beating against the windows slowed to a patter. Sam's attention returned to the helicopter's interior as Shaira brushed against his legs. Walter signaled to him to switch channels on his headset.

"Two minutes out," his father said once they were connected. "We've picked up the dive boat's call."

Sam nodded, but kept his eyes on Rox.

"That healer has proved she can take care of herself. And even if she can't, that's what I'm here for. You focus on Val, and I'll take care of the healer."

His father was right. Rox could hold her own. *But against men like they were about to go up against?* Sam shook his head. It didn't matter. None of them had a choice.

He took a deep breath and noticed the scent of

recently manufactured interior. Everything smelled new. There was still plastic covering parts of the control panels overhead.

Walter followed Sam's gaze. "Fresh out of the factory. Just taking it for a quick spin."

Sam wasn't sure it was a great idea to fly a brand new helicopter into a tropical storm as a test drive, but then again, they had to accept help from where they could get it. And the pilot was a friend of Walter's from when they were active. Like all bonds forged during combat, time did little to weaken them.

Static sounded through his headphones just before the pilot announced they were above the drop site. Sam gazed at Rox, and she was visibly shaking now, but he had to give her credit because she hadn't complained once. In fact, she hadn't said a word since they boarded. He wanted to tell her that everything would be all right or that they would protect her, but he doubted there was anything he could say to assuage her fears given they were about to lower themselves from the helicopter onto a boat in the middle of the night. During a storm.

Sam leaned over and tried to peer straight down through the window. Darkness had swallowed the waves as well as the sea.

Walter tapped him on his shoulder, and Sam sat back as his father slid open the door. Curtis did the same to the other door Rox had been staring out of, and despite Curtis's darker complexion, he looked pale with fear. They exchanged a brief nod before Curtis checked his harness, then backed out of the helicopter and lowered himself down the rope.

Silent lightning brightened the sky, and they watched as the wind forced him into a swirling pattern until the darkness swallowed him too.

The helicopter dipped, and Sam grabbed the handlebars to steady himself. He looked out the door and realized that they were lowering. Walter tapped Sam on the shoulder and nodded towards Rox. She was breathing heavily now, perhaps on the verge of hyperventilating. They were going to need to distract her, get her out of her own head.

There wasn't enough room above for Sam to stand to his full height, but he crossed the interior somewhat faster than normal to reach her. He couldn't deny the attraction and reminded himself that it wasn't to her per se, but to the energy she emitted.

She jumped when he touched her, but then a calmness spread over him that he knew she felt by the fall of her shoulders.

He switched the channel on her headset to break their silence. "You're going to be just fine. Remember, if you're going too fast, pull up. Lower your arm down below your hip to keep going."

She didn't respond right away, but then she slowly nodded.

"I'm going to go first so that I can catch you when you're down there. Walter will make sure your line is secure and he'll send you after me. Follow his instructions. Understand?"

She nodded again, but he wasn't sure how much she actually retained. That's why practice was essential for missions like this. Fear was a necessary part of the human psyche. Lowering oneself out of a helicopter wasn't a good idea on a clear day, but in the middle of a storm had to be insanity. Her mind was doing what it was designed to do: protect its body. The only thing that could override this kind of fear was a habit born of practice. Muscle memory took care of what the nerves couldn't. He had seen the look in Rox's eyes before, and if time wasn't of the essence, he would have told her to sit this one out. But they needed her. Val needed her, and so either Rox was going to snap out of it or she was going to panic and put them all at risk.

"All right, that's one down!" His father's voice cut through their headsets. "Need to pick it up, ladies. We're wasting too much damn fuel trying to keep this bird steady."

The helicopter swayed, and Sam reached out to grab Rox from tumbling back into Walter.

"I got her!" Walter mouthed, but his voice was swallowed by the roar of the wind outside.

Sam nodded and grabbed the rope that Walter had already worked into Shaira's clip. He had repelled from a helicopter only once with his wolf. It was a training exercise they had done just for fun. Shaira didn't like being suspended in mid-air and he had a nice scar running down the length of his right bicep to prove just how much she disliked the experience. But he sensed a calm about the wolf that bespoke experience. The first time was always the hardest.

"Ready?" his father asked.

This was the worst plan he had ever put into action. But

sometimes, bad plans were your only option. The last thing Sam saw as he sat back into darkness was the look of terror on Rox's face. Fear was something she obviously couldn't heal.

Options

Rox was on her hands and knees taking in sand with each breath. Her head was pounding, her ears were waterlogged, and she was certain that the burning sensation in her eyes meant she was going blind. But she was alive.

That was the most dangerous thing she had ever done. And the most stupid. Who the hell lowers themselves out of a helicopter in the middle of a storm? She wasn't sure what scared her more – falling to her death, drowning (another death experience she had not had) or being struck by lightning. The hairs on her arms rose with each charge of electricity that flew between the clouds. She wasn't sure if the adrenaline surge was her body's way of preparing for certain death or if she was somehow feeding off the storm's energy – either way, that was an experience she never wished to repeat.

A wave crashed behind her and sent the surf up her legs and around her elbows. She crawled forward until she was out of the water and collapsed on her back. It wasn't raining as hard as it had been, but she still had to turn her head. The others moved around her, but she ignored them as the first signs of shock hit. Her teeth clattered, and she shook despite the warmer temperatures of the

Caribbean. She should keep moving to stay warm, but curling into the fetal position and taking a nap sounded more appealing.

Rox rolled to her side and was about to give in to exhaustion when the uncontrollable urge to laugh burst through. She hadn't died. On some level, that made her feel bad ass. She had repelled out of a moving aircraft onto a diveboat and swam ashore. Josh would never believe her capable of that. Hell, she hadn't believed she was capable of that. She giggled until she snorted, and then she threw her head back and let the mirth of being alive take her. Tears rolled down her face, and she reached up to wipe them only to get sand in her eyes.

She wasn't sure how long it took her to pull herself together, but when she sobered, she realized that this was just the beginning. Things were going to get tougher from here.

The waves crashed to shore as if on a schedule, and Rox timed her breathing to its return in an attempt to calm herself.

Lightning cracked over the horizon, and the ocean's kinetic energy struck her like a live current. Her head arched back as an unseen force spread across the nape of her neck to run beneath the waistband of her cargo pants. Goosepimples sprouted along her skin and her fingers curled into the sand as if searching for a lifeline.

When she syphoned energy from a person, it was like she tapped into their unique frequency, which required both concentration and effort. But this was different. This energy was just sitting there, coiled with anticipation and eager to be absorbed.

The pain at the back of her shoulders where a wave had struck her lessened, and the tension in her forehead eased, allowing her vision to focus. The fatigue in her muscles lightened and her lungs opened wider. Her stomach lurched to expel the seawater and sand she had swallowed.

It burned just as badly coming back up as it did going down, but instead of feeling weak, Rox straightened and rolled her shoulders forward like she had awoken from a nap. The ocean's energy continued to pour into her like a cup that had reached its capacity. Her eyes slid close as she swayed to the rhythm of the tide and the kinetic energy warmed her. On instinct, she lifted her hands to redirect the excess to the others and her fingertips tingled as if circulation had been cut off.

"Is that you?"

Rox jumped at the sound of Sam's voice. She lowered her arms, feeling self-conscious about her actions.

"It's like I feel lighter," Sam said. "Is that how your ability works?"

Rox pushed to her feet. "I guess. It's like I feel other people's energy and sometimes, I guess you can say I help it flow right. Or maybe better."

"Bethany said your heart stopped. Back at Halo."

Rox wasn't sure how to respond, or if she wanted to. She didn't like to talk about her ability. Mostly because there was so much about it she didn't understand. Josh had always been afraid to take her to a doctor, and when she had left him, she too carried that same fear.

"I'm sorry about what happened back there," Sam said.

It took her a moment to realize he was talking about when they were back at Halo.

She nodded like she understood because in some way she did.

Sam took a bag off his shoulder and lowered it to the ground. Her toes curled into the sand as he pulled out her shoes and dropped them beside her feet. She had completely forgotten that Walter had taken them from her before she left the helicopter. Her shoes looked ridiculous compared to his boots that came up past his ankles. Hers were obviously recreational, serving fashion's purpose more than function's. But they were the only pair that the shelter had that fit.

The sound of a gun's chamber clicking back into place caught her attention. Sam placed the weapon into a holster and then knelt in front of her. Rox raised her arms as he secured its buckle around her waist, and she became conscious again of the pulses that they exchanged. She wasn't sure arming her in this particular set of circumstances was a great idea. For one, she was having trouble concentrating given the way she reacted to his energy.

Sam's hands slipped between her thighs and her breath caught. She would have stumbled backwards if he hadn't reached out to steady her. "Just another sec and I'll be done." A sheath hung from the belt and he grabbed the two straps at its end and looped it around her thigh, pulling the velcro between her legs to hold it into place.

Yes. Arming her was a bad idea. Aside from a lack of concentration, there was the fact that she never had much luck with her aim on a stationary target. And she doubted it would improve with a moving one. She was about to say as much when Sam pulled out a knife from the bag. It wasn't large, but it looked well cared for and its edge caught the sliver of light that broke through the clouds. The handle was made for someone with her palm size.

A knife she could handle.

He pulled it from its carry sheath and slipped it into the one secured to her thigh. His hand circled the back of her leg and the heat from his hand made her flinch. They looked at one another as he pushed the snap in place to prevent the knife from falling out.

A part of her brain told her to step back out of his reach, but his touch rooted her. She realized just how tall he was when he stood. Her head only came to his chest, which meant she had to look up to maintain eye contact. It was hard to make out his expression given the darkness, but she didn't move when Sam reached up to push a few strands of hair out of his way and slipped an earpiece in her ear.

Her eyes slid closed when his knuckles brushed her cheek. The waves silenced and the rain stopped as she leaned into his hand. His fingers cradled the side of her face and she exhaled so deeply she wanted to lie down and take that nap on the sand.

His thumb wiped a tear off her cheekbone, and the gentleness of his touch snapped her back to reality. The sound of the ocean raised a few decibels as the clouds rumbled across the sky.

"Ready?" He had to shout to be heard, but his tone was sympathetic.

Rox gave a sharp cry the moment they broke contact. Pain shot from her ear canal down and around her jaw. She burned the tip of her finger as she yanked out the earpiece and dropped it on the sand. She held her head against the pain radiating throughout the right side of her face as the scent of burning plastic filled her nostrils.

A flashlight blinded her, and she turned away from the light towards the ocean. Raw energy sped through the air and up her arm, weaving its way to the ruptured ear drum and immediately began lacing the delicate tissue back together. On instinct, she opened her mouth wide a few times, trying to scratch an itch there was no way she could reach. She moved her lower jaw side to side until she heard a pop, and then she could hear in surround sound again.

"Well, alrighty then," Walter said. "Hadn't planned for that. You got extra?"

Sam reached for his pack to look for another earpiece, but Rox shook her head. "It won't work."

She had gotten so caught up in Sam's touch that she forgot about the effects electronics had on her. Its energy hurt. It created a vibration at the base of her skull like its frequency was trying to find a direct pathway into her brain, but what surprised her was she should've felt the discomfort long before Sam was able to put the earpiece in.

Walter pointed a finger at her. "You stay on my ass, you hear?"

Rox didn't like his tone, but she had a feeling there would be other, more pressing concerns before the night was over.

"OK. Time check," Curtis said. "We got until sunlight before things get real, people. So I'm gonna find us a more reliable way than our feet to get the hell away from this place once you have her."

Rox wanted to breathe a sigh of relief that their return trip didn't include a swim back to the boat, but the realization that they hadn't already mapped out an escape plan gave her cause for new concern.

Sam extended his hand to Curtis. "If we're not back by sunrise, you head to Cabarete. Just ask around for a guy named Yosemite. Tell him Sam Gray sent you. He'll get you back to the States, no questions."

"Gray?" Curtis asked as he pulled Sam in for a brief hug.

"No questions," Sam said.

Curtis nodded. "If it comes to that, I'll tell Mika and we'll come get you."

"No!" Walter said. "Tell him to tell Harry. He'll know what to do."

Rox felt her panic rising to helicopter-jumping levels again. One, who the hell were Mika and Harry? And two, if they didn't find Val by sunrise, their only transportation out of this nightmare was instructed to leave them? "Wait!" She turned to Walter. "That's not what we agreed to. You said you'd help me find my identity if I helped you get your daughter back."

"And we will," Walter said. "But I'm not risking the only person who knows where we are," he pointed at Curtis, "by telling him to take on a solo mission to get us out. If it comes to it, Harry will help you uncover your identity."

"And if he doesn't? It's not like Harry and I have even

met!" This wasn't their deal. Halo was supposed to *help* her. Harry was some guy she didn't know and therefore didn't trust. In fact, she hadn't made up her mind if she actually trusted these guys.

"Tell him I sent you," Walter said.

Rox held his gaze until tears threatened to spill. If jumping out of a helicopter was stupid, then attempting to breach this Watership Down with their only mode of escape instructed to leave them if they were late was downright imbecilic. But what choice did she have? She couldn't change her mind now. They were already here. She had been instructed to leave her ID and passport back at Halo, which was fine because her ID was fake and she didn't have a passport to begin with. But it left her totally reliant on them. She had left one bad situation only to find herself in one much worse.

What was so important about her past that she continuously risked her life to find out? Why couldn't she just be satisfied with Josh? And if not with Josh, then at least be satisfied on her own? People started over all the time.

But how do you start over when you're running from someone with Josh's resources? It was only a matter of time before he found her, which meant her only hope was to find out who she was. But then what? She discovered she had a family, were they just supposed to miraculously take her back? She'd been missing for at least four years. People moved on. If she were married, her husband would surely have found someone new by now. There was a good chance that her parents were dead or old enough that seeing her again would give them heart failure.

And kids? Would they even remember her? Because she damn sure didn't remember them.

Rox felt a hand on her shoulder and its touch was warm. It wasn't the same sense of calm as when their contact was skin-to-skin, but it was enough. "We can't stay here. We're too exposed and time is literally running out."

Rox nodded and wiped the rain out of her eyes. She turned around to face Walter. "OK, look, I never was a fan of guns and so if I have to draw this thing, I'm telling you now that my bluff is better than my aim. My best bet for defense will be this." She unsheathed her knife and tested its balance. "This is my best chance if things get ... hostile. But I don't have any formal training. You guys seem military or at least trained for something ... hostile. I'm more trained for self-preservation, you know, strike and run."

"Well, that's better than nothing," Walter said. "You know how to take the safety off and reload?" He pointed towards her hip where Sam had placed the gun.

Rox nodded.

Walter had to wait until the roll of thunder dissipated before he continued. "Sam's taking point on finding Val. So that means you're with me."

Shaira gave a low bark and turned in a circle before loping a few paces away. "And the wolf?" Rox asked. She had forgotten the animal was there.

"She's with Sam."

Rox looked from Sam back to the wolf. She would have laughed at the absurdity of it all if her life wasn't on the line. "How are you gonna get her out of here?"

"Same way we got her here. Illegally."

Thunder and lightning

When Walter said they would be penetrating a highly secret, highly secured research facility, Rox had found it difficult to focus. There was talk of schematics and sunrise and armed guards, to which she now wished she had paid more attention. But what *had* grabbed her attention at the time was Sam's reaction. A stillness had settled over him, and she was unable to discern whether he was scared or simply preparing himself. As she followed on his heels, she noticed how his head swiveled in a rhythmic pattern, like he was trying to take in everything. Walter was a few yards ahead of them, almost out of sight, but still visible so they knew in which direction to follow.

Watership Down had two facilities, the dormitories and the laboratories. The dorms were situated in the main house on the top of the bluff that rose about eight storeys out of the ocean they had just climbed out of. There were two access points from the beach up to the facilities – one was a narrow road formed from frequent vehicle use nearby to where they had swam ashore, and the other was an overgrown climbing path with steps carved into the actual rock face.

Walter said that before the Dominican government had sold it, the land used to belong to descendants from plantation owners during the slave trade, and the path down the cliff was how slaves would escape. In the dead of the night, against a dark cliff with naturally darker skin, they would be hard to spot. Sam had been skeptical about using that as their access point given it had been centuries since the path had been used, but Walter said that was their best bet for getting onto the property undetected.

The labs were underground and divided into color-coded sections, each requiring a different key. Technology had been reduced to a bare minimum, which Rox had thought was good news until Sam explained that less technology meant more guards. People patrolling noticed a hell of a lot more than someone sitting in a comfortable chair only occasionally glancing up at security screens.

As they neared the base of the bluff, Sam held up his hand for Rox to stop while Walter looked for the path. He hadn't turned on his flashlight so she had no idea how he was able to see given she had stumbled a half dozen times.

Sam turned to her and pulled her close so he could whisper in her ear. "Keep your eyes open and let us know if you see anything. But stay quiet. Surprise is our only advantage."

The wind blew sand from the beach into their faces, and Rox sensed that he was also affected by their proximity, but neither of them moved.

Something landed in the sand next to them and they both jumped. They looked up and could just make out Walter waving at them. He was trying to get their attention without making noise.

"When we get to the top, stay behind my father," Sam said. "He'll keep you safe."

The hillside was covered in a dense shrubbery that had

learned to survive in the harsh sand. It was some sort of perennial flora that grew tall in certain places and thick and dense in others. It had dark, fragrant leaves as large as her hands with sharp edges.

Rox looked at the sky and could just make out the clouds rushing by. She closed her eyes and let the rain spill down her cheeks and run into the space between her shirt and chest. How hard could a rescue mission be? They had gotten this far without incident. Plus, they had the element of surprise. And it was raining. The guards would be seeking shelter and not watching for some unlikely threat.

Walter set a pace like he knew the terrain, which made Rox curious about his ability. He found the beginning of the path about a quarter of the way up the hillside. Shaira darted past her and stopped in front of Walter. The wolf sniffed the air before making a sound that was between a cough and a snort, then turned around and ran past them along the beach.

The "path" up the cliffside was nothing more than naturally formed rock protrusions. A few times Rox thought she got a foothold, but would slip backwards and have to grab onto one of the nearby shrubs to keep from tumbling backwards. The thorns along the branches and the sharp edges of the leaves sliced into her hands more than a few times, but the ocean's energy healed them before it impeded her ascent.

Sam's step gave way and she turned her head as pieces of the cliff crumbled and fell past her. When she looked up next, he was looking down at her, waiting for her to signal she was all right. She waved for him to continue and fought back the giggles of her predicament. She could add rock climbing to her list of adventures since awakening four years ago. Rock climbing in the rain, tarred and feathered in sand while she attempted to infiltrate a secret government facility especially designed for dissecting her kind.

Goosepimples formed over her back and the hair on her arms moved as if something was crawling on her. Lightning flashed and the path ahead lit for a split second before the clouds threw the night back into darkness.

Rox lifted the sleeve of her shirt as the hair on her arms resettled. A strong gust of wind threatened to dislodge her, but a strong hand pushed her safely back against the cliff.

"Lean in," Sam said. "You want to keep your body as close to the wall as possible."

The irony of her situation was not lost on her. She had finally found someone to help her, but she was probably going to get blown off the side of the cliff and break her neck as she tumbled down. The fall, of course, would *not* kill her. No, she would lay there in writhing pain, temporarily paralyzed while her body mended itself. And if those weren't happy enough thoughts, she was hungry. She felt her blood sugar dropping and all she could think about was a rack of meaty barbeque pork ribs with a side of carbs. And a milk shake.

The wind howled, and she paused for a moment before she realized that it was Shaira. A short burst from an automatic weapon fired a couple of hundred yards above them. Walter and Sam hurried their pace when the path finally levelled out. The roots of a tree growing out of the side of the cliff made an archway over the path. She leaned against the cliff and scooted sideways underneath the roots, but her braid snagged in one of the smaller branches.

By the time she pulled free, a healthy chunk of her hair was missing, and Walter and Sam were clearing the summit. She started to jog after them when she felt a shift in the energy. She looked up at the clouds and was surprised that the rain had lessened, but it was the electric charge in the air that slowed her steps.

The sky roared and the hair on her arms rose again. Her skin felt like ants were setting up a nest inside her body. There was a sharp pop just behind her jaw and then lightning snaked from the sky and splintered a tree jutting out from the side of the cliff just ahead of her. Splinters the size of carpenter nails sliced open her neck and face before she could turn back under the protection of the archway of roots.

The pop in her ears started a ringing that drowned out all other sound. Fire leapt to life where lightning had struck the underbrush. Smoke filled her lungs as the wind blew the flames in her direction. Her only choice was to go back down the side of the cliff. Blinded, peppered with splinters and flames licking at her back, Rox turned around and lost her footing.

CHAPTER FIVE

Watership Down

She knew the moment her finger broke. A searing pain radiated up her wrist and seemed to set up residency in her chest. She wanted to let go and cradle her hand, but if she released the root, it was going to be a long and much more painful way back down.

Rox cried out as she pulled herself up to solid footing. She placed her full weight on the balls of her feet as she balanced on the narrow ledge. Her finger grew hot, as if the flames from the fire were on it, and there was a crack as the storm's energy healed her finger.

Rox wasn't sure how long she hung there, but when her thoughts took form again, she restarted her climb back to the top. The rain had quelled the flames, but she moved quickly underneath the canopy of roots and past the burnt remains of the underbrush.

She crouched at the edge of the cliff, afraid to move as she tried to figure out what the hell to do next. The skirmish from earlier appeared to be over, but Sam and Walter were nowhere to be found. She picked her way up onto solid ground and reached out with her energy. Nothing responded to her except the storm making its away across the sky. She crept forward a few steps when she felt something coming at her hard and fast. She fumbled with the holster and pulled her gun free.

A pair of glowing eyes appeared in the distance as the familiarity of the energy set in.

"Oh, thank you." Rox re-holstered her weapon and fought back the tears of relief when Shaira's shape took form. "Almost got yourself shot," she said and tentatively reached down to pat the wolf.

Shaira circled her legs and nudged her forward before running back in the direction from which she came.

Rox hesitated. Was she supposed to follow? Did Shaira know where Sam and Walter had disappeared to?

Shaira trotted back towards her, but stopped. Rox studied the animal. In any other situation, this would be absurd, but she didn't see any other choice.

"Hope you know what you're doing," she said.

They crept along for a few minutes before Shaira stopped. Her growl wasn't loud enough to carry, but Rox knew that it meant trouble. She reached out with her energy and sensed two people coming towards them.

"Shit!" Rox spun in a circle. The cliff top wasn't exactly teaming with places to hide. There was a bench situated directly below the only tree she could make out in the darkness. It didn't look like it had many leaves, but it would have to do. She used the bench to catapult herself up the lowest branch. She kicked out her feet once to get the momentum to pull herself up. She wasn't overly high up and the foliage did very little to hide her, but she was out of options.

She scooted against the tree trunk and focused on slowing her heartbeat. She doubted they would be able to hear her over the rain, but she took deep slow breaths just in case.

The two guards were close enough to make out in the dark. One of them stopped when he spotted Shaira sitting on the bench, not even attempting to be discreet.

"Is that a ... a dog?" one of the guards said.

"What?" The second guy asked, and followed his partner's stare.

The first guard fumbled for his weapon, and Rox reached out. His energy slammed into her with such force she lost her perch. His legs buckled just as she hit the ground.

The second guard looked from his fallen partner to Rox and then Shaira. By the time he galvanized into action, it was too late and Shaira was on him. He didn't even scream, but Rox heard the tearing of his skin. Energy poured from her, and she scrambled to get out of range. Her ability to heal was an extraordinary gift, but it wasn't always voluntary. Minor scrapes she could easily stop herself from healing, but wounds like the ones Shaira had just caused would latch onto her like a lifeline and drain her dry.

Rox got to her feet just as the guard took his last breath. His pull on her gone. But just because he was dead didn't mean she could relax. When someone died, their energy had to go somewhere. Abrupt deaths were the worst because the energy was potent, like it was hyped up on adrenaline and desperate for a new host.

It slammed into Rox with enough force that she stumbled. She felt the sudden urge to get down on all fours and howl, then get up and attack the entire compound. She could do it. With so much energy coursing through her, she felt like she could run laps around this place, dodge bullets, break through walls and tear off handcuffs.

Shaira gave a low growl, and Rox narrowed her eyes and bared her teeth. She was the predator now and for the first time in a very long time, she wasn't afraid. Rox would have advanced if Shaira hadn't lowered herself to the ground, resting her head on her paws. Rox fought against her instinct to attack and closed her eyes. Her breathing drowned out all other sound until she felt like she was in control again. When she opened them, Shaira had inched closer, but still remained low to the ground.

A small wave of involuntary energy swept from Rox to wind itself around Shaira. Rox cautiously walked over and held out her hand, palm down, hoping that her actions would be understood as an apology. They needed to work together. It was just them, against who knew how many more guards, in search of Sam and Walter, not to mention a woman she had never seen. Literally. So even if she came across her, Rox would have no way of knowing she was the woman they were looking for.

Lightning followed by thunder rolled across the sky, and Shaira waited until it ended before she got up and led the way. In a perfect world, they would hide the bodies, but this was far from perfect. Hell, they were barely on the border of functioning, so Rox just left them there. The guard whose energy she stole would wake in a few hours with a horrible headache. He would notice his partner's body and would definitely call for back-up. Time was not on their side.

They crept along for ten minutes before the outline of the main house appeared through the darkness. They were much closer than Rox would have preferred, but it was hard to gauge distance in the rain. A stone wall about waist high bordered the main house on the northwest side and acted as a natural barrier between the house grounds and the rest of the clifftop. They made their way over and crouched with their backs pressed against it to catch their breaths.

Shaira's ear flicked, and Rox was beginning to learn that meant trouble. She reached out with her energy and felt three guards approaching. Rox drew herself into a ball and sank as low to the ground as she could, hoping the wall would provide enough cover to keep her and Shaira in the shadows.

"You think we got 'em all?" One of the guards asked as they drew nearer.

"How should I know? I'm here just like you."

"I'm just asking."

Rox held her breath and glanced at Shaira. The wolf was lying belly down in the mud, her head once again resting on her paws.

"Two don't seem like enough to come rescue nobody from a place like this," said the guard who hadn't spoken.

One of them inhaled like he was drawing from a

cigarette. "Well, we got this place locked the fuck down now. So nobody getting in or out."

"Connor said they came up the cliff side. That must be where our defenses are the weakest."

"It's also a cliff, Jermaine. A natural fucking defense against anyone."

"Suppose. But they must be pretty desperate for them to try and break in this place, just the two of them," he chuckled. "Shit, man, that wouldn't be me."

A lighter struggling to ignite filled their silence before it was tossed over the wall. "Damn rain."

"Conner catch you doing that 'n he'll have your balls, you know that, right?"

"Jermaine, stop being such a pussy."

The other guy laughed. "C'mon. Let's get to the end and then circle back. I don't think anybody else is coming or they'd have showed by now."

Rox rested her head back against the wall as cold fear settled in. Sam and Walter had been captured, and the only other person who could help them was Curtis, who was busy working on an extraction plan and under instruction to leave them at sunrise.

The rescue plan now entailed rescuing the rescuers.

What was she going to do? Sam hadn't shared with her *how* they planned to get Val out. She looked over at Shaira as fresh tears ran down her face with the rain.

"What are we going to do?" Rox whispered.

Shaira stared back at her as if waiting for Rox to take the lead. But Rox had spent so much time running, she never thought of herself as a leader. Maybe now was her chance.

There was a woman being held against her will somewhere in the main house. Maybe Rox was Val's chance at escape, and sitting there with her back against the wall, crying because she was afraid wasn't helping anyone. The longer she waited, the higher the probability she would be found. And she wasn't alone. She had a wolf. A wolf which had to be evolved. Or maybe wolves were just naturally intelligent. It didn't matter. Sam and Walter would be able to take care of themselves. She would focus on Val.

"I guess it's up to you and me," Rox said as she rubbed Shaira's head.

She was about to get up, when Shaira gave another low growl. They stopped and waited for another trio of guards to pass. When they were well out of eyesight, Rox lifted her head to formulate a plan to get them inside the main house.

In the end, it was dumb luck they didn't get caught when they sprinted from the wall to the side of the house as a pair of guards exited through the front door, looking the wrong way.

Rox and Shaira clung to the side of the house and waited until she couldn't sense their energy anymore. Shaira ran up the steps with Rox close on her heels. Rox cracked open the door and stuck her head inside, and upon immediate reflection realized that it was probably not a good idea. But lucky for her, an exit sign provided enough light for her to see that no one was in the foyer.

Shaira slipped in between her legs and sniffed the air. Rox shut the door behind her, making sure to twist the handle to ensure it didn't click when it closed. Rox leaned against the wall to catch her breath. A round table sat in the middle with a vase of fragrant flowers. Its juxtaposition against the true nature of this place caused Rox to shiver.

Shaira's nails were silent against the carpet as she crept forward. They made it to the end of the entryway where a dim light allowed Rox to make out the layout of the building. Straight in front of her was a grand staircase that curved up and disappeared to the left, where muffled sounds of a conversation trickled down over a balcony. To the left and right of the staircase stretched a single, long hallway with doors at both ends.

Shaira pushed past her and took the hallway to the right, staying in the shadows. Rox followed, thinking it was best to stay together. Just around the corner was an alcove that she guessed served as the main office. There was a guard sitting behind the desk, his feet propped up and reading a book.

Why couldn't he be listening to music? With headphones.

Shaira slipped passed him unnoticed and stopped in front of the door at the end of the hall. Rox laid on the floor and peered into the office again. This was going to be difficult. Go too quickly and he might catch the movement in his peripheral vision. Too slowly and he might look her way.

She could take his energy. But then she would be amped up on adrenaline whilst trying to go unnoticed, and that was always a recipe for failure. Her stomach growled and she scooted back from the door frame. Using her abilities burned through calories like a high intensity workout. She would have to eat something soon or she would be good to no one.

Rox stood, took a deep breath, and crept in three big strides past the main office. When she got to the other side, she kept going and pushed open the door at the end of the hall.

A kitchen. She wanted to cry.

There was an industrial-sized refrigerator and stove top. Cabinets without doors lined the walls so no one had to guess where anything was kept. It was meticulously clean and smelled of disinfectant. Twin, deep, stainless steel sinks sat beneath a window overlooking the back of the house that faced the cliff. Rox walked over to look out when two guards walked past, their backs to the window.

She dropped into a crouch.

A back door was off to the side of the sink. The top half was made of glass and was covered by a sheer curtain. In the kitchen's center was a large, rectangular table. A basket of fruit was the centerpiece. She crept over and grabbed an apple before she realized there was no way to eat that quietly, so she took a banana instead. She peeled it and finished it off in two bites. She grabbed two more and started to munch on one when Shaira signaled to her with a low snort.

There was a set of stairs off to the right of the refrigerator. Stairs or refrigerator? But, damn, she was hungry and those bananas had done nothing. She peeled the third one and started eating it as she reached for the handle, then stopped. There was a list clipped to a magnet on the door. It looked like some kind of rota.

She slipped her fingers between the rubber of the door and the rest of the refrigerator and pried it open just a sliver. She used the light to read. It was a meal schedule. She skimmed down the names looking for Val.

Valence?

It was close enough.

Shaira ran up to her just as she heard someone cleaning their boots at the back door.

"Shit!" Rox closed the fridge and followed Shaira up the steps before she realized that she was leaving a trail of muddy footprints directly to her location.

The door knob turned and Shaira sprinted up the steps, her nails lightly tapping on each one until she disappeared around the corner on the second floor where her nails silenced. Rox stopped midway, the kitchen down behind her and the second floor up and to her right. She pressed her back against the wall and waited.

The voices she had heard from the foyer were clearer up here. Two guards were talking soccer, or football as Josh would say. She took each step slowly until she reached the top. The hallway was dark, the wall sconce dimmed to provide almost no light. There were four rooms between her and the voices at the center of the hall. The scent of mildew rose from the carpet, and the air felt old and heavy from the sea. A few paintings hung on the walls on the staircase as well as between the rooms, but it was too dark to make out an image.

There was another exit sign just above her and she used its light to read the list she still had in her hand from the refrigerator. Valence was in room 208. Rox looked at the numbers on the door nearest her. 201.

Brilliant.

Whoever had come in the kitchen was rummaging in the fridge, and Rox hoped that he wouldn't draw the attention of the two guards talking at the center of the hallway – or the guard looking for a snack wouldn't decide to come and join them.

Sitting there waiting felt like an incredible waste of precious time. She peered down the hallway and noticed Shaira standing in the middle of the floor, her tongue out, waiting. If either of the guards stepped back and looked their way, they would see a great big wolf standing in the middle of the hall. Rox laid her head back against the wall and thought of what to do next. She assumed there were another four rooms on the other side of the hallway. If she were on the 201 side, then Valence had to be on the other side. There was no way Rox could sneak behind them without being noticed. The hallway was too narrow. They would sense her whether they had special abilities or not.

Time was ticking and she began to panic about sunrise. She squatted in the shadows and just stopped short of banging the back of her head against the wall in frustration when a scream brought her to her feet. The conversation between the two guards stopped, and Shaira moved against the wall. Rox turned and crept back down a few steps as she heard one of the guards step back from the railing into the hallway.

"203?" the guard said.

"Who else could it be?"

"Fuck, I hate that woman. I'm not going in there. It's your turn."

Another scream sliced through the hallway. Someone

from another room joined in, but the sound was different. A male.

"Shit, she's going to get them all riled up again."

"I hate working in here. These people ain't right," said one of the guards. "What do you wanna do?"

Rox pressed her chest to the floor and peered around the corner.

"Shut her the hell up." The guards started towards 203, walking slowly, like they were half expecting someone to jump through the door.

Shaira was no more than ten feet away from them, low and ready to attack if necessary. She waited until the two guards passed her before she continued down the hall to the other side of the staircase.

Rox would have laughed if the guards weren't drawing closer. Then she remembered the guard in the kitchen and spun to look down the steps. All was quiet that way. He must've left.

The sounds in room 203 stopped, and Rox peered back around the corner to see that the guards had also stopped.

"She gives me the creeps. What's her ability?"

"Bitch can hear a bat shit in a cave." Had she heard Rox and hoped that she was there to help? Or was she trying to warn the guards that they had an intruder?

The screams started again.

"I'll go downstairs and get the doc. Maybe he can give her something to help her go back to sleep."

"We'll only have to hold her down while he tries to stick her. And last time she bit a fucking chunk out of my arm. Shit, I still got a scar from her. We'll get the doc afterwards."

He holstered his weapon and pulled a heavy ring of keys from his pocket. "*Goddammit*, turn on the light, Martin."

Martin hesitated. "You sure? I don't want to wake up the others."

The guard with the keys stomped towards the steps, and Rox pushed to her feet. Surprise was her only advantage and a gun firing would alert the entire compound, so she put her hand on the handle of her knife. Rox reached out with her energy and started to syphon some of his. Her heart picked up its pace as she took more from him. She saw the moment it began to affect his coordination because he stumbled into the wall.

"You okay?" Martin shouted.

"Yeah! Damn light." The guard stopped just shy of the stairwell and held up the keys towards the exit sign. He found the key for room 203 and retraced his steps to unlock the door.

"Shut the hell up," he growled as he disappeared inside.

Rox looked back towards the kitchen again and then back to the second guard, Martin, who was still standing in the hallway. Beyond him, Shaira was quietly sniffing the floor outside of each door in search of Valence.

There was the sound of skin meeting flesh, and the scream wavered.

Rox felt her anger peak. She took a single step, but then stopped. The guard in the hall would spot her before she got in range to do much of anything. The screaming started again, but this time it was reinforced with base, like 203 had something to prove. A smile spread across Rox's face.

But then a thick crack and the scream turned into a cough.

"Hey, we're not supposed to interact with them," Martin said as he crept closer to the room.

"Stay in the hallway and tell me if you hear someone coming."

Ever since waking up with no memories, Rox had this feeling that she had, at one time, *belonged*. It wasn't something she could put her finger on, let alone explain. But she knew in a way that defied logic she was a part of something bigger than herself. And it drove her to action, to make silly mistakes, trust the wrong people, and make awfully bad choices. But whoever she had been, she never wanted to be the person hiding around the corner.

It was just the two of them, and she had surprise on her side.

Rox stood on the top step and breathed in as much oxygen into her lungs as she could. When she turned the corner, she pulled. Martin's energy fled his body and slipped along the invisible tentacles leading back to her. It hit with such a force she stumbled backwards. Her vision narrowed as her pupils dilated. She could do this.

Martin's knees gave out, and he fell face-first onto the carpet. Rox froze, but the adrenaline wouldn't allow her to stay still. She pushed some of the energy towards the opposite end of the hall where Shaira was up on her hind legs, her front paws raking against the door as if she could scratch through it. No way the guard downstairs would stay put. They were making way too much noise. She needed to hurry.

Rox entered the room fast and quiet, but her rhythm broke when she saw Martin's partner straddling the woman.

He was tightening a belt around her neck, and 203's face was purple, long past red. His thighs pinned her arms by her body, and she was using what little strength she had left to try to buck him off.

The guard sensed Rox's presence and turned to look over his shoulder straight into her punch. It threw him forward and his head bounced off the headboard. Rox grabbed him by his hair and smacked his face against the headboard once more before she yanked him off the woman.

She was going to have to finish him quickly because he was big. Rox aimed for his face and kicked him hard. She heard something pop, and she was fairly certain she had just broken his nose and her toe. When she put her foot down, pain lanced up her leg and she stumbled. That delay was all he needed. Martin's partner yanked her off her feet. Her back slammed against the floor before her hands could break her fall.

The guard pulled her towards him, and Rox kicked out again with her good leg. The heel of her shoe cut the skin just under his eye and he fell back into the lamp bolted to the nightstand. When it broke, it left jagged edges of plastic sticking up. The guard recovered much too quickly and reached for the gun Rox had forgotten she carried. Adrenaline did that. It sped up the action processes and slowed down the thinking ones. Her foot connected with his groin and pain shot through them both. She stumbled into him and he grabbed her. They wrestled for a brief moment before his sheer size overpowered her. He had her up by her neck and her back was pressed against the wall when the barrel of her gun slammed into her jaw. Another blow to her stomach stole her breath, and her focus.

The safety clicked off just as 203 slipped the belt over his head from behind. The gun fell to the floor as his fingers raked at his neck. Rox slumped forward as 203 placed her foot in the small of the guard's back. He was strong, and she was lifted off her feet, but she used the ends of the belt and his back as leverage. 203 was a small woman, not as tall as Rox or as broad, but there was a grim determination in her like she knew this was the moment she had suffered for. And the guard somehow knew it too. Panic made him erratic as he swung at her without connection.

Rox moved out of his reach and aimed her kick at his knee. It made an awful sound, and he went down, but 203 didn't let go. Instead she spun around, using the extra leverage she gained from being higher. Rox wasn't sure if 203 had been trained in hand-to-hand combat or if the woman had been on the receiving end of too much abuse, but when the guard's body went slack, 203 continued to hold on for a few seconds more. When she released his body, he fell to the floor.

The room was silent for a good long while before 203 finally exhaled. Rox lowered her hands to her knees and exhaled a sigh of relief. This was *not* part of the plan.

A second wave of death's energy slammed in to her and her legs gave out. She sat down hard on the floor as her entire body was engulfed in pain. She had no idea her nose was broken until it popped back in place, followed almost immediately by her toe.

Stars formed behind her eyes as the room tilted. Nausea gripped her, and Rox threw up the bananas. 203 came over to her and reached out a hesitant hand just as healing energy seeped out of Rox to engulf 203 around her throat where the skin was raw and bruised. 203 stumbled, uncertain about what just happened.

"I'm looking for someone named Valence," Rox said. "You know her?"

203 swallowed a few times before she responded. She nodded and pointed down the hall. "Get the keys."

Keys! Of course.

Rox turned back to the guard, and her hand shook when she reached into his pocket. It wasn't that she regretted what happened to him – he had been beating a defenseless woman so he hadn't deserved kindness. But Rox knew death. She knew the moment when the brain could no longer formulate a scenario in which it survived. She knew the feelings of confusion. And sorrow. Sometimes, there was anger, but sometimes death was too swift for anything but its arrival. And still there had been other times when Rox hadn't realized she had died until she woke from its embrace. She had felt death's touch more times than anyone should, and it was cold and indifferent. Death did not care if you were fighting for a good cause or if you had just one more thing you needed to do.

Rox swiped at her tears with the back of her hand, and the pain from a recently broken nose brought her thoughts back to reality. She didn't have time for this right now. She needed to get to Valence before others came. She scooped up her gun and half expected the hallway to be filled with armed guards, but when she stepped out of 203's room, it was empty. Even Shaira was gone.

Rox jogged down the hall to room 208 with 203 close on her heels. "This Valence's room?" She asked her new companion.

203 nodded. Rox looked down at the keychain and groaned. It was too dark to read the writing on the keys. She crept to the exit sign on this side of the hallway. A staircase very similar to the one she had come up was at the end. She leaned her head around the corner. It was dark, and thankfully empty, and Rox breathed a sigh of relief.

The door opened quietly and Rox dropped the keys in her pocket as she slipped inside. It was dark. And quiet. She reached out with her energy and found that someone else was in there, but their energy was ... sedate, like they were asleep, but the bed was empty. The only sounds were the steady tick of an invisible clock and the *dinks* from the rain as it beat against the side of the house. Thunder rolled across the sky and the room lit up for a brief moment when the flash of lightning cut through the curtainless window.

A woman sat in the corner next to the window with her back to the door and her forehead running sideways against the wall in a back-and-forth motion that made a soft swishing sound.

"Valence?" Rox whispered.

The swishing stopped. The woman lifted her head and brought it down forcefully against the wall before she resumed swishing.

This was not a good sign. Rox wasn't sure what she had expected, but it had been something along the lines of gratitude. A smile. Loads of thank-yous. Worst case, someone who was scared to leave and would require a brief pep talk.

Rox took a step forward. "Look, Valence, you don't know me—"

Her head shot up again to smack down against the wall. This one harder than the last.

Just then the floorboards creaked behind Rox and she spun around. It was 203, and she was still carrying the guard's belt. Shaira came trotting in just then, her nails clicking out of rhythm against the hardwood floors.

Energy slipped free from Rox along an invisible pathway following the wolf. Shaira brushed passed her and sat in front of Valence. The wolf barked softly and the woman stopped. Her head turned slowly in their direction. Shaira licked her face, and Valence started to scream.

"No, sh!" Rox ran over to calm her.

"Not real! Not real!" Valence squeezed her eyes shut and then started to hum.

"They experimented with her brain," 203 said softly.

Rox closed her eyes and tried to get a sense of what was wrong with her. Val's energy was weak, but not from an ailment. There was nothing for Rox to actually heal.

"I-I'm afraid … " Val whispered.

Rox opened her eyes and scooted closer. She reached out her hand like she was going to touch her, but decided against it. "Yeah, I've not been here that long and this place scares me, too."

Valence shook her head. " … that you're not real."

Rox didn't know what to say to that. How long had Sam

said she'd been missing? Eight months? That's a long time to have someone experiment on you. Especially your mind.

Rox extended her hand, letting Val determine their level of intimacy. "How about we get out of here? Your brother, Sam, brought me. With your father."

Shaira barked.

"And her." Rox couldn't help but smile.

Valence's fingers dug into the wolf's fur, and for a moment Shaira just sat there, somehow knowing not to move.

"We need to go," 203 said from behind them.

"Please be real," Valence said, softly.

"We are," Rox said. "C'mon, Shaira. We need to get out of here."

Shaira stepped out of the embrace and licked Valence's face once before she turned and padded towards the door, her nails resuming their rhythmic beat. She sniffed the air and trotted down the hall, stopping every now and again to make sure the three ladies were following.

"Hey, wait—" Rox whispered, as loudly as she dared when Shaira turned left to go down the grand staircase to the lobby, but Shaira just kept going.

The guard who had been reading now lay halfway up the steps, his throat open and his blood staining the carpet.

Rox's energy reached out to heal him on its own accord, and she had to force her legs to keep going. She had just thrown up the only sustenance she'd had in hours, which meant she was running on pure adrenaline. Her only options were to continue to steal energy from others or find something hearty to eat. She couldn't afford to waste anything on healing someone with injuries as severe as his.

She kept going and followed Shaira into the kitchen, which thankfully remained empty. Rox grabbed the last three bananas from the fruit bowl. She passed one to 203 and another to Valence. 203 shook her head, but Valence took hers and peeled off the skin before taking a bite. Her hands were bloody, and that's when Rox noticed Shaira's fur was matted in blood. But Rox looked no better. The sections of her clothes that weren't spotted in blood were caked in mud. How she had survived this far without Sam or his father was nothing short of miraculous.

Rox went over to the window and looked outside. The rain had picked up, making it harder to see. She hoped that meant the guards had sought shelter and would wait for the storm to pass before they resumed patrol.

Curtis said he was going to find them transport. Transport meant wheels. Wheels meant a car. Rox remembered there had been a small road leading up from the beach. That's where they needed to go. She needed to find that path and follow it to a main road. Or at least as close to a main road as she could without being spotted.

And then what?

Shaira would protect 203 and Valence until Curtis arrived. 203 had a belt. Rox looked down at her holster. She'd also leave them the gun. Then Rox would go and look for Sam and his father. It'd have to be a quick look because time was running out.

Daylight was coming.

Dead zone

Meita opened her laptop and her fingertips flew across the keyboard at such a pace Josh wondered if she were human. "You said there was no network."

She nodded. "There isn't. I'm just checking a few things before I shut it down."

Josh glanced down at his watch. It was the middle of the night, no more than an hour or two before dawn, and he was walking into an illegal research facility pretending to be someone he wasn't. He had his ability, which would put the odds in his favor to make it out alive, but just barely. First rule of being an EO: never rely solely on your ability.

They had passed a security checkpoint about a half-mile back and their driver was told to keep straight until they reached the main house. The road was narrow and carved its way through a dense forest. It was obvious that the road was designed with unnecessary twists and curves to ensure no one could approach at top speed – or leave at one. This was private property, yet technically it belonged to no one. This place wasn't on a map – printed or electronic. It was just a dead zone.

A chill ran down his back. Josh reached out with his mind and felt for anyone in the woods. He couldn't sense anyone, but that didn't bring him any comfort.

Meita said there were no networked systems. Not even a closed circuit one. Watership Down was old-school. Surveillance was conducted by guards who roamed the perimeter at regular intervals. Logs and files were handwritten and then stored in fire-proof cabinets. Information was relayed with a walkie-talkie. No cell phones, laptops or tablets above ground. Guards had to be recommended for an assignment here and the vetting process took a year.

Employees at Watership Down were on a two-by-four rotation: on for two weeks, off for four. And they received full pay and unparalleled benefits. It was the ultimate gig if you didn't mind saying goodbye to civilization for a couple of weeks. And your conscience. You had to say goodbye to that if you could accept being a warden at an illegal prison for unlicensed and unethical human experiments – even if those humans were evolved.

Josh didn't like their plan, but he was short of options. He reached out with his mind again and still came back with only the driver's.

"That's a new look on you." Her laptop was closed, and she was staring at him.

He had watched a video that showed him how to look ten years older by adding gray highlights to his temple and some more on top. He then used concealer to add wrinkles to his face and some eye shadow under his eyes to give the appearance of bags.

"We're walking into the unknown, with only one another for backup. We won't be able to signal anyone else for help," he said.

She nodded that she understood his concern, then asked, "Who are you?"

"My name is Jan Brotzeit, and I'm in charge of Special

Projects at Coffee House." God, he hoped her information was accurate. Coffee House? That sounded like a cafe and not some organization involved in human experiments.

"You know if this goes south, I'm as good as dead too," she said.

The car pulled beneath a carport situated about five hundred yards from the main house. Someone yanked open the door, and the long muzzle of a gun was pushed inside. "This is a restricted area."

They both raised their hands, but Meita was the first to recover. "The guardhouse up the road told us to come this way."

"What?"

"The guardhouse—"

"I heard you, but we're on lockdown." The guard seemed genuinely confused. "Nobody in, nobody out."

Josh cleared his throat, coming out of his shock. "But I have an appointment. Look, my name is Brotzeit. Jan Brotzeit."

The guard stepped back from the car and reached for his walkie-talkie. "Hey, I got a Brotzeit here. A Jan Brotzeit. I seem to remember something about a visitor, but I thought we were on lockdown."

There was a moment of radio static before a voice came through. "Yeah, his name's on the log. Hang on."

"Sorry about this," the guard said, and his hand shook a little.

Lockdown, Josh thought. Something must have happened because the guard was clearly on edge. Josh used that to his advantage and made a move to get out of the car.

"Hang on, Mr Brotzeit—"

"I shall not hang on." Josh continued to get out of the car, and the guard planted his feet and raised his weapon.

"Sir, I said—"

The radio crackled. "Hey, Connor said let him in."

"But we're on lockdown," the anxious guard replied.

There was a moment of radio silence, and Josh thought they might be forced to leave. His ability wouldn't be enough at an armed facility like this. They would have to think of something else, and fast, because he wasn't leaving without Rox.

The radio barked to life: "He's one of the benefactors or some shit. Just escort him, okay, and don't let him out of your sight."

Josh pinched the bridge of his nose and closed his eyes as he breathed a sigh of relief. He reached out with his mind, and it took a few seconds for him to quiet his own thoughts enough to hone in on the guard's.

... rich asshole. Love how the rules never apply to these guys. My head's about to explode.

That's when Josh noticed the guard's black eye. Someone had attempted to break onto the premises tonight. They were apprehended, but not easily. The guard's face connected with the less deadly end of a pistol. His thoughts were scattered and his adrenaline was still spiked because he was struggling to focus.

"Turn around," the guard said, and Josh turned and placed his hands on the roof of the car. The guard began to pat him down.

"Busy night?" Josh asked.

That's one way to put it. Two nut jobs sneaking up the cliff-side to break someone out. Nobody gets out of this fucking place. Only way out is to stop breathing. And even then, they'd just revive your poor ass. Hell, even death's temporary in this place.

"I have my assistant here with me, she accompanies—"

"Not tonight, she don't. Clearance is for you only. I don't need to radio in for that one."

Josh knew the guard was serious so he didn't push the issue. He told Meita that she would have to wait in the car and then turned back to the guard. "My umbrella's in the boot."

Dude, I will shoot your ass after the night I just had. "No!" The guard barked. *We just lost six men tonight. And Rick was a beast! Whoever took him down was no fucking joke.*

Lightning flashed across the sky as the guard led Josh to a nearby golf cart. Once they were in, the guard rolled down a sheet of clear plastic tarpaulin that would cover the sides of the cart as they drove through the rain.

As they made their way towards the main house, Josh couldn't see much, but he sensed at least half a dozen men out on patrol. They were also nervous and counting the hours until sunrise.

The guard parked at the base of the front steps to the main house, but they were both drenched by the time they entered. "Wipe your feet," the guard instructed.

Josh wasn't sure how much difference it would make, but he did as told. The guard rounded the corner as Josh recognized the tart smell of copper in the air. Josh slowed and reached out with his mind. Something was wrong. The foyer ahead was empty, but there were people upstairs. Some of their thoughts were caged, like they were incapable of finishing a thought.

Drugs. The people upstairs were being drugged to keep them docile.

"Oh shit!"

Josh saw another guard halfway up the steps. Blood covered his face and it looked like a chunk had been taken from his neck.

The guard turned in a circle like he wasn't sure what to do next. Then he reached for his walkie-talkie and stepped straight back into Josh's arms. Josh kicked his legs out from under him and the guard fell forward into a chokehold. When Josh felt his muscles relax, he yanked up and put all his weight on the side of the guard's neck. The snap sounded much like dry wood breaking apart in the heat of summer, and it reverberated through the hall, killing the silence. He dragged the body into the office and closed the door behind him. Josh scooped up the walkie-talkie the guard had dropped and ran up the stairs. His mind already reaching for Rox.

CHAPTER SIX

Rescue attempt

Shaira took the lead once they were out the back door. She led them along the side of the house, between the wall and the bushes that bordered it. It wasn't a lot of space and they had to crawl through the narrow opening, but the shrubbery was dense enough to provide good cover.

They were about to make a run for it across the opening between the house and the wall when 203 instructed them to wait. A pair of guards were out on patrol, but these two were a lot less talkative.

When they had moved out of earshot, Shaira was the first to cross and Rox was the last. She leaned her head back against the far side of the wall and had a renewed sense of hope that they were going to make it. They were still a long way from the US, but at least they were out of that house, and that had to be a good sign.

Just as quickly as she settled into that hope, Rox had to let it go when she noticed that Shaira wasn't with them. She wouldn't leave them, and if she had been discovered, they would have heard.

Val tapped Rox on the shoulder and pointed in the direction of glowing eyes fast approaching. Shaira stopped in front of them and motioned with her head to follow.

Rox took a step after her, then remembered her earlier resolve to find Sam and Walter. She was so close to escaping this place that the temptation to keep running felt sweet. She had found Valence and she had also rescued someone else. It would be foolish to risk her life to go back to look for Sam and Walter. Besides, she wasn't trained for this. She'd been lucky to survive this long. And it wasn't like she knew where they were being held.

Well, they weren't in the main house, which meant they had to be in the labs. But that could be anywhere in a place like this!

No. The smart thing to do was to locate Curtis, and he'd get them to Yosemite. They would get back to the US and then devise a plan – a proper plan – to save Sam and Walter.

But how long would that take? Sam's face materialized in her mind and she could have sworn she felt one of his energy pulses. Her breath caught and she battled between screaming in frustration and sobbing with indecision. She stamped her foot against the ground, splattering mud across all of them and let out a string of silent expletives.

Rox got down on one knee in front of Shaira. "I need you to take them to Curtis. I'm going to look for Sam and Walter." She wasn't sure when speaking to a wolf like a person became sensible, but it was clear by the fact that she was going back to look for them that she had lost all common sense.

"We're splitting up?" 203 shared her concern of separating.

Rox reached for her gun and passed it to her. "This is how you take the safety off." She wrapped 203's fingers around the grip. "Plant your feet. Eyes open. And squeeze."

203 shook her head. "I've only fired a gun once, when I was a kid."

"Shaira will protect you."

"How?" 203 looked unconvinced.

"Just follow her lead. When she crouches, you get low. When she runs, you run." Maybe this wasn't such a good idea, but she couldn't just leave Sam and Walter here. All she had to do was look at these two to see how horribly this placed treated evolved ones. "Look, I've got to go back. I need you to take Valence and follow Shaira."

Shaira circled them before loping a few paces away.

"Find your way to the main road. I'll meet you there. Wait for a man named Curtis. He'll know what to do." Rox was about to turn around but stopped. "If you don't see him, then ... then make your way to a town called Cabarete. Ask for a man named Yosemite. He'll get you back to the States."

"I'm Canadian."

"Close enough." Rox wasn't sure why, but she pulled 203 in for a brief hug. "Now go!"

Rox watched until they disappeared into the darkness. She hopped back over the wall and wondered how the hell she was going to find the labs. It wasn't until she was halfway back to the kitchen that she realized she should have asked 203 for directions.

Since waking, Rox hadn't been particularly religious. She'd seen some things, had some things happen to her that could be easily explained with or without the existence of a god. But she offered up a silent prayer that Shaira would lead them to safety and another that she would find Sam and Walter before it was too late for them.

Despite the rain, the sky was brightening. She didn't have long before dawn put in an appearance, and she had no doubt that if Curtis found Valence, he wouldn't wait for them. She didn't have the time to take things slowly anymore. She picked up her pace and the ground tilted like it was rising in front of her. The excess adrenaline she had from taking other people's energy was almost gone.

She felt three guards approaching and slipped back into the bushes. She siphoned a little of their energy until their radios erupted. The rain made it hard to make out what was going on, but she assumed that someone had found Martin and his partner. Or the guard who had been bleeding out on the steps. Or perhaps the two guards lying by the bench near the cliff. She didn't want to think about the possibility of them finding Shaira. The wolf would put up a fight. But no matter how intelligent or evolved, she couldn't stop bullets. She wasn't invincible. And neither were 203 and Valence.

The three guards made a hard left and ran past the back of the house in the direction she had come. Rox had a choice to make – keep going forward or turn back.

She was about to turn around when she saw movement straight ahead. It was a little shed just beyond the house on the side of the kitchen, about two hundred yards away from her. She would have overlooked it in the rain if it weren't for the guard exiting.

Could that be the way down to the laboratories? Her head said to go back and check on Shaira, but something was pulling her in the opposite direction.

The door was locked, but Rox smiled at her wisdom for keeping the keyring. Her luck held because the first key worked, and she slipped quietly inside. She turned and walked straight into another guard. It took them both a moment to register each other as a threat. He recovered first and reached for her. She quickly sidestepped him but didn't see the desk until she was lying sideways over it. His fingers scratched along her neck as he pulled her up by the back of her shirt. She reached for his energy, but his fist bloodied her nose before she could get a grip, and that really hurt because it was still sore from earlier.

A boot connected with her ribs and pain exploded down her left side. She heard Josh's voice shouting to get to her feet, and for a moment she wasn't sure if it was his actual voice or if she were reliving one of their training sessions. She was kicked again, but this time she held on. The guard lost his footing and fell back into his overturned chair, his back arched upwards, causing his head to slam against the corner of the filing cabinet. For a moment, she thought she might have killed him when he didn't move, then a huge wave of energy drained from her.

"Shit!" Rox turned in a circle, searching for the keys. She had to get out of range quickly because she was involuntarily healing him.

She grabbed the edge of the desk for support when

another wave of her energy left. There! The keys were by the guard's hand. She stepped over the trash can and made it to the door. She looked for the keyhole, but there wasn't any. "Ah, come on!" She spun around just in time to avoid the downward thrust of the guard's knife. Her ability had just healed the man trying to kill her.

She backed away and attempted to hop onto the desk, but banged her ankle on the edge and went down painfully on her side. He brought down the blade just as she slid out of the way, and its tip sliced into the wood of the table top. She grabbed the nearest thing and slammed it into his head. His head whipped around and she was able to hit him twice more before he went down.

She pulled the knife free as more energy seeped from her. She didn't have long. She stood over him trying to decide what to do.

This place was bad. And everyone who worked in it had to be evil. Why else would they allow such horrible things to happen? Evolved ones were human. Why couldn't everyone see that?

Tears flooded her vision as she shuffled closer to him. His convulsions stopped, but his body continued to pull at her. She wanted to justify her actions by saying he would be dead anyway. But the truth was she didn't know how long he had. The fact that he was taking from her meant there was still hope for him.

Another wave of energy left her, making her knees give out. She thought of Josh, his son, Jay, and of the family she was desperately searching for.

Why did it have to be kill or be killed?

Rox lifted the knife. If she were smart, she'd just get it over with. But what she was about to do was wrong, even if it was for the right reasons, and he deserved that one moment to defend himself.

She didn't know his name, but this was a man's face that would stay with her for as long as her memories held. Tears flowed freely, and she lowered her head in shame. What kind of healer had she become? She had the ability to end suffering, give people second chances. Yet ...

Death's energy engulfed her. It was fast and heady. She knew she didn't have long before it would dissipate, so she had to ride the high and the feelings of invincibility while they lasted. She went back to the door, and without the imminent threat of attack, she noticed the palm print panel.

The tingling of her nose distracted her, and she cried out as the bone snapped back in place for the second time. The throbbing in her ankle eased as she pulled the guard over to the door. It was awkward and difficult, but she placed his right hand on the panel and the name Connor Chatsworth scrolled across the screen. A soft click sounded when the latch released, and the door opened. She squeezed through the small opening and looked through. About a half-dozen steps led down into what she hoped was the underground laboratory.

Rox stepped through and was about to pull the door closed when she realized that the other side also required a hand print. She would have no way of getting back out this way, so she settled on using the nearby trash can to keep it propped open.

Satisfied that the door wasn't going to close, she crept to the bottom of the stairs and tried to get her bearings. This area was different from the main house. Up there, the look and feel was rustic and the air was heavy with the scent of sea and mold. But down here, things were shiny and new. The hallway smelled of antiseptic. The lights were too bright to be natural. Doors dotted both sides of the hall, and each one had a small window positioned at eye level. She looked up for surveillance cameras, but didn't see any, and she wasn't sure if that was a good thing or not. Down here, things felt … off.

This was the laboratory.

She went to the first door on her right and looked through the narrow window. A man was lying on a table that looked too uncomfortable to be called a bed. There were straps across his chest and legs. He looked dead, and Rox instinctively reached out with her energy. He was alive, but barely.

She stepped away from the door, hoping she wouldn't start to heal him. Then shame filled her when she realized that she was choosing to leave him there, all of them – people no different than her – to be experimented on.

Rox backed into the opposite wall and scared herself. She had to focus. Dawn had to be just over the horizon, and she still needed to find Sam. She would grieve later for those she couldn't save. She crept down the hall and looked through the window of the door to her left. She'd found them!

Her luck held when the door opened without the need for a key or a handprint. She couldn't believe it, but they were going to make it. Sam and Walter were tied to their chairs with their backs to one another. When she stepped through the door, Sam stopped struggling and looked up.

A wave of his energy pulsed through her, and she smiled. "Some rescue—"

A sharp pinch and a sudden build-up of pressure just underneath her recently healed cracked rib made her look down. Rox watched in confusion as a blade slid free. *Where had that come from?* A hand tangled in her hair and yanked it back and to the side. Her throat itched like a row of mosquitoes had lined up neatly along her neck in a coordinated attack.

Her lips moved, but no sound came out as warmth spread down her chest. Was she bleeding? She touched her throat and pulled her hands away, but her vision wouldn't focus. Her legs gave out, and she wondered how she got on the floor. Her eyes closed as the sound of someone shouting grew in her head.

～

Absence

Sam screamed behind the tape over his mouth until he started to choke on his own saliva. The air felt sucked from his lungs. He couldn't breathe and was beginning to hyperventilate. His father was shouting, but Sam couldn't hear him over his own muffled cries.

He locked eyes with hers, and his breathing slowed. An ache started in his chest as he watched her still. She was a healer, but there was no way she could heal herself from this. She wouldn't have enough blood.

He couldn't feel her anymore. It was like a dull ache had settled in his chest. He lifted his head and looked at the woman who had just killed her. She was leaning over Rox with a sick smile on her face, like she had won a round of cards and not just taken someone's life.

He promised her he was going to kill her. She may not be able to understand a thing he said with the tape over his mouth, but he knew she understood he was issuing a threat. And a mortal one at that. It was in his eyes and the tears that blinded him.

Dammit! He had just met Rox. He didn't even know her last name. All she wanted was to find out if she had a family. If she had belonged somewhere. She didn't deserve this. None of this even made sense. Maybe he was cracking under the pressures of leadership. He always thought his brother, Mika, would take over after their father retired. Sam had never been interested in running Halo.

The woman stood up and shoved Rox's shoulder with her foot. Nothing. She took Rox's knife from the sheath and then set about checking her pockets. Sam channeled his rage and waves of energy began emanating from him as he focused on the different spectrums of color forming, colors he had no words for and had only seen when he used his ability. He struggled against his restraints in frustration when he realized that no matter how far ahead in time he jumped, he was still trapped in the chair.

Abdominal pain broke his concentration and he was brought back to the here and now. His right arm felt numb under the weight of his body and the chair. He had jumped to the time when the woman was standing over him with the knife he had given Rox. Sam screamed behind the tape and pain exploded throughout his stomach when she kicked him. His nostrils felt like they might rip as he tried to pull in more air. He attempted to curl away from the next blow, but it landed on his shoulder. The next few were across his chest and one landed on his chin. His chair slid backwards across the floor from the next blow and the room faded for a brief moment.

She stooped down over him, the knife back and ready to strike. Sam braced himself as if coiled muscles could stop a sharp object, but then her radio sounded. She paused as voices shouted through the walkie-talkie at her hip. He tried to listen, but the sounds of his heavy breathing made it impossible.

The woman's boots spun around and fled from the room. Guilt racked Sam's mind when he looked at Rox. She hadn't moved since she had fallen to the floor. Halo had done this to her. *He* had done this to her.

Sam allowed the pain to shut down his body. He would sleep for a few minutes. Just long enough to gather his strength, because when he awoke, he was going to kill a lot of people.

Desperate

Consciousness slammed into Rox just as quickly as it had left. Her eyelids felt like they were sewn shut as she reached out to the first energy source she could, and drew. The thing about healing deep wounds was that it was excruciating. The stitching of tissue and ligaments, veins and arteries felt like hundreds of thousands of ants nibbling at her skin. The urge to scratch was undeniable.

After losing consciousness twice, the pain finally eased and her muscles lost some of their tautness. She gained a semblance of coherent thought, but nearly lost it when she tried to take a deep breath. She hadn't even known it was possible for her pores to hurt. And she was brutally cold. Her teeth chattered.

She thought about turning her head, but slipped back into unconsciousness when moving her neck felt as if it had been tethered to a chain of molten lava. She stayed in that in-between place, between death and life, until the worst of the healing had finished.

She attempted to open her eyes once more, but her right one wouldn't cooperate and the blinding light in her left eye forced her to shut it again. The memory of exactly what happened eluded her, but she knew she had died. Nothing felt like coming back from the dead. Every nerve ending reanimated as blood flowed through her veins. Every cut and broken bone from the past few hours tore at her consciousness. The first thing she was going to do when she could stand would be to turn on the heater.

A bolt of energy slipped beneath the cold, and Rox shivered as it washed over her like a recovered memory. She wasn't alone. She felt the hairs on her arms rise, and the shiver along her spine was only partially caused by the room's temperature.

Sam.

Her skin grew warm and her teeth stopped rattling. For a moment, she felt like she was floating. She lifted her head, and her memories from the past four years fell into place with the weight of certainty. Her stomach rumbled. It was so empty that it hurt, and the putrid smell of her own blood made her gag. Acid burned its way up her esophagus only to get stuck in her throat, and for a moment, the pain made her forget how to breathe.

The sound of movement pulled Rox back to her surroundings and her thoughts centered on Sam. He had seen her die, and he was witnessing her revival. She wanted to curl away from him, but lacked the strength. The only person who had been privy to that was Josh. She always felt exposed when she returned to life.

More sounds of shuffling and a bit of moaning once again broke her concentration. She pushed herself up to a sitting position and realized just how low on energy she was. Each pulse from Sam helped, but she needed more than just drips; she needed to *consume* energy. Or eat. She would give anything to eat.

It took a moment for her vision to focus after she pried her right eye open. Sam was lying on his side, half his face swollen and bruised. He was holding his head up off the floor because that was all he could move. The rest of him was zip-tied to a chair.

"S—" Rox thought breathing hurt, but when she tried to speak, the room disappeared behind a tunnel of blackness.

Pain was sobering. It focused the thoughts and cleared all doubt. It was precise in its purpose and Rox knew that they were in trouble. Serious, life-threatening trouble. Whoever killed her had slit her throat. While she didn't have the exact memory, she had the pain.

Right now, their only advantage was the fact that she hadn't stayed dead. She was famished and low on energy, but she was their only hope of making it out of there alive. She had to get up. Keep moving. Remaining in one place made for an easy target. She knew the routine: one foot in front of the other, don't stop, and don't look back.

Rox pushed up to her feet and slipped. She whacked her knee, but it was the ache in her side that stole her breath. That was a stab wound still in the midst of healing. Muscles remembered. Her body might heal quickly, but the soreness, fatigue and the pain of recovery were something her ability couldn't alleviate.

It took all her concentration not to scratch.

Another wave of energy hit her, and Rox looked up to see Sam still grunting behind the tape covering his mouth. But she couldn't afford to focus on him, not if she wanted to get up off the floor. She managed to keep her footing this time and reached for one of the counters running around the room's perimeter.

She ignored her pool of blood on the floor and looked at Walter. He was sitting with his back to them. His head was angled up and to the side in the hopes of catching a small glimpse of what was happening. And just like Sam, he was zip-tied to his chair.

She needed a pair of scissors. Or a knife. Basically anything with a sharp edge. She looked around the room, and the enormity of their situation hit her again. Valence had survived in this place for months. How could there be people who thought it was okay to do this to another human being?

Tears spilled down her cheek, creating a trail through the blood. She wanted to curl into a ball and wait until the healing had completed. Maybe, if she closed her eyes and took a nap, when she awoke she would discover this had all been a very horrible nightmare. She hadn't died twice. Josh wasn't chasing her, and her memories were intact. She knew who she was. Her name was … Sandra. Sandra sounded like a good name. Nothing exciting ever happened to people named Sandra.

A nap was all she needed.

Rox slowly slid down the side of the countertop until she was sitting on the floor. When she woke up, things would be all right. She was worrying for nothing. This was just a horrible dream.

She chuckled; Sandra might lead a boring life, but she had one hell of an imagination. Jumping out of helicopters? People trying to kill her? Actually succeeding at killing her! Yes, a dream made a lot more sense than reality because people who had their throats slit stayed dead.

Her eyes slid shut as the man's grunting grew louder. Rox smiled. In her dreams, she bet she named him Sam because that was her father's name. Maybe her grandfather's? Anyway, it sounded old and strong. Just like him. Actually, the more she thought about it, the more certain she was that this *was* nothing more than a dream. And Sam was the hero, right? Tall. Strong. Attractive. He had the bright blue eyes and copper hair thing going – speaking of which, why did all heroes have to be fair? In fact, if she created a hero, he would have a lot more muscles. Bullets would bounce off his biceps. And he would have black hair. Thick and curly. But bald was also attractive. A smooth head for a sensitive heart. And he would be dark!

Her eyes flew open.

Sam stopped moaning and held her stare.

If she had the energy, she would have laughed, but she was too hungry to laugh, and so very tired. She slowly pushed back to her feet and started to search through the cabinets for something sharp. Nothing about her plan to uncover her identity had gone right. It was time to stop lying to herself. She had no clue what she was doing and the fact that she had just died – again – was all the proof she needed. It didn't matter who she was because chances were they weren't making it out of this alive. She would be experimented on because who in their right minds wouldn't want to understand how to heal. Sam and Walter might just die outright if they were lucky. She wasn't even sure Sam had an ability. Maybe he just sent his energy out to people. Most abilities were banal anyway. Either way, they were all dead.

Rox didn't need to look at Sam to know that he had been following her around the room. She felt his eyes on her the entire time. She wanted to say something, but what?

Rox stopped. Why hadn't she removed the tape from their mouths?

She threw up her hands in self-frustration and almost lost her balance. She steadied herself against the chair Walter was tied to and said, "This is going to hurt."

The edges of the tape were secure, and her hands were shaking too badly to get a good grip on the first try. She scratched his cheek and drew blood with her nails before she was able to peel back a corner far enough to yank it off.

When industrial-strength tape adheres to skin, ripping it off can do serious damage. It was best to go slowly or use a solvent to weaken the adhesive, but they didn't have the time. Or a solvent.

"*Goddammit!*" Walter said. "Didn't anybody ever tell you that the first thing you do is take the tape off someone's mouth?"

A sizable strip of skin just above his top lip was hanging from the edge of the tape. Rox shook her hand until it fell to the floor.

"And where the hell have you been? You just came barging in here like—"

Was he angry at her? What could she have possibly done to make him angry? She was in the process of saving him!

"—and go take the tape off Sam!"

Was he ordering her about? Walter definitely didn't seem like the sensitive type, but she was expecting a little more gratitude.

"This is going to hurt," she said, as she knelt beside Sam.

His came off easier, but it was still painful. There was no blood or chunks of flesh – but it was raw and red.

"You find anything?" Walter said over his shoulder, then grunted in frustration. "Did you get it off him? Turn me around so I can see what the hell is going on."

"Please!" Rox said. "Turn me around *please ...* " *so I can see what the hell is going on*, she mumbled.

Walter was silent for a moment and then he started to laugh.

"Dad, stop." Sam pulled against his restraints. "The drawers were empty?"

Rox nodded and noticed her bloody handprints on every surface she had touched.

"We need to find something to cut through the ties."

The person who had slit her throat had also relieved her of her knife. The gun wouldn't have helped in the situation anyway, but that knife was just what they needed. "I passed a room on my way in here," Rox remembered. "Plus there's an office just up the steps." There had to be a pair of scissors lying around somewhere. "I'll be right back. Wait here."

"Oh, she's a genius, that one."

Rox kept walking. It would take too much energy to turn around anyway. She was going to untie him last.

The dried blood on the soles of her shoes made each step sound like tape ripping off its dispenser as she crept through the hall. As far as she could tell, it was empty, but sound traveled, and so she tried to walk as quickly and quietly as possible. After about the fifth step, she just gave up and took big strides.

The door she had propped open with the trash can was closed. That could only mean someone had found him. Maybe the same someone who had killed her. She tried to remember the specifics, but she was struggling to piece together the last few moments leading up to her death.

Her hand closed over the door handle to the room she had passed when she was looking for Sam and froze.

Rox!

No one was behind her.

Where are you?

She had spent the last eighteen months running, hiding, and basically failing at every turn. She had cut herself off from anyone who could help Josh find her, which meant anyone he could buy. And when you don't have money and you're on the run, that's everyone around you. It wasn't that everyone she encountered was bad. In fact, she was humbled by the generosity of those who had nothing. They seemed the most willing to give and always without requiring anything in return. It was just that without the benefit of time, it was impossible to know who to trust. And without the ability to trust, it was impossible to make a connection. And if she had learned only one thing in the past year, it was that people needed people.

She hadn't been prepared for the loneliness. She doubted Josh wanted to hurt her. In fact, she understood that in his own way, he probably still loved her. His ability wasn't a one-way street. The more he invaded her thoughts, the more she could experience his, but she never had any control over them. She felt his love in his thoughts. But then again, he could have been manipulating her mind into thinking that. And that was the root of the problem. How was she ever going to trust him again when he could control her thoughts?

Are you in the lab? Stay where you are; I'm coming.

Rox pushed open the door with the certainty that she was done playing the victim, she would rather die than go back or remain here for a moment longer. She stopped short. She had forgotten about the man lying there. He still looked as if he was only asleep, though Rox was pretty confident that his rest was anything but voluntary. His energy lacked the fluctuations of someone still tethered to consciousness. Most people's energy ebbed and peaked like waves – sometimes sharp and sometimes peaceful, even while they slept.

She hated herself the moment she realized that she was going to draw from him. She wouldn't kill him, but she would leave him lacking the energy to protect himself, which wasn't terribly different from his current state. Guilt consumed her, but not as much as her desperation.

Shared enemies

Removing Sam's zip ties with a flathead screwdriver was messy and painful, but her body healed each of his cuts. What she took from the man in the other room wasn't enough to bring her to full strength, but it did take the edge off the hunger.

"That the best you could find?"

Both Rox and Sam looked at Walter.

"You're not helping, Dad."

It took a full two minutes to make a hole through the tie and another minute to widen the hole so that it weakened the integrity of the plastic enough to break it. While he was freeing his hands, she set to work on the tape around his torso and then the zip ties around each ankle.

Sam and Rox worked together in silence to get Walter

free. He stood up and almost immediately fell over, but Sam caught him. That's when Rox noticed his leg. She leaned closer. There was a hole in his trousers, but she didn't see any wound.

"You healed me," Walter said.

"You're welcome."

But Walter had already turned his attention to his son. "I'm not leaving her. Not when we're this close."

Rox slapped her forehead and instantly regretted it. How could she have forgotten? "She's alive."

A look of pain crossed Walter's face. "Where is she?"

Rox shook her head. "We had to split up. I sent her to Curtis."

"You did what!"

Sam stepped between them.

"What is your problem?" Rox shouted. She had died trying to save them. Literally. "I saved your daughter and could've followed her, you know."

"We don't have time for this," Sam said.

"Where is Valence?"

"You're right. We don't have time for this. Valence is with Shaira and 203. I sent them to Curt—"

"203?"

Rox spun away from Walter and headed for the door. "The other woman I saved. After fighting off *two* guards bent on beating the crap out of her." But her hand hovered above the handle. She hated it when logic ruined a perfectly good rant. She could be prideful and walk away from them, but she needed their help to escape. Surely it was daytime by now and Curtis would be gone.

"Shaira is with her?" Sam asked.

Rox nodded. "The way I got in here is closed now. You need a handprint to access the door."

They stepped out into the quiet hallway. "We came in from the southwest entrance. Down the hall on the left and through a few doors thataway," Walter said.

Rox's broken footprints showed the path she took to find the screwdriver. She tried not to think of the man she was leaving behind. She had taken his energy and now she was leaving him to who knows what. She wanted to be above that type of cowardice, but she had died once already, and dying again wasn't going to help anybody.

"Go," Sam whispered to her. "You take point."

Their progress was noisy. Between Rox's shoes and Walter's heavy breathing, someone was bound to hear them. She stopped to remove her shoes, but Sam told her to leave them. "When we get topside, you'll need them and you may not have time to lace up. Never take off your boots unless they're making you drown."

Walter snorted. "If they're making you drown, you ain't kicking hard enough."

They came to an intersection, and Walter leaned against the wall and rubbed his eyes.

"You okay?" Sam asked him.

"Bright light." He pointed up to the ceiling. "It hurts my eyes."

Really? Mr Tough Guy was going to complain about the lights being too bright?

He must have caught her look because he exhaled and banged the back of his head against the wall. "Look, there's a chain of command in these types of situations and you fall out of it. That's real dangerous ... "

She couldn't believe his audacity. "I just saved you!" If they weren't escaping certain death from a locked underground facility that they didn't know how to get out of, she would have shouted her frustration at him.

He nodded like she said something that was obvious, but was still somehow irrelevant. "Sam and I have been in this situation before and niceties don't cut it. Do what we say, when we say it."

Was that supposed to be some kind of an apology by way of explanation? She had risked her life to get his daughter to safety. And she came back for them! Tears of frustration welled. She wanted to walk away and leave his sorry ass for the sick psychos to experiment on. But the likelihood of getting out of this alive exponentially increased if they stayed together – she didn't need "experience" to know that.

"Which way?" she asked, disdain clearly in her voice.

He pointed to the left.

Rox reached out with her energy now that she had a little more strength. There were definitely people this way, but not close enough that they would see them. Something was blocking their direct flow of energy, so she peered around the corner. There were three doors on the right and a set of stairs leading up at the far end of the hall.

"H-how was she?" Walter whispered.

She hated the vulnerability in his voice because she wanted to stay angry at him. But a part of her understood that he was just a man worried about his daughter. And with good reason. Valence was not in a good way. The woman's mind had shut down, and that was something Rox couldn't heal.

"She recognized Shaira." Which meant that her mind wasn't totally broken, right? "And 203, the other woman, she helped me. They'll make it to Curtis."

Walter inhaled deeply, like he was trying to get control. He opened his mouth as if to say something else, but Sam stopped him. "We can see for ourselves later."

Rox felt a surge of energy as they neared the first door and it took everything she had not to just inhale it. She never studied the different types of energy people put off – she wouldn't know the first way to go about something like that – but she had enough experience to know that someone in that room was in a lot of pain.

She peered through the narrow slit of glass on the door. A man was tied to some kind of reclining chair and a woman in a white lab coat spoke to him while she injected something into his IV bag. He was definitely conscious because he was screaming behind a strap that was secured around his mouth. Another guard, dressed in the same black uniform as Conner, stood with his arms crossed against his chest. He shifted his weight like he was uncomfortable, but he held his position.

"What?" Sam mouthed.

How did she explain it? Torture? Treatment? Another experiment of some kind? It seemed that this entire facility was dedicated to taking people's lives away from them. Had she been a prisoner at a place like this? Is that why she was still no closer to remembering who she was?

Rox siphoned energy from the guard and the woman in the white coat simultaneously. She didn't want to alert them by taking too much, but she kept up a steady pull. It was going to hurt like hell when Rox came down from all the "borrowed" energy, but until then, she was going to take as much as she could.

Sam lowered Walter to the floor once more and signaled that he was going to sneak past and scout the other rooms. Rox nodded and continued to draw from the two inside. She knew she had hit the maximum she could take from the guard when he wiped the sweat from his brow.

She turned to Walter and slowly lowered her hand over his leg. "I can't take the bullet out, but each time the wound opens, I'll automatically heal it." The reconstituted skin would prevent it from moving about with the blood flow, but it would mean surgery when they found a doctor to reopen the wound to remove the bullet.

"Don't. Save your energy," Walter instructed her.

Rox rolled her eyes. "Trust me, I don't want to. And stop scratching. You'll just tear the new skin."

Once she was sure he wasn't going to give in to temptation, she made her way past Sam to check the final room. She was about to peer through the glass when a man in a white lab coat walked out looking down at his tablet.

For a moment they both just stared at one another, but then instinct took over and she struck him. People often hurt themselves when they throw a punch. Especially those who had never done it before. It takes practice and form, and Josh made her practice enough that she had both.

Fear made her fast and muscle memory ensured she

put her entire weight behind it. The tablet fell to the floor just moments before he did. No one moved. The clatter followed by a solid thump seemed to scream in the hallway, but the only thing louder than their brief altercation was the muffled cries of the man in the room behind.

"Here," Sam said as he moved beside her. "Help me get him up the steps."

There was a door ahead of them that was similar to the one she had come through. If they could get him up there, they could use his handprint to get out of the area. Rox nodded, but almost fell on her face when she tried to lift his legs. Her adrenaline levels were dropping again. Healing Walter had taken more than she thought, and then she had just put a lot of power behind a physical assault.

"You okay?" Sam asked.

She was starving, that was what she was.

The man's energy came to her on the barest of commands. She hated taking from people, especially if they hadn't given their consent, but she hated the prospect of being trapped there even more.

"Let's go," she said, and grabbed his ankles.

The name Dr Kevin Lim slowly ran across the screen; the light turned green, and the lock released.

"Bring him in," Walter said, as he hobbled through the door. "Lie him down here."

That was a good idea. If anyone was trying to come after them, they would have a hard time pushing through the door with Kevin's body lying up against it.

Where the passageways and the rooms behind them were clinical and white, this hallway had puke green walls.

The industrial floor tiles of the labs gave way to ecru-colored carpeting. This was the administrative wing, the place where paperwork got filed.

Up ahead was silent and much darker than the area they left behind. This was the nine-to-five section because whoever worked in these offices had gone home for the day. At the far end of the hallway was another door, but something about it made Rox think it was the last one before they went topside.

The room to the right had a light on and a name was stenciled onto the door's glass. She was about to peer in when an intense feeling of rage settled over her. The urge to scream started in the pit of her stomach and if it hadn't been for the lingering pain already pulsating around her neck, she would have roared.

Where are you?

Josh opened up his thoughts and nothing short of anger flooded her. He had found the room where she had died. He had seen her blood, and he was scared for her.

Rox reached out to steady herself against the wall, but instead accidentally rested on Sam's chest. It was like a switch had flipped and all the rage was gone. The tiny electric impulses that had shocked her whenever he was near had ceased. The hum that sat at the base of her skull no longer strummed as the tension in her muscles eased.

"You okay?" he asked.

She was far from okay. They were trapped inside an underground laboratory of unknown dangers, she had just died, she was so hungry that her body was beginning to consume itself, and the man she had thought she loved but ultimately had to escape was on the other side of the door, down the corridor, and around the corner from a man they had left to be tortured and another unconscious man from whom she had stolen energy.

This was more than she could handle. She was about to lose it, and even though she knew that this was not the time to come apart, she wasn't sure she would be able to stop herself.

Sam led her away from the door and lowered her to the carpet so she could sit down.

"Deep breaths," he said to her, and they breathed together for a while.

"I'm starving," she whispered when her heart rate slowed.

"Are you often hungry after?" Sam asked.

Rox nodded.

"Low blood sugar," Walter said.

Sam stood up and peered into the room, while Walter took his place. "Steak. Medium."

"With English mustard," she said.

"And horseradish mashed potatoes."

Rox wasn't sure if she ever had horseradish mashed potatoes.

"Side of creamed spinach," Walter continued and smacked his lips together.

Rox lifted her hand and it trembled as if with fear. She closed it into a fist and laid her head back against the wall. She just needed to breathe through it. In a few minutes, the intensity of it would pass. It would inevitably return, but for now she needed to focus on making it from one moment to the next.

"You like wine?" Walter whispered.

Rox snorted. "No. I actually hate it." Josh used to buy expensive bottles that they would drink together.

Walter nodded like she had finally said something he agreed with.

Rox glanced up at Sam, but his eyes were closed and even in the dim light of the hallway, she could make out a crease in his forehead. Waves of energy pulsated off him in a frequency much higher than before. She pushed to her feet, but Walter held her back. Could Walter not feel the pressure change? She looked down at him, but he didn't seem to take notice. She turned back to Sam, but there was only empty space.

"C'mon. Let's go," Walter said, as he pushed himself to his feet using the wall for support.

A sound came from inside the office, and then someone shouted, "Wait!"

Walter yanked open the door, and Rox stepped in behind him. Sam had someone bent over the top of the desk, his hand squeezing the person by the back of the neck. The man was dressed in a white lab coat that had red streaks running down the front lapel. He looked up as they entered and let out a high-pitched scream.

Then Rox remembered the blood. Hers. And with her skin tone bordering on waxen, she was sure the poor man thought he was looking at a zombie.

"Look, I didn't do anything," he said. "I don't even want to be here."

"Shut up," Sam said.

Rox stepped closer, and the man all but body-slammed

himself back on the desk to try to break free. "Wait! Wait, wait-wait-wait, look, I can get you out of here," he said.

And everyone stilled.

"Look, I'm on your side. I swear. See, look, here … " He tried to reach into his pocket, but Sam kicked his foot out from under him so that all his weight was on his torso. "It's just a slip drive, man, it's just a slip drive!"

Sam reached into his coat's pocket and pulled out a small circular plastic case about the size of a coin.

"What's that?" Rox asked.

"A file copier," Sam explained. Inside was an automatic data retrieval program designed to do only one thing: copy files. They didn't need to be physically inserted like an external drive. They just need to be within range.

"You a reporter?" Walter asked.

He shook his head, but kept his eyes on Rox. "I'm, I'm really a paramedic."

"What?" Sam and Walter said simultaneously.

The man shook his head. "Long story, but if you let me up, I can help you get outta here."

"Why?" Rox asked. No one helped without expecting something in return.

Sam eased his hold on him and the man lifted up a bit. "We can help each other. I can get us through the doors and you can take care of anyone who tries to stop us." His lip was swelling to match the size of his cheek and his teeth were red tinted with blood.

Rox fought against the pull of her energy to heal him. It wouldn't require a lot, but she didn't want to waste any of it, especially on someone who may not be an ally.

"Who are you?" Walter asked.

"Kamal Sheppard." He tried to come around the desk to shake hands, but Sam gave him a look that made him rethink that.

"What are you doing here?" Rox asked.

"Nuh-uh." Walter waved his hand. "All we need to know is how he can help us get out?"

"Well, Walter, he could be planning to blow this place up," Rox said with frustration. "And that could impact our ability to 'get out'."

"No!" said Kamal. "Look, you don't know half the shit that goes on in this place. If you just let me copy what I'm supposed to, then I can get us out of here."

"'Supposed to'?" Rox said. "What do you mean?"

Walter waved his hand again. "Another thing we don't have time for." He turned his attention back to Kamal. "You help us get out of here and we won't kill you. Deal?"

It was hard to believe that Walter was one of the good guys. And, apparently, Kamal was feeling the same way. He looked at the three of them with a scrutiny that said he really didn't want to answer that. His eyes settled again on Rox, and he shivered. "W-what happened to you?"

"She died," Walter said.

Kamal shook his head and tried to step around the desk, but Sam grabbed him by the back of his neck again and held him still.

"Look, man, I won't say anything." His voice cracked. "I don't know you. You don't know me. I just, I just want to get out of here."

Rox couldn't control it anymore and a little bit of

her energy leaked out and healed his broken nose. She stumbled forward onto the desk. "Do you have something to eat?"

Kamal looked at her like maybe he hadn't heard her correctly. "Like a sandwich?"

Rox nodded.

"Look in the drawers," Sam told him.

"There's nothing in them but paperwork," Kamal said. "I just checked."

"We can stop at the cafeteria later," Walter quipped. "But for now, we gotta keep moving. Bring him with us."

"And then you'll let me go?" Kamal asked.

"I doubt it," Walter said, as he peeped out of the door and then signaled for them to follow.

Hard choices

There were two other rooms between them and the next set of stairs. Sam took the lead, but pushed Kamal along ahead of them. The carpet masked any sounds from Rox's shoes as they crept along single file, bodies pressed up tightly against the wall.

Sam couldn't believe she was alive. He knew she was a healer, but to witness her rebirth from something like that was remarkable. Rox was powerful. He could slip forward a few seconds in time, but the ability to hold onto life like that was … he struggled to find any word other than extraordinary.

Sam knew the look of pain, had experienced it himself

and had done his fair share of dishing it out, but Rox had handled it well. A part of him was afraid of her. Someone with that ability could do a lot of bad things. There were moments after he and his father were captured when he thought she was in on it.

But then she died. And no one could fake that. He had seen death up close, witnessed the look in a man's eyes when their final heartbeat had come and gone. Good men who just needed a few more moments to get things sorted, and evil men whose final thoughts were trying to accept that they had been bested. To see death is to be a part of it. He thought he had felt her life slip through him when he held her back in the clinic at Halo. But to feel it ripped from her, taken so callously and with such malice caused a stirring in him he hadn't been prepared for.

It was in that moment Sam knew she told the truth. Only someone desperate would have agreed to accompany them, and then die trying to save them. Knowing that she had found Val was more than he could process at the moment. In all his years of living, he had never met anyone so giving. She had the perfect opportunity to escape with Val. Back on the beach, they had already told her how to get back to the US, so it wasn't like she had much to lose by leaving them, which was exactly what he would have done. The mission parameters had been simple: get in and get out with Valence. She had done that.

Yet she came back. Shame filled him at how they had used her.

"You guys are the ones who broke in, right?" Kamal whispered as they neared the final office.

"Great, another genius," Walter said. "Just shut up."

"Sh!" Sam brought up his hand. "Someone's in that office."

He signaled for Kamal to look through the window, and Kamal jumped back like he saw something that didn't agree with him.

"Sheppard?" the voice called from inside.

"Shit, man. He saw me. What do I do?"

Rox accidentally brushed against Sam, and a tiny pulse of electricity from Rox slid up his back and around to the center of his chest. It was jarring and soothing all at the same time. He shook his head and then grabbed the doorknob. "You'll think of something," he told Kamal and shoved him in.

"We're going to leave him, right?" Rox asked.

Walter shook his head. "We need all the help we can get."

"And if he tells whoever he's talking to in there about us?" Rox asked.

"Then I'll snap both their necks," Walter said.

Sam leaned as close to the door as he could without being seen through the narrow pane of glass. The door was thinner than those in the labs, but still thick enough to prevent anyone from eavesdropping.

Rox reached out to steady herself, and Sam caught her before she made contact with the wall. The electric pulses between them ceased and he felt calmer. Perhaps more in control, like the next few seconds were just a fingertip away.

"I just need to eat," she said. "I've spent too much energy."

And it dawned on him just how valuable she truly was. Sure, studying her ability could be the key to immortality, but she was also the key to getting everyone out alive. She could heal the injured and steal the very life force from the enemy.

"Take some of mine," Sam said softly.

Rox shook her head and stepped back until she was up against the wall. "We need you at full strength," she said.

"I'm not sure I'll be much use in a fight if I'm carrying you," he countered.

"She'll be fine," Walter said and stepped between them. "Won't you, Buttercup?"

Rox's stomach replied for her and then the office door opened. Kamal exited and turned around, propping the door open with his shoe. "Yeah, you're lucky. This place is going to be insane over the next couple of days, trying to uncover who leaked our location," he said.

"Luckily, we got word or it could have been a lot worse," said the voice from inside. "Hey, you sure you want to drive home in this storm? It's pissing out there."

"Yeah, I want to get out of here," Kamal said, pointing to his face.

"Glad you got away and they only roughed you up a bit. Catch you next time, bro."

Kamal closed the door and walked towards them so that he was no longer visible from the doorway. His smile almost broke his face in half it was so wide. The blood from his nose had dried around his nostrils, but the stain around his mouth and on his lapels remained.

"And this," he whispered as he pulled something from

his pocket, "is for you."

A candy bar. Chocolate covered.

Sam looked confused at first, but then he saw Rox snatching it out of his hand and ripping open the wrapper.

"Guess no one ever told her about folks bearing gifts," Walter snorted. "Shit, girl. Not so fast. You'll choke."

"I guessed that her ability consumes a lot of calories," Kamal explained. "That's why she was asking for food."

"That door lead out of this hell hole?" Walter asked as he pointed to the top of the stairs.

Kamal nodded. "We need to hurry. Morning shift should be here."

They exited the underground lab into a shed. Steel lockers with mesh door frames lined the walls. There had to be at least twenty of them, and they all held weapons. Sam yanked the handles before he realized that they were locked. "Do you have a key for this?"

Kamal shook his head. "Med staff don't need weapons. Besides, we don't have time, come on."

"We need to make time," Walter said.

Rox started searching her pockets, and Sam assumed she was looking for the keyring the guard had taken from her. He explained to her that she no longer had it.

"Yo, I wasn't exaggerating." Kamal held up his arm and turned it out so that they could see his watch. It was too small and the room wasn't bright enough, but his point was taken. "We have literal minutes before the 'changing of the guards'. We gotta get outta here!" There was panic in his voice and he was taking small steps towards the door.

"I'm not leaving without Val." Walter was looking at

Sam when he spoke.

Sam rested his fists on the desk and lowered his head. "Sheppard, stop moving." And the man froze a few paces from the door.

He didn't want to leave without his little sister either, but they had been compromised. Somehow, Watership Down knew they were coming. It was a miracle they weren't executed on sight. They couldn't save anyone if they were dead, and so their best hope – no, their only hope – was to escape.

"They'll move her," Walter said as if reading Sam's face. "They'll shut this place down and move or kill everyone in it."

"I got her out!" Rox all but shouted.

"But did she make it off the property?" Walter spun around to face her. "This place is situated on the edge of a cliff, miles away from town. Getting out of this place isn't as simple as walking out the front door."

His father was right, but time wasn't on their side. Rox said that Shaira had gone with her, but a wolf against a semi-automatic wasn't a fair fight. Especially when there would be more than one. And Val didn't have any abilities.

"I am truly sorry to interrupt, but we are out of time," Kamal said. "And I'm your best shot of getting through that main gate."

He was scared. Whatever he had copied onto that slip drive would probably get him killed if anyone found out.

"Son, you take them and get out while you can. I'll stay and make sure she got away."

Sam was shaking his head before his father finished.

"What's your exit strategy?"

"Son, we—"

"What's your exit strategy?" He repeated the question, his voice teetering between annoyance and restraint. He was no good to anyone if he lost his head. Sam knew that anything could go wrong on a mission, and often did, but it was a level head that got everyone out, alive.

He understood why his father didn't want to leave without Val; hell, he hated himself for what they were about to do, but what choice did they have? Sam was a father – *had* been a father. He understood that parents would sacrifice themselves for their children, but what if sacrificing yourself was the wrong choice? What if dying for your child was a waste of your life and theirs? Remaining to look for Val was a death sentence.

"We. Don't. Have. Time. For this shit!" Kamal was past freaking out and headed for the door again, but Rox stepped in front of him.

"There're patrols everywhere," Rox said, looking at Walter. "And they walk in pairs, sometimes in threes. It's only a matter of time before they realize that we've escaped. There's nowhere to hide if you stay behind."

"You broke onto our property in the dead of night to ask for our help, you're hardly the one to offer advice on decision-making," Walter retorted.

"And look where it's gotten me? I've died. Twice."

"Wait. What?" Kamal said.

"You help me find my identity, and I'll … I'll offer my healing to her in any capacity she needs."

Rox had already lived up to her end of the bargain.

They would help her no matter what; she had more than earned it. But Sam sensed that she was trying to get his father to see reason.

The phone on the desk rang and everyone jumped.

"All right, let's go," Kamal said and tried to step around Rox, but she stopped him once more.

"Let me see if anyone's out there first," she said. A few seconds later, she shook her head that no one was waiting for them beyond, allowing Kamal to walk out like he was just ending his shift and on his way home.

Lots of killing

Dawn had breached the horizon, but the dark clouds and heavy downpour made visibility tough. They might have looked less conspicuous if they had umbrellas or ponchos, but there wasn't time for that now. They had to keep moving. Kamal took the lead and the three of them formed a staggered horizontal line behind him.

The wind blew the rain in their faces, and Rox hoped it would wash away some of the blood. She reached out with what little energy she had just as the ground shook with thunder. They exited the shack on the east side of the property. Kamal said he would take them to the carport where they would get into a buggy and drive to the main gate. There, he was hoping to explain that he was getting them off the property as they were valued guests who had gotten attacked during the breach. No one was confident the plan would work, so Rox was preparing herself for a fight once they got there.

The sky lit up a few moments later and gave them their first view up ahead. A surge of energy cracked through the air and Rox reached for it on instinct. The lethargy she was feeling moments ago was replaced by a renewed sense of vigor. It was like she had consumed death's energy, but without the darkness that usually accompanied it.

She reached towards the sky and took more. Her breath caught, and she wondered how she could have spent the past four years without realizing that all this energy existed. She had been drawing off people, but this ... this was like the energy from the waves on the beach. It was just sitting there, waiting to be utilized.

Rox opened her eyes and stumbled forward. Her hands sank into the mud as the realization hit her that she had all the energy she needed. She was about to laugh, but the urge to sit down consumed her.

Just wait for me, goddammit. I'm almost there.

"What's wrong?" Sam said. He was trying to get her to her feet.

"He's here," she said.

"Who?" Sam wrapped her arm around the back of his neck, and the urge to wait dissipated. This wasn't the first time that Josh's ability to control her suddenly ended when Sam was near. Could it be Sam's energy? Could he somehow block Josh's ability?

"Take what you need from me," Sam said.

She shook her head. Energy was all around her and for the first time she knew how to access it. But the storm wouldn't help her from Josh. She wasn't sure how he found her, and she wasn't going to waste a single moment trying to figure it out.

"Hang in there for me." Sam took her hand and pulled her into a run. As they picked up pace, they let go of one another.

Walter and Kamal were quite a distance ahead of them when thunder rolled and lightning flashed. The hair on Rox rose. For a brief moment, she could make out the carport ahead of them and a little shed that she assumed housed more guards.

Did you hear me? They're coming. Black limo. Now!

Flood lights lit the entire compound as a siren went off. The front doors to the main house swung open and two guards rushed out, their weapons raised. Another one came from the far side of the house and still two more came from the shed that Rox and the others had just left.

Keep moving. I've got the two trailing you.

Shouts erupted behind her as he made contact with the guards. Josh wouldn't be able to maintain his mental barriers while he fought multiple opponents, so she slipped between the cracks in his mind to find out why he was risking his life to help her escape.

Rox was unprepared for the onslaught of emotions his thoughts triggered. She saw things from his perspective. She couldn't exactly understand everything because too many of them were in Spanish and incomplete and went by too fast for her to interpret, but settled just beneath his more immediate thoughts about combat were ones rooted in fear and regret. He felt responsible for an entire group of people, his people. He believed failing her was somehow indicative of his ability to save all evolved ones. He wanted to help her piece herself back together so she could rediscover the simple pleasures of living again.

Josh was not her enemy. In fact, he had become her family. And Jay ... Rox stumbled at the thought of his son. She had become his surrogate mother, and he filled the empty hole that kept her up at night whenever Josh wasn't near.

Rox slowed. But Josh wasn't a friend either. He had helped her, but he had also lied to her. He manipulated her mind and thoughts to serve his purpose instead of helping her find a purpose of her own. He didn't care about her family. He cared about his, and how *he* felt. He had taken advantage of her vulnerabilities and given her the certainty she craved, but it was all for his benefit.

But did he deserve to die? At a place like this? Because that was going to happen if she didn't help him. It could still happen even if she came to his aid, but that didn't sit well with her. And then there was Jay. He had already lost a mother ...

Sam grabbed her arm and pulled her after him, but she wrenched free. There wasn't time to explain it all to him. It was complicated, and she doubted he would understand anyway. Somethings you had to live through to fully comprehend.

Rox stopped and told Sam of the black limo. "Find it and get in."

"What?" Sam looked confused.

"Find the limo," she said. "But, don't let him touch you. It's easier for him to control you that way."

"We can discuss this later. Let's go!" His tone reminded her of Walter.

Rox felt Josh take a hit that brought him to his knees, and she responded on instinct. He was about a hundred yards behind her and outnumbered. Luckily, no bullets had ripped through her flesh yet and so she kept her head down as much as she could and reversed her direction toward the man she had spent well over a year running away from.

Lightning branched across the sky, and she remembered that all the energy she needed was right at her fingertips. She was surprised at how much of it hit her at once. It was almost too much for her to handle and it stopped her mid stride. She watched as the guard closest to Josh went rigid and then fell. The other one pulled the trigger on his taser, and Josh dodged its probes at the last minute.

As soon as she regained control of her limbs, Rox closed the distance between them at a speed that surprised her and transferred all the weight of her next step into a left hook. The guard absorbed the full force of her blow, and she felt his jaw shift as he crumbled to the ground.

Josh plunged a knife into his chest and death's energy slammed into her.

"Incoming!"

She turned in time to see four guards sprinting towards them. They were in a line, the fastest out front, his weapon in one hand and the other pumping up and down with each stride. Despite the perimeter lights, it was still difficult to judge distance because of the rain, but she knew that all any of them had to do was stop, take aim and fire.

She remembered the taser and stooped to retrieve it.
Catch.

Josh caught it with ease, but without another gas cartridge, he could only use it as a club.

The first of the guards was no more than five paces from striking distance, and all the flaws in her plan became crystal clear. There was no way that they were making it out of this alive. It was four against two, and in top form she could only handle someone if she caught them by surprise.

Josh pushed her out of the way as the first guard's rifle came down in a vicious arc designed to knock her unconscious. She scrambled to her feet as the second guard joined the fray.

Fight!

Rox grabbed the knife out of the guard's chest and crouched for the first attack. It was fast and it was powerful. She back-stepped, alternating her lead foot. They needed to end this quickly before more guards arrived from somewhere, but fear kept her on the defensive. The guard attacking her was big, at least more than half her size. And she definitely didn't have the element of surprise.

Rox reached towards her attacker and yanked. More energy than she could contain slammed into her, and she began to shake. The guard wobbled as he took a step back, and then collapsed. She wouldn't be able to do that again until she'd used up some of what she took.

She turned back to Josh just as Sam tackled one of their attackers. The fourth guard was standing on the edge of the fight, his gun drawn and his aim shifting between Josh, Rox, and now Sam.

Why hadn't he taken a shot? Rox had been the most easy target given she had spent the last few seconds relatively stationary.

"Shoot something!" The guard pinned beneath Sam shouted.

The fourth guard swiveled his aim to Sam and pulled the trigger a second after the tip of Rox's blade slid into his stomach. The shot went wide, but grabbed everyone's attention. Sam jumped off the guard just as Josh tased him.

The fourth guard stared at Rox in disbelief before his knees buckled, but then froze mid fall. He righted himself, and Rox wanted to shout at Josh to release him, but that wouldn't solve anything. Everything froze when the guard took aim at his partner and squeezed the trigger.

"C'mon." Rox grabbed Sam's hand and hurried him towards the limo.

Sam hesitated. "What about him?" He was pointing to the guard under Josh's control. "Wait, what the f—"

Rox knew what was coming, but she still flinched when the guard turned the weapon on himself.

"Let's go." She pulled Sam closer to her. "Remember what I said." But the look on Sam's face said that he was having problems processing what just happened.

Bright lights hurtled towards them, and the car hydroplaned a few feet before it came to a complete stop.

Rox froze.

"They're with me," Josh said as he ran ahead of them to meet the car. "Keep moving," he shouted over his shoulder.

The door swung open and a woman stuck her head above the window. "You are twenty minutes behind schedule. Twenty minutes!"

But Josh kept his eyes on Rox, whose energy high was fading.

You're starving. I can feel your hunger. Get in.

Her hands were shaking and her body was seconds away from shutting down. She was beyond hungry. Tears flooded her eyes as the car went over a speed bump too fast. The suspension moaned and they rocked inside the limo. Glasses shattered and the smell of expensive alcohol filled the interior. The woman reached down to move the shards and cursed as she pulled her hand away.

Rox waited for her body to heal the cut, but nothing happened.

I didn't have time to get you anything.

After all she had been through, she had simply wound up right back where she started.

The silence stretched as the tension in the limo grew.

You're not an easy woman to find.

Rox was visibly shaking now. Her body was shutting down and without sustenance, there was nothing she could do about it. Sam reached for her hand and pushed some of his energy to her, and she wondered how he did that.

The window separating the back of the limo from the front lowered. "Think there's trouble ahead. Looks like two guards, weapons drawn and two men on their knees. What do you want me to do?"

The driver's voice sounded steady, like he was giving a traffic update and not about to drive them into a hostile situation.

Sam stiffened. "Shit, stop the limo. They're with us."

"A bit late for that," the driver said.

"Proceed as planned," Josh said, still staring at Rox.

Sam released Rox and pulled at the door handle, but it was locked. "No! Stop, that's—"

"And the other two?" the driver asked.

Do you know them?

And there it was. She had to ask for his help or he would keep going. She wasn't sure if he wanted to prove that she needed him or if he was simply asking if she knew the identities of the two men being held at gunpoint. She was beginning to wonder if she could trust her mind anymore.

"Yes," Rox said quietly. She laid her head back against the seat, too tired to mount any defense. Josh would be able to read her mind as easily as if she were speaking aloud.

"We've room for two more," Josh announced to the driver.

Sam stopped trying to open the door with his shoulder, and Rox closed her eyes. She would have to sit this one out. They should be able to handle the two guards at the gate. They would think of something to save Walter and Kamal. She wasn't sure she liked either one of them, but they didn't deserve to die in this hell. No one did.

Her head rolled to the side and stopped on Sam's shoulder. The car slowed, and the last thing Rox remembered was the sound of Josh's voice.

"Let me handle this."

CHAPTER SEVEN

Turbulence

Josh used his ability to help them release Walter and Kamal from the guards at the main gate. Sam's father hadn't wanted to come, but he had lost the argument given the intensity of the situation. The look on his face said he hated himself for it, but Sam's consolation was that they were all still alive, for now. They would rescue Val when they regrouped.

It was raining hard still and Josh had their driver take them to an airfield that catered to private aircrafts. They passed a helicopter that looked like it was on its last few trips before the car rolled to a stop in front of a private jet. The door lowered and the staircase unfolded onto the tarmac.

Sam was grateful for Josh back at Watership Down, but his instinct was telling him that Josh wasn't a man he should trust. They were far from safe. When one had toed the line between life and death for as long as Sam had, one knew when to keep his hackles raised. The look on that guard's face back at Watership Down had said it all. He hadn't wanted to kill himself but had been powerless to stop it. Josh was a powerful EO, and the fact that Rox had spent the last year and a half running from him was a source of major concern for Sam.

Rox's head rolled against Sam's chest as he gathered her from the back seat of the limo. That she had managed to avoid Josh for so long spoke volumes about her resourcefulness. He wished there had been time to hear her entire story. Why was she running? What did she mean when she said her memories only went back four years? Did she have glimpses of the identity she was searching for or was she just running on instinct?

Rox stirred and turned her head into the crevice between his arm and body as he pulled her out into the rain. They were only a few paces from the stairs, but she would get good and wet by the time he got them aboard.

Sam expected her to open her eyes, but she didn't make another move. She had come back for him and his father, and that was something he would never forget. He grew up with the motto of never leaving a man behind, but he sensed that hadn't been drilled into Rox the way it had been into him. That wasn't something she had learned – that was instinct, and he respected the hell out of her for it.

A blast of cold air greeted them when he stepped into the cabin, and she woke. Her stomach growled and he hoped there was a bag of peanuts or some other confectionary for her.

She was confused by her surroundings, but he watched as awareness settled in on her, and she moved to get down from his arms. He wanted to tell her that he was fine carrying her – it was only a few more steps to a seat – but he kept silent and released her.

Sam looked around the cabin and had to admit he had never been on a mission where they flew in a plane like this. There were three rows of two premium-smelling leather seats situated on either side of the aisle. Just behind the last row on the left was a small couch, big enough to sit three people if comfort wasn't a priority. The rear of the plane had two doors, one on the left and another on the right with a painting separating the two. Another set of seats beneath the painting would have made the most practical sense, but instead there was a counter.

Rox spun away from him and inhaled like a bloodhound that caught a scent. She strode to the back of the plane and ripped off the lid to a platter of food sitting atop the counter. Sam stepped closer because, truth be told, the food smelled good.

Sam heard Josh's voice just before the engines started. "Anything you can tell me about your friend?" he asked her.

"Don't let him touch you," she said around a mouthful of chicken.

"I remember. Anything else?"

"His name's Josh Mendez."

He'd heard that before. Josh ... Josh ... "The wealthy EO activist?"

She nodded.

Shit! Josh had been in the paper a few times. Never a television appearance, though. Sam remembered catching the end of a radio interview Josh did a few years ago when he said he wasn't interested in building a public profile. But the company he owned with his father – no uncle – was known for their donations to EO causes.

Under normal circumstances, Sam should feel at ease being saved by someone like Josh, but the fact that Rox had spent such a long time running from him, coupled with the fact he had just witnessed Josh force a man to take his own life, well, that made Sam a bit nervous. Most EO abilities were benign; but mind control? That was definitely leaning towards malignant.

Sam's ability allowed him to slip forward in time by a few seconds, and up until now, that was the most extraordinary gift he had ever encountered. He had been like that since he was a teenager, and he still didn't properly understand how it worked. Sure, he could ask a geneticist or perhaps a physicist to break it down for him, but that meant trusting someone with the most valuable information about himself. All Sam really understood about his ability was that it required a deep level of focus and an accelerated heart rate, then he could step out of reality and reinsert himself after a few seconds. Anything longer and it was like a rubber band snapping, and he was sprung back to reality against his will. People didn't stop moving while he used his ability, he was just able to see their actions from the outside. Outside of where, he had no clue.

Sam had spent the better part of a decade helping his father and Halo relocate EOs who were in danger, and while they made it a point never to ask about abilities, he knew they had never come across anything so extraordinary as Rox's ability to heal or Josh's ability to control a person's actions.

His father's ability allowed him to see in near darkness yet now that seemed trite compared to what he had just witnessed. There was a lot of money being diverted into grants and other forms of research to uncover why some humans evolved and others didn't. But the problem was test subjects. Human trials were frowned upon by governments, but there were no animals they could safely test upon. Scientists said that experiments were crucial to further understanding the human genome, but there weren't a lot of evolved ones volunteering for such programs. Instead, they were mysteriously disappearing, and it seemed that the federal authorities were slow to react.

That's why places like Watership Down continued to exist. Non-evolved humans were waging a war against evolved ones. It was a silent one that left EOs unprotected and scared. The only recourse they had was to flee. There weren't enough of them to stand and fight, not when most abilities served no value in war. Besides, most of them were like ordinary humans in that they lived an average existence in an average job and had no hopes of ever amassing any type of wealth that could fund a war even if they wanted one. But a few more with abilities like Josh and Rox, coupled with a small team of EOs like his brother and father? Maybe if they could work together, then EOs everywhere could stop running.

Rox ripped off the other chicken leg and passed it to him. He preferred breast if he was honest, but he also knew that food was food. Preference was a luxury often denied in the field. He couldn't mistake this for anything other than what it was: a mission, one that had failed and left them uncertain and definitely unsafe.

Information was his best bet at the moment, and so he

took a deep breath and began to question the one person who seemed to have any answers. "You two ... have a thing?"

The way she turned away from him said that at one time, their thing must have been huge. "He hurt you."

She cleared her throat and shook her head. "Not like that."

"He hasn't stopped looking at you since we got in the limo." And Sam had to admit that kind of "undivided attention" given their circumstances bordered on obsessive.

"I, ugh, I didn't leave on good terms," she said.

There was obviously a lot more to that story, and he was surprised by just how much he wanted to know, but his first priority was to establish if Josh was a threat. A man who could control your actions wasn't someone you wanted on the opposing team, but if he was honest with himself, he probably wasn't going to like Josh much anyway. And it had nothing to do with Rox. OK, it had everything to do with Rox. A man shouldn't chase a woman for almost two years, leaving her afraid and defenseless.

"Why's he chasing you?"

He could tell she was tired. The area underneath her eyes were darker than the rest of her face and the way she was leaning against the seat was a sign that she was struggling to remain upright. Or awake.

He turned around as the woman from the limo stepped onto the plane. She was dressed in an expensive suit that retained its shape despite the downpour it had just been exposed to. Kamal followed behind her, and he looked a lot like Rox. Walter stopped at the entrance and gave a low whistle.

"He must be some kind of de Sade evil," his father said.

"Excuse me?" The woman from the limo turned around to face his father.

Walter pointed to Rox. "She been running from what? This? A man's gotta be into some freaky shit to chase a woman away from this kind of money."

A part of Sam wanted to laugh at his father. His ability to say the wrong thing at exactly the wrong time wasn't the easiest thing to adjust to when he was growing up. Especially after his mother died, but in the end, it was his father's unwavering sense of humor and his infallible will to take nothing seriously that had saved Sam.

"Dad," Sam cautioned him softly, even though he had to admit he thought his father had a point.

Josh boarded the plane last. "We got followers. Buckle up," he said and closed the door.

Sam waited for Rox to choose a seat and sat beside her. He still had a few more questions he needed answering. He hated pushing her when she was clearly exhausted, but he had a feeling he needed more information if they were going to make it back to Halo.

Josh's voice came through the speaker. "Prep for take-off."

Rox got up and grabbed the tray of chicken as the plane started to taxi. She wobbled, but angled herself so she could fall back in her seat, the food still firmly in her grasp.

"You going to share that or is it all yours?" Walter said.

Rox considered it before she handed him a big chunk of white meat, and his father laughed at her hesitation.

"Can I have some, too?" Kamal said.

They were all seated at the back of the plane, nearest the counter because that's where Rox and Sam had chosen to sit. Kamal and the woman from the limo had chosen the three-seater lounge. Everyone had their belts firmly pulled across their laps.

Rox waited until they were airborne before she released her seatbelt and retrieved the plates and cutlery. It was obvious she had been aboard this plane before, and old doubts of her being part of some greater scheme began to resurface. But who would willingly die like she had to save them? Someone who knew they wouldn't stay dead, the darker side of his mind answered.

Rox disappeared into one of the doors at the back of the plane and returned with a bowl of cellophane-covered cheese. Once everyone had a plate, she took her seat again.

"I'm Meita," the woman from the limo said and smiled warmly at everyone.

"I'm Kamal."

They shook hands, and then Meita turned to Walter who put the last piece of his chicken and cheese in his mouth together and nodded his hello.

"I'm Rox." She placed her empty plate in the compartment below the counter, but made no move to shake hands. "And thanks for your help back there."

Meita nodded. "I know who you are. Josh hired me to find you."

That confession took everyone by surprise. Sam watched as Rox swallowed her next mouthful carefully. "How did you know I'd be at Watership when I had made no plans to go there?"

A broad smile crossed Meita's face. "Based on what Josh saw when he connected with you. Then it was down to algorithms, probabilities, and personality traits."

Walter turned his seat around so that he could face Meita a bit easier. "And who'd you share the results of those analyses with?"

Meita pointed to the front of the cockpit.

"Anyone else?" Sam asked.

"No. Why?"

"Because someone knew we were coming, and—"

"Ah yes. I saw that. That's why we changed our plans to arrive much earlier than originally scheduled," she said.

"What do you mean, you 'saw that'?" Walter asked.

Meita popped a piece of cheese in her mouth, and despite the fact that she had been drenched like the rest of them, she carried herself with a poise and confidence that made her immediately untrustworthy. "I charge people for that type of information. But the good news is, I just successfully finished a case," she pointed to Rox, "and my time will be available again after we land."

"What *do* you do?" Rox asked, and the two women stared at one another for a moment that slowly began to turn awkward.

Sam got the impression that Meita wasn't all she presented. There was an agenda behind her friendly demeanor and warm smiles.

"That is information I rarely volunteer," she said.

"Well, let's consider this a rare occasion," Walter said.

Meita had answers they needed, but now wasn't the time to press for them. She had a connection to Josh, which meant she was on his team, and they were on his plane, and he was flying them to an undisclosed location, which meant until Sam knew more, they shouldn't get on anyone's bad side. "Dad."

Walter let the silence linger before he reclined his seat and switched off from the conversation.

Neither of them had forgotten about Val. She had Shaira and Shaira had Curtis, and Curtis would get them to Cabarete. Yosemite owed him, so he would ensure they got back State-side.

Sam should call Halo to give them an update, but when he asked for a phone, Rox cautioned him against it.

"He'll have your call recorded," she said.

"And traced," Meita added.

This was beginning to feel like anything but a rescue. "Any idea where we're going, Meita?"

She looked at Rox before shaking her head.

The seatbelt sign chimed off when the plane leveled.

"Ok, I just have one question," Kamal said. "Does anyone know what the hell is going on? 'Cause I gotta be somewhere—" he looked down at his watch, "like in twenty minutes."

Walter snorted.

Meita chuckled.

But Rox remained quiet, like she was retreating inward. Sam wasn't sure if it was because Josh had found her or if it was because she had died twice since she had arrived at Halo. But either way, they all needed to rest. It had been an epic night, and they needed to lick their wounds and plan for the day ahead.

Sam felt the familiar pulse pass through him as Rox reclined her seat. He couldn't get the images of her death out of his mind, so he turned to look out the window. They were above the clouds now and the sun shone brightly through the window. He pulled down the shade and was surprised when he felt Rox's touch.

"He won't hurt you." Her voice sounded weak from exhaustion.

"What makes you so sure?" he asked.

Her eyes drifted close, but the sides of her lips curled up. "Because I won't let him."

She fell asleep with her hand still on his arm, and Sam wasn't sure why, but he left it there.

"Buckle up," Josh announced. "Turbulence ahead." And then the seatbelt sign chimed back on.

Why

There was nothing more comfortable than hotel bedsheets. She wasn't sure what they did to them, but since waking four years ago, her best nights of sleep were always had in a hotel.

I love you.

She turned to her side and stroked his cheek. *I love you too.*

Shall we order room service?

Mm, I'm starving.

Josh laughed and reached for the phone beside the

bed. *When aren't you starving? It's only been like two hours since you last ate.*

She sat up behind him and placed a trail of kisses along his back while he ordered. She dipped down along his side and nibbled at the tender spot just below his ribs, and he squirmed. She continued around to his belly button and went lower. He sucked in his breath as he told them to bring it in an hour's time.

Aren't you confident, she teased.

After a few minutes, he pulled her up and kissed her deeply. Rox pushed him back on the bed and straddled him, rocking her hips back and forth without giving him access. He reached up and cupped her breast, squeezing her nipple between his fingers, and she moaned her pleasure.

Her eyes flew open at the remembered love-making. Her lips felt swollen, like they had just been kissed. It took a moment for her to realize she was on the plane. She looked around, hoping that she hadn't moaned aloud. Luckily, Sam remained asleep beside her.

They had to leave the food outside the door.

Rox took a few deep breaths to slow her heart rate. Tears flooded her eyes as she pushed the button to return her seat upright. The tray of chicken had been cleared and in its place was a bowl of grapes and bunch of bananas.

You can't avoid me forever.
I was trying my best.
Do you love him?
Rox snorted. *I just met him!*

OK. Good. Maybe I won't make him kill himself.
Not funny.
He feels something for you though.
Get out of his head.

Rox wondered if what she felt with Josh had ever been real or whether it was nothing more than a part of his construct. In the end, it didn't matter. Love without trust was nothing more than desperation.

Even when he's asleep, his thoughts are hard to zero in on. It's like they keep moving between now and ... I don't know. But he does feel something.

Gratitude. I just helped him rescue his sister. And probably a good dose of fear after seeing what you can do.

A suicide mission if I ever heard one. I thought I taught you better than that.

He had. But being away from him for so long had allowed her to discover the parts of herself she had no idea existed. A year ago, she would never have offered to help Sam. But a year ago, she still had hope she could do things on her own.

What are we doing, Rox?
I'm *trying to find out who I was. Am.*
I can help you.
No, thanks.
Why?
Because when you had the opportunity to, you didn't. Instead, you made me think things, feel things that don't feel real to me now.

I was trying to protect you. I only wanted you to move forward. You were so stuck in the past. You still are. Did you ever stop to think that finding out who you were could get you killed all over again?

She had. *A risk I'm willing to take.*

Sam was snoring lightly, and she thought about reaching for his hand again.

Are you really not going to ask about him?

Her hand halted. Guilt shook her fingers and for a moment she was lost in the memories of his laughter. Jay would be sixteen now, and she knew without asking that her leaving had crushed him.

Sam turned in his seat, but didn't wake.

He thought someone took you.

The tears she was fighting began to fall in earnest.

He called me in a panic when he discovered you were gone. I took the first flight back. He swore that one of the anti-EO groups had taken you.

Rox wasn't his mother, but she and Josh's son had taken an instant liking to one another. It was like they were filling each other's void.

I never meant to hurt him.

No. Just me.

I needed some time to think! Without you in my head telling me how to feel.

Is that what you think? She felt his rage and it excited hers.

Then what would you call it? You made *me feel things, Josh.*

That's a very black and white way of looking at it. I simply helped you untangle what you were already feeling and brought those feelings to the surface.

But that wasn't your right! I had a right to work through my emotions on my own. Maybe what I had felt for you could have grown into a real love on its own. Maybe it would never have, but you took the choice from me.

I love you, and I'll be damned if I have to apologize for that. And I know you loved me. I could hear it. Hell, Rox, I could feel it every time we made love.

She used the back of her sleeve to wipe her face. Yes, she did love him. But who could say how much of that was real? Didn't he understand that? Everything would be so much easier if it was real. But he had broken her trust in a way she wasn't sure was reparable. Besides, she might already have a family, and she didn't think she could move forward with anyone until she had answers.

You died back there.

Rox sighed. *Yeah, I know.*

Why'd you agree to help them? Did you think that your past was somehow connected with Watership Down?

She knew her explanation wouldn't make sense to Josh. She wasn't sure how much sense it made to her. *They were looking for someone they had lost, and I guess I knew what that felt like.*

And that was worth getting yourself killed over? Twice?

They promised to help me find my identity.

Rox heard his laughter in her mind. *If I hadn't showed up, they wouldn't be helping you find anything. Because they'd be dead and you'd be coming back to life in some fucking cell. Again! Why would you do something so insane?*

Because I understood what he was going through! I know what it feels like to—

What? Lose someone you love? Go crazy trying to find out what happened to them? And then fight like hell to get them back? I understand more than you think I do.

I'm not going to let you make me the bad guy in all of this.

His sigh was physical. *I don't want to fight. I just found you.*

He had caught her off guard with that one. She chuckled at the idea that he had taken the moral high ground after chasing her for so long.

So, you found his sister?

Yeah, but they knew we were coming.

If she was in the main house, then they were close to selling her off. Whatever experiments they wanted to do with her, they'd finished.

How do you know?

I've known about places like Watership Down for years. I've been trying to find enough stuff on them to shut them down, but that facility is just one of many. We can't afford to close that one until we know where some of the others are located.

A wave of Sam's energy pulsated toward her. His ginger stubble was coming in thick and had covered the lower portion of his face. She was caught by the sudden urge to give it a scratch.

A small sensation bubbled in the pit of her stomach, and she reached for him, but Josh stopped her.

He misses you.

It took her a moment to realize who Josh spoke of.

He doesn't understand why you left.

I never meant to hurt him, Josh.

I told him that.

She wasn't sure what to say.

He's gotten taller.

A smile slipped across Rox's face.

He's filled out, too. You wouldn't recognize him.

Kamal stretched as he sat up from the sofa and grabbed one of the bottles of water from the counter with the fruit. "You slept?" he asked her.

Rox nodded.

"Yeah, me too." He took a long drink. "Any idea where we're headed?"

Josh's voice came through the speaker. "This is your pilot speaking. Wake up. We're landing in twenty."

Once we touch down, your guys can contact whoever they need to.

Thank you.

De nada, corazón.

∽

"Woman"

"The initial report says a female intruder was killed. But you're telling me you can't find the body?"

"Ma'am, we are only just getting the initial reports. Reports are typed and then sent—"

"Do not attempt to *remind* me about reporting protocol." Katherine needed a minute to calm herself. But holy hell, Watership Down was a huge pain in her ass. She had finally gotten a name and location for facility WD-11, thanks to the hard work of one of her agents – her favorite and most talented agent – but now Katherine was being told that not only had the drone tasked with following Meita malfunctioned, but a female intruder had been killed. Katherine hoped to hell it wasn't Meita.

No, she was too resourceful to be dead. She was alive. Katherine decided that until someone presented her with evidence to the contrary, she would proceed as if her best agent was still in operation.

Technically, Watership Down was one of her facilities now that she was the head of GFO, but there was a lot that went on inside WD-11 that Katherine was clueless about.

The guard on the other end of the phone cleared his throat as if he was about to say something, but Katherine spoke over him.

"The latest report I have said that one of your guards, a woman named Mila, confirmed a kill of one of the intruders. She slit a throat and then left the body with two of the five intruders in one of the transit rooms. But according to the protocols you so eagerly referenced, all unauthorized people are to be immediately incapacitated, tagged, and then put in separate isolation cells until you received instructions for processing."

"Yes, ma'am, that is correct. But Connor's in charge of security—"

"Then why am I not speaking to Connor?"

"Because he's dead, ma'am." The rest of his explanation came spilling out like he had been holding his breath. "Connor and ten others were killed, ma'am, and so we had no way of knowing what was going on—"

Katherine laughed. It was a genuine laugh. A comedy of

fuck-ups usually made for good humor.

"Right. So can anyone confirm the identity of any of the intruders?"

"Ugh ... "

Katherine was fully aware of what people said about her when her back was turned. She knew her reputation. And she didn't care. She wasn't a lady, and she never pretended to be one. She was a goddamn woman and it was up to everyone else to figure out the difference.

"Ma'am, Connor—"

If Meita was right and First Lieutenant Walter Watts was there, then chances were his son, Major Sam Watts, was there as well. And if something went wrong, Meita would see them as assets, so she would ensure that Josh teamed up with them. And if they had the healer – provided she was indeed a healer – that could tip the odds of a successful escape in their favor.

There were a total of five intruders: Meita, the Watts, Josh, and this healer. That meant the female Mila killed could have been the healer. As the head of a global research facility that contracted for the US government on all EO-related matters, Katherine knew that the healer held more value than one of her agents, but as a woman who had been in this line of work for over half her life, if she had to choose a survivor, she would choose her agent each time. Good women were hard to find.

"Ma'am, I'm sorry, I think our connection is poor—"

"No, it's fine. I'm just ignoring you." Katherine would have loved video surveillance, but apparently WD-11 was a bit of a luddite when it came to surveillance and security.

Perhaps that's why Meita's drone failed. Katherine would check with the engineering team to see if a jamming device could bring down a quarter-million-dollar piece of government property.

Katherine looked for something from the report that would help her identify the dead body. The dead body that was no longer there! Then it came to her.

"Get me three thirty-milliliter samples of that blood. I will send my courier to collect it. You will give it to him only. Is that understood?"

"Yes, ma'am."

"My courier's name is Richardson."

"Richardson. Understood, ma'am. Should we have a password or something so that I know it's him?"

She took a deep breath, held it for a count of three before she exhaled.

"Ma'am?"

"Sure, because you never know how many Richardsons are going to show up with the same request. Password: zero-dash-one-one."

"Thank you, ma'am."

She laughed another genuine laugh.

"Oh, and one more thing, ma'am. What blood?"

Katherine stopped and took another deep breath. Sometimes, it felt like she spent entire days only moments from slipping into unconsciousness from the many deep breaths she took. Whoever said to take a deep breath never held a real job. "Son, what is your name again?"

"Henry."

"Henry. You're a fucking idiot and I'm going to fire

whoever it was that hired you. To say that I'm wholly unimpressed with you would be an understatement. And I know I sound like some evil bitch to you right now, but that's only because you cannot fathom just how frustrating it is for someone with my intellect to have a conversation with someone with yours. Now. I'm going to ask you a question and I want you to think really hard about it before you answer. Whose blood do you think I'm speaking of?"

There was a long pause before she started to count. If he didn't answer by the time she reached ten, she was going to have him killed.

His voice sounded like he hadn't yet reached puberty when he finally spoke. "The intruder's we took down?"

"Correct, Henry. The report says that your colleague, Mila, slit her throat, and I'm not sure if you've ever seen a person's throat slit, but it's quite messy. Blood gets everywhere, Henry. And so, you should have more than ninety milliliters of blood to work with, but I'm only asking for a small fraction of what's there."

There was another long pause, and she wasn't sure whether to laugh or scream this time.

"Do you understand, Henry?"

"Yes, ma'am, but, but, you see, well, without Connor and his team, ma'am, you see, they're the real leaders here on the ground and the rest of us just follow orders—"

Holy hell. She was trapped in some parallel universe and talking to Henry was her punishment for all the wrongs she had done. She feared that if she hung up, her phone would ring, it would be Henry, and she would be forced to have this conversation all over again.

"... and so, since we didn't know what to do ..."

"Oh my god! Henry, if you tell me you've cleared up that blood I will have your balls. And please don't misunderstand, I am not making a pass at you, Henry. I want you to take everything I say quite literally."

She heard him swallow. She took the phone from her ear and held it to her chest. Her perineum contracted as she roared in frustration.

Katherine Louise Cheung was a second generation citizen. Her family fled their home in the middle of a civil war and washed up on the shores of a first-world democracy in a sinking boat with more holes than passengers. They took trains, buses, and finally a plane before they were given the opportunity to start a new life in some other country that claimed they wanted immigrants – until they arrived. Her parents went from being a doctor and a pharmacist to working in a goddamn laundromat. Her father washed and pressed the clothes of people too lazy to do basic housework and her mother cleaned public transportation toilets on the nightshift. Katherine grew up being teased for looking different. Her eyes were never quite right. Her accent, though better than any native speaker, always made her classmates laugh. The good thing about not fitting in is that she developed a keen sense of observation. And with that observation came the belief that if she could survive the teasing, the isolation, and the disappointment that threatened to suffocate her, good things were in her future. But only if she could manage to rise above it and have a healthy level of self-esteem despite the gum stuck in her hair at recess, the black eye that she knew wasn't an accident on the hockey field, or the one white guy who was nice to her for a week – so nice in fact that she kissed him – but then later found out he told everyone her mouth tasted like soy sauce. If she could survive that, then she had no choice but to be smarter. Unfortunately, at this precise moment, her patience for morons like Henry, who made up the very country she swore an oath to protect, was strained.

"... and so, ma'am, I'm afraid it's all gone."

Her other phone rang, and for a moment she thought it was Henry. So she ignored it and focused on the phone already in her grasp.

"Listen to me carefully, Henry. You have twelve hours to find me a sample of her blood. An undiluted, uncontaminated sample of her blood. If you don't have it ready by the time Richardson gets there, he will kill you. And because it's your parents' fault that you're an idiot, I will tell Richardson to kill you quickly. I may be a bitch, but I am a merciful one."

She hit the end button and threw the mobile phone across the cabin.

She picked up the other and took a deep, calming breath before she answered. "Your name had better not be Henry."

CHAPTER EIGHT

Crossroads

They touched down in a small airfield that looked like it belonged in the days of first flight. None of them had spoken much since leaving the Dominican Republic. Rox assumed that everyone had something different on their minds. Walter and Sam would be worried about Valence. Kamal seemed the most skittish, probably still uncertain if Walter was going to kill him. Meita was the only one who seemed undisturbed. She sat with her legs curled up and her laptop open, her fingers flying across the keyboard nonstop. At one point, Kamal asked her what she was working on and although her answer was polite, it was empty.

Rox stared out at the blue sky and wondered what her next steps would be. She felt no closer to finding her true identity and now Josh had found her. While she was grateful for his help, and the food, she was preparing herself for any mental control he might try to exert. It scared her how easily he had invaded her dreams, but she took solace that he hadn't tried anything else.

The wheels met the tarmac in a hard punch. Rox recognized the landscape as the plane slowed. She wanted to tell everyone that they were at a safe place, but the truth was it was hard for her to know that. For one, she wasn't sure if those who ran Watership Down knew their identities or only knew that "someone" had been coming. And while she seriously doubted Josh wanted anything to do with Sam or Walter, the truth was she wasn't sure where that left any of them. She was counting on Halo to uphold their end of the bargain, but what if they reneged because they weren't sure if Valence had made it out? And what could she do about it if they did?

Rox was still staring out the window when Josh opened the door to the cabin and lowered the stairs so they could alight. Warm air and the scent of outside rushed in.

Meita closed her laptop and slipped it into a black leather bag as she followed Josh outside without looking back at them. Kamal looked at Walter for instruction, and the old man nodded that they should follow. There wasn't much of an alternative.

"Anything you can tell me about this place?" Sam asked as he followed behind her down the steps.

"Not much; I've only been here once. Just do what they say and they'll help us," she explained as she descended the steps.

"And if we don't?"

Four men stood in a semi-circle around the bottom of the steps. Three of them had their guns raised and the one who didn't held his arms crossed over his chest.

The man without a drawn weapon spoke. "Welcome to Crossroads."

"We appreciate your hospitality," Josh said.

"Been here before?"

Josh nodded.

"Well, then you know the rule. Since you're the first to speak, I'm anointin' you the leader."

Again Josh nodded.

"Follow me." He tipped the front of his hat back and wisps of white hair stuck to the thick lines on his forehead. His energy came off him in hesitant waves, and Rox was tempted to wrinkle her nose. He was sick. Something terminal if she had to guess. She pushed a little energy his way, and his aura devoured it like an addict. Healing him would require more strength than she possessed at the moment, and the truth was who knew if it would work. She had healed those with terminal illnesses before, and more often than not they eventually died. She took a step back to maintain a safe distance.

The other men stepped aside and allowed them to pass before falling in behind them.

"What kinda package you looking for?" the old man asked Josh.

"Conceal and transport."

"You paying?"

Josh nodded.

"And the aircraft?"

"She'll need room and board."

"All right. You gotta tail?"

"No."

"How certain are you?"

"Ninety percent."

The leader stopped to study Josh like the answer to his

question was somehow imprinted on his body. "All right then. Put all your phones and electronic equipment in that container over there." He pointed towards a metal box that was pushed up against the hangar door. "You can call me Moses." He nodded back towards his other three men, but kept his eyes on Josh. "You can call them Abraham, Noah, or David."

"Which one's which?" Walter asked.

"Don't really matter. They'll answer to all three of 'em."

Walter stepped up to Moses. "Mind telling me what kind of place you got here?"

Moses placed his hand on the handle of his gun. "Thought you said you'd been here before."

Josh put up his hands. "Yes. Two of us have, but this is the first time for the rest."

Moses looked over each of them and stopped at Rox before he turned back to Josh. "I suggest you two explain to them the rule. Now go on in and Mags'll take care of you shortly."

Crossroads was an out-of-the-way airstrip known for its discretion. There was only one large facility, which was nothing more than two or three aircraft hangars built adjacent to one another. A smaller building tacked on the side of one of the hangars functioned as the main office and looked the most cared for with a fresh coat of paint that announced it as a new – if not a hasty – addition. There wasn't a control tower and there weren't any trees or fences. Just open space and the late morning sun. In some ways it was peaceful. There were no surveillance cameras – or at least not any that Rox had ever seen – and very little in the way of computer systems. Guests at Crossroads were referred to as "Hey you" and those who worked there responded to any name, as long as it was biblical.

They followed Josh inside where Mags greeted them with a tray of lemonade and iced tea. Her holster was strapped to her hip, and she had a knife sheathed and tied at her thigh. "Welcome to Crossroads, travelers. Take your drinks and make yourselves comfortable over there."

The inside of the office area was open floor plan. It reminded Rox of a showroom with different areas cordoned off by design instead of ropes. The area that Mags was referring to was the "guest area". It was furnished with two leather sofas that converted to pull-out beds, two matching recliners that went back far enough to be makeshift cots, and a family dining room table that no longer had its original chairs.

"I'll have some food made shortly. Y'all first timers?"

"Some of us," Josh answered.

"OK, you're the leader I see. Make sure your flock here don't stray and share the rule with everyone. Anybody needing medical attention, now's the time to speak up." Mags looked at Rox.

Rox had healed both Sam and Walter when they were escaping from Watership, but she couldn't do anything about their appearance. She had taken care of Kamal's lip and the few scrapes and cuts that Josh had when they were aboard the plane. Meita looked as if she had stepped out of a fashion magazine in her heels and skirt instead of escaping a government facility conducting experiments on evolved ones. But Rox's ribs were still sore and she'd gotten used to the itch running along her throat. Her body had healed all her major injuries, but she needed proper rest before she would fully recover.

"I can see no one's in a rush to meet their Maker, so I'll have Ruth see to your food," Mags said. "And I'll be back with my med kit. I just need to know about any allergies to any medicines or food?"

Everyone shook their head, except Kamal. "Well, I mean, it's not an allergy per se, more of an intolerance."

"To?"

"To dairy."

"Since I ain't sleeping with you, son, let's keep focus on the shit that can kill ya." Mags chuckled. "All right then. We'll give you two separate sat phones when we feel it's safe to do so. 'Til then, sit tight and I'll be back."

The guest area was in the center of the warehouse, and Rox sensed that wasn't by accident. In the far corner near the back was a sign denoting the restrooms.

Josh dropped his bag and took one of the recliners by the dining table.

Might as well get comfortable. We won't get out of here before morning.

She felt the energy pulses from behind and then the shock of peace when Sam briefly touched her. Her connection with Josh was broken, and Rox felt the tension release from her shoulders.

"What's the rule?" he asked.

Rox sat on the edge of the table and tried not to scratch her throat. "This is only my second time here and I don't know much, but don't ask them anything that's not related to what you need during your stay."

"And if we do?" Kamal asked.

"Son, what is it you said you did back at Watership Down?" Walter looked like he might actually laugh, and it rubbed off on Rox.

"Dad," Sam said, and she assumed he was telling his father to leave Kamal alone.

"Just don't ask any questions," Rox said.

"They mentioned giving us a sat phone?" Walter said.

"Yeah, but probably not until the morning," Josh said.

"Why?"

Rox shrugged. She wasn't really sure, but she assumed it was mostly to protect the Crossroads more than anything else.

"I'm still trying to decide whether we can trust you," Walter said, and it took everyone a moment before they realized who he was addressing.

"Save you the trouble," Josh said. "Don't. I'm here for one thing and one thing only."

"And if you don't get the one thing you're here for?" Sam asked.

Rox placed her hand on Sam's chest to stop him from advancing. For a moment they simply looked at one another before she stepped back from him and let her hand drop.

"If you want to go with him, tell me now," Sam said quietly, but still everyone heard.

That was a very easy question to answer, but the truth was she couldn't afford to pay for Crossroads. And Moses and Mags didn't seem like the type who would take installments.

Rox slowly shook her head and whispered, "But neither can I afford this place."

"Let me worry about that. It's the least we can do." Sam cast a quick glance around the large room before he turned back to her. "Are we safe here?"

"Yes." Rox nodded. "As long as we follow the rule."

"I'm sure I can do that," Sam said. "Now, tell me what happened with Val."

Rox filled him in on what he had missed after they got separated on the cliff. But she left out Connor. She wasn't ready to face that memory just yet.

"Who's 203?" Sam asked.

She should have asked the woman's name, but it didn't seem like an important detail at the time. Rox explained how she entered the house and the state in which she had found Val.

"Shaira would've found Curtis, and Curtis would get them out." He spoke with a certainty that surprised her. The only interaction she had with Curtis was back in the clinic at Halo, and that had been far from pleasant, but no one deserved what would happen to them if they didn't make it.

Trouble in paradise?

Rox looked at Josh before she could stop herself.

Sam followed her gaze. "Is he in your head?"

She nodded.

Aw, is he jealous?

Rox grabbed Sam's hand without thinking.

"Did he make you stay with him?"

That question caught her off guard, and she was tempted to let go, but he tightened their grip.

"Did he manipulate your thoughts the way he did those guards?"

No, because she didn't want to admit she had ever been that vulnerable. Yes, because the moment his control on her weakened, she had this undeniable instinct to find out who she truly was.

"If you don't want to go back, then I won't let him take you."

She felt Josh's eyes on her, and she tried to pull away, but Sam held on. This was all too much. She was back at Crossroads with Josh, which made the last year and a half of her life feel like one big circle. She was still no closer to finding her identity, but she tried to take comfort in that she had Halo now. She had Sam now.

Rox wanted to look at the photo she had been carrying around since leaving Josh, but she didn't have it anymore. While she had memorized each freckle, each angle of the smiles, and the placement of every mole, that photo was the only tangible connection she had to her past.

She hadn't felt the tears running down her face until Sam brushed them away. "I won't let him hurt you."

"You quiet the hum." It tumbled out before she could stop it.

"The hum?"

She shook her head, embarrassed. "It's nothing. Just, it's just the energy. You know, sometimes it builds up and gives me a headache." Of epic proportions.

He nodded like he understood.

Fighting words

Mags walked back in carrying her medical bag. Abraham – as Sam decided to call him – followed behind her with a tray of clothes piled on top. She placed her bag on the table and signaled for Abraham to do the same. Mags put her hands on her hips and gave each of them a long once-over before she spoke. "Well, all righty then. Honey, you look the freshest of the group, so you go on ahead and shower first." Mags was talking to Meita, who looked at Josh before she grabbed some clothes and headed for the showers.

Sam looked at Josh, but he was already staring at him. Well, at least he wasn't looking at Rox anymore.

You're blocking me from her.

Sam winced against the pain in his head. His muscles grew heavy as the images of Rox's death played in his mind. He was tied to the chair, unable to stop it. What kind of man was he if he let his woman die? He didn't deserve her. But a man like Josh, someone who could—

Sam sucked in his breath and leveled his stare at Josh. That son of a bitch was playing with his thoughts.

"Honey, you and your boyfriend here look like you survived something that'd be a mighty interesting tale." Mags gestured for Rox to sit.

"Someone needs to look at her neck," said Josh. "Her ribs are broken. They're on the mend, but still need to be taped."

"Well, all righty." Mags opened her bag and took out a pair of surgical gloves. "I didn't want to say anything, but you look like you had your ass handed to you. But given you're still breathing, I'm assuming you gave as good as you got."

"She always does," Josh said. His lips were turned up in a smile that issued a challenge Sam wanted to be mature enough to ignore, but was beginning to doubt he was.

Sam wondered what would happen if he knocked that smug look off of Josh's face.

He thought as loudly as he could, *What do you want?*

Josh looked surprised, but then smiled.

Mags whistled as she tilted Rox's head to the side and shone a penlight on her neck. "Sweetheart, you are one of the most luckiest gals on the planet. That there's a professional cut. Whoever tended to this must've been damn fast and knew what the hell they were doing. No way you could survive a cut that deep."

Who said she had?

"Sit up as straight as you can for me." Mags put her hands in one of the tears in Rox's shirt and ripped it open. Rox was in a sports bra that at one time had been white. The skin beneath it was tinged red and covered in fading black and blue splotches.

Sam's stomach knotted at the thought of how she got those. She must have taken some heavy blows to crack a rib. He knew because he had one himself before Rox healed him.

You can't tell right now by looking at them, but her breasts are like a chai latte. The first time you get one in your mouth ...

Sam knew he was playing right into Josh's plan, but this was primal. With two strides, he was on top of the wooden coffee table that separated them. His father stepped in front of him, but Sam jumped through time. He was a second from launching himself at Josh when he suddenly felt in control again.

"Don't!" Rox wasn't pleading or begging. It was more of a command and that made him pause.

Whipped already?

"Get out of his head," Rox spoke to Josh, but she kept her eyes on Sam.

There was a long moment of silence, and he realized that Josh and Rox were doing their telepathy thing again, and that pissed him off even more. She was standing there in front of everyone with her shirt ripped open, and her body bruised and beaten. Every muscle in his body wanted to lunge forward, but it had been her touch that held him back.

"Agreed." Rox broke the silence.

"Well, now. Since y'all were able to resolve that there on your own, no need for me to get involved." Mags eased the hammer back in place and holstered her gun. Abraham kept his out, but lowered it.

Sam hadn't noticed Mags, and that was a problem because he doubted she would have hesitated to shoot any of them if she felt it was necessary. This was her family, the way that Halo was Sam's.

His father released his arm as Rox guided him back to the table to stand beside her.

Sam looked over at Kamal. The poor guy looked like he

was about to have a heart attack. He had his feet curled up in the chair and his arms wrapped around his legs. He was a loose end that they would have to fix at some point, but first they had to get out of Crossroads. Alive.

Rox sat back down, and Mags continued like the threat of violence was an everyday occurrence to her.

"Honey, these ribs feel a bit tender, but you'd know if they were broken." Mags said. "Besides, by the way you just hurried over there to stop them two fools from fighting means you're going to be just fine."

"Thank you," Rox said softly.

"Go on and take your shower. Who's next?"

"Sam." It was the first time Rox had said his name, and it made his stomach rise like he was stepping out of the helicopter again. He wanted to look back at Josh and tell him that it wasn't over, but he didn't want to break eye contact with her.

"Son, I need you to get this shirt off."

He winced as he pulled the shirt over his head. "Holy shit, and I thought she had the living shit kicked out of her."

Mags had a heavy touch, and he gritted against the pain. "Well, the good news is I doubt anything's broken, which means you must've been a milk-drinking lad growing up by the size and coloring of those bruises."

Sam knew that the rapid healing of his ribs was due to Rox. He had felt the itch that came with her healing.

"Thanks," Sam said, and grabbed the largest set of clothes in the pile.

"Be careful with them cuts on your wrist when you're

in the shower. They've scabbed over, but they'll still be tender," Mags added. "There's two shower stalls in the bathroom. Your fashion model friend should be done before your girlfriend, so you can go in when she comes out."

Josh took Sam's seat next to Mags as she looked him over. Sam was surprised at his reaction to Josh. No one got to him that easily. He shook his head to clear the feeling of Josh from inside. He needed to wash off the blood and dirt, have a decent meal, and a cup of coffee. Then he would develop a strategy to get them out of here.

The problem was he had no idea where they were. Without seeing the flight plan or knowing their destination, he couldn't pinpoint their location. When they landed, it felt midday, maybe closing in on noon. Crossroads had a midwestern feel to it, which made him think north of Texas or somewhere in Oklahoma or Tennessee. Their flight time would make any of those locations a possibility.

"Son?" His father called to him when they were far enough away from the others. "You all right?"

No, he wasn't. His thoughts were scattered and they kept returning to Rox. "When I touch her, it's like the energy inside me calms," Sam said.

Walter grasped his hands behind his back and rocked forward on his toes. "I was talking physically, son. Like does anything hurt? Do you feel concussed?"

Sam stared at his father. Did he not understand what it meant for him to react to someone like this? Ever since he developed his ability, he had to work hard to control it. *She* made it easier.

"Look, son," Walter began. "I'm sorry. We're out of our element here, dependent on someone we aren't sure we can trust. Talk to me."

All of a sudden he didn't know what to say. How do you describe something you don't fully understand? Every EO he had ever met struggled with the same limitations: how to find out more about their abilities without winding up restrained on a table with their freedom taken away.

"I mean, just the way you launched yourself at Josh back there. You're usually a lot more careful with yourself," his father said.

He was right. It was stupid to let Josh into his thoughts. Rox had warned him about Josh's abilities, but a man stalking a woman for over a year just didn't sit well with him. And knowing that he had manipulated her thoughts for longer, made her do things … Sam swore under his breath.

"You sure you're alright?" Walter asked.

"Yeah, it's nothing."

Why wasn't Rox more angry with Josh? If someone had kept him prisoner for three years, forced him to do things, he would be a lot more volatile. And she had said, "Agreed." What had she agreed to?

"Son, I want you to be careful here." His father's tone had become serious. "I'm sure she cleans up nicely and all that, but what's happening here is messy. A man like that," he nodded towards Josh, "doesn't just chase a woman for as long as he has for no good reason. Unless, of course, he's psycho, which might be the case, but until we know more, we need to play it safe."

Sam knew his father was right. He had just met Rox – what? – two, three days ago when she showed up at Halo unannounced. But every fiber of his being reacted to her. And the guilt of blackmailing her into helping them find Val wasn't helping. He couldn't get the images of the knife sliding across her throat out of his mind. But neither could he forget that she went back to help Josh. Sam had watched her toss Josh the taser without ever looking at him. They communicated in a way that lay evidence to their relationship. They had been partners. Lovers.

"What are you thinking, son?"

Sam wasn't ready to give voice to his insecurities, so he said the next thing to pop into his mind. "She pulsates, Dad. And I can feel it. It's like a sonar. Her body sends out, I don't know, an electric shockwave and it clashes with mine. And the farther apart we are, the weaker the waves get, but when we're close, it's like … Do you feel it? I mean do you feel anything when she's near?"

It was the look on his father's face that answered his question. Maybe this was what Josh felt. Maybe this was why he couldn't let her go and had chased after her for so long.

Sam looked over at Josh, but his back was to him. Mags was telling him something, but he was too far away to make it out.

"I'm definitely grateful he showed up when he did," Walter said. "Whatever his motive. But I'm ready to put as much distance between us as possible."

Sam nodded and looked at Kamal, who had just sat down in front of Mags. "What about him?"

Walter chuckled. "I'm surprised he hasn't gotten himself killed by now."

Sam smiled. Kamal was definitely in over his head. Sam wasn't sure what kind of information he had been trying to steal, but he knew that they had saved him just as much as he had them. "I don't like the idea of leaving him with Josh."

His father was quiet for a moment. "Perhaps after we get away from here, Rox'll take him with her for company."

Sam looked confused. "We said we'd help her. I said we'd help her find her identity."

This wasn't like his father. He didn't back away from a challenge and he never went back on his word. If he said Halo would help, then they would.

"I don't know that I trust her. And I definitely don't like this mind reader thrown into the mix."

"She died in front of me. She saved Val. What more do you want from her?" Sam couldn't hide the anger in his voice.

The shrill of a whistle cut through the warehouse and bounced back off the walls. "Old timer!" Mags shouted. "Your turn."

CHAPTER NINE

I. Am. Rox.

Her stomach growled and pulled her from the depths of a healing sleep. It was eerily quiet so she reached out with her energy to confirm that she was alone. The first energy pulse hit her, and her memories flooded back into place. For a moment, she just laid there and breathed in the fact that she was alive.

She wasn't sure how long she had slept, but she knew her body was done healing. Everything was sore, but nothing itched. She sat up and got her bearings before she stretched to standing. Her fingers ran across her neck where a scar would have been on a normal human.

Good morning.

She turned and looked at the table. Everyone had stopped eating and was watching her.

"Good morning," she said, feeling immediately self-conscious at the attention.

Seems they made your favorite.
Everything?
Everything.

She hadn't meant to smile, but the fact that she ate just about anything, everything became a running joke they shared.

The smell of bacon made her stomach growl as she sat down in the last empty space beside Kamal.

"You can't be hungry," Kamal said. "I mean, you had like three servings last night. She had to bring out an extra jug of gravy just for you."

Walter burst into laughter, and that broke the tension and everyone relaxed. A part of her felt embarrassed, but she was a healer, and that required a lot of energy transference.

Rox stuck out her tongue at Walter, and he did the same to her. If things had been different, she could have grown to like him. But she sensed his distrust, and she couldn't blame him. Rox hoped Shaira had helped Val and 203 find Curtis. That reminded her ...

"Hey, you said that when they were in the main house it meant they were done experimenting," Rox said to Josh. "What did you mean experimenting?"

Josh put down his fork and picked up his coffee. "Don't know much. I mean, we've always known about the facility and that they did experiments, but the types? No clue. Ask your boy here." He signaled towards Kamal.

Kamal looked up from his plate.

"How long have you been working there?" Sam asked.

"Just nine months."

"What kind of work did you do there?"

Kamal was nervous, and it was more than being the center of attention. He was hiding something.

"And why'd you help us escape?" Rox asked.

"I needed to get out of there as well," he looked at his unfinished eggs and placed his fork against the plate. "My former roommate used to work there. He got himself in some trouble and he disappeared about a year ago. My cousin works in the FBI, so I got him involved."

"And?" Walter said.

"And then a day later he's taken off the case and I'm meeting with two guys from 'the government'." Kamal used air quotes.

"What?" Rox said. That didn't make sense.

"They said that my roommate, George, was more than likely dead and his body would never be recovered. That he had gotten himself involved with some shady anti-EO organization."

"Let me guess, and you were so eager to avenge his death?" Walter said.

Kamal looked away, but not before his eyes told them all they needed to know. "I agreed to help them, and they told me to reach out using George's contacts. My credit was altered and I was given some sob back story so that I looked unscrupulous enough to work there. I mean, the interview process should've scared me off, but …" He swallowed and drew in a shaky breath. "He didn't deserve to die. No matter what he did or didn't do."

"And all you had to do was copy those files you were stealing when we ran into you." Rox began to piece it together.

Kamal's laugh was nervous. "They probably think I'm dead now. I was supposed to report in hours ago. Hell, I don't even know what day it is."

"Any idea what you got on that slip disk?"

Kamal shook his head. "Instructions were to find out where they kept the files for experiments. Took me awhile to figure that out. People there aren't exactly trusting." He snorted. "Then I just had to put the disk next to the computer, wait until the red light turned green, and then get the hell out of there."

He sipped his coffee with a shaky hand. "I'm just a paramedic. They had me posing as a medical doctor with advanced degrees in genetics. I'm amazed I was able to fool them for as long as I did."

The table was quiet as everyone absorbed Kamal's story. Living on the edge like that for nine months was hard. Rox understood what it felt like to always look over your shoulder, but to have to deceive people who were already doing despicable things must have worn him down. She was impressed he lasted as long as he had.

"What do you want to do?" Walter asked.

Kamal looked like he hadn't been asked that question in a long time. He shrugged his shoulders and picked up his fork. He moved the eggs around on his plate like he might eat them. "Turn in this slip disk. Get my good credit back. It's hard as hell living on bad credit." He laughed, and this time there was a hint of humor in it. "Find out what they did to George. I mean, he wasn't a saint, but he and I had known one another since high school. We weren't even the best of friends, just similar stories. You know, two people trying to find their place in the world."

"We know a few people who can help you," Sam said.

"You can come with us when we leave here."

"Hope it's not the same people who 'helped' you find your sister," Josh said.

Mags walked over carrying a heavy plastic case. She dumped it on the coffee table and signaled for Josh. "Here's your two encrypted satellite phones. So far, no one's been on your tail that we can tell and the money cleared last night. Make your calls and we'll drop you off first thing in the morning."

Sam and his father took one of the phones and moved to the far side of the room.

Decision time, corazón.

Rox was starving but suddenly lost some of her appetite. She forced down a bite of sausage that tasted as if it had come straight from the pig.

Follow me, Rox said.

Josh tossed the phone to Meita and gave her a number to dial before he followed Rox out the front door.

The sun wasn't high enough in the sky for it to be noon, but it warmed the cool breeze that blew across the open field. For a while, the only sounds were their footsteps against the packed sand. Rox wasn't sure where she was taking them. There wasn't anything but the three buildings, but she wanted to stretch her legs after a night of healing.

She also didn't have a clue what she wanted to say to him. She hated him and didn't hate him all at the same time.

Look, I know what you're going to say.

"No, I don't think you do."

I found you in a facility much like Watership. It was

called Mockingbird. I had no idea what I was getting into. I hadn't realized just how organized or extensive their network was. I just wanted to do some good. Protect my people, you know.

Many EOs thought they could just hide in a life of anonymity, but that was dangerous. If the wrong people discovered you, then there would be no one to come looking for you once you went missing. Who would alert the authorities or the media? You just simply disappeared into a life of experiments and subjugation. Ever since she had known Josh, he was committed to using his ability and influence to do something about that. To let those who threatened EOs know that someone would make them pay.

I came across a room with a few people lying on a table. I tried to read their minds. I was thinking maybe I could make them get up and follow us out. Perhaps help us if we got caught or something. But their minds were ... I've never felt anything so ...

"Empty."

No, expansive. Like I could get lost in there. There were no walls, no compartmentalizations. I knew they weren't coming back. A mind needs parameters, babe. Pathways, sections to help it process and store all its information. Theirs were just this never-ending road that ... I don't know.

They reached the end of the third hanger and Rox stopped, but he kept walking. *So I left them there. Then I came across a room, and I don't know, instinct led me inside. You were just lying there. I thought your mind was like the others, so I didn't even try to connect with you, but then all of a sudden I felt this energy. I had hurt my ankle jumping down from a maintenance ladder, but when I came into your room, I felt this wave of heat encircle it and all of a sudden I could put my full weight on it again.*

"And so you took me with you?"

Josh nodded. *Took you a fortnight to wake up. And the first thing you said to me was—*

"I'm hungry."

You are a powerful asset, Rox. Your ability changes everything. To heal and take life is an ability that people would kill for. And if they ever found you, they would put you back in another facility and do whatever they needed to replicate your abilities.

"So that justified—"

No, it didn't. Josh turned to face her. *But I'd do it all again. In the beginning, it was about getting you to stay to help me. But then the more I sifted through your mind, the more I felt attracted to you. Genuinely so.* His thoughts started to flow with a sense of urgency. *I've followed you to say I'm sorry. To look you in the eyes and make this right. I just want to make it right again, babe. How do I get us back to where we used to be?*

Rox started to walk again.

You don't hate me. I'd know if you hated me.

Rox knew she didn't need to respond. He would just read her thoughts. He only brought it up so that she could think about it. His ability was powerful, but like all abilities, his had its limitations too.

They had walked past the reach of Crossroads' electricity grid. Out here, Rox felt a different kind of hum. It was more harmonious and less invasive.

How'd you learn to block me out?

For a moment, she thought about not replying, but knew he had already read her thoughts. "Math. Nonsense. Anything random. You need patterns."

Rox—

"Don't. It was easy to manipulate me because I was scared and vulnerable. I woke up without a single memory. Rox isn't even my real name; it's something you came up with."

Suits you though, doesn't it?

Tears pooled, but she was too tired to give in to them. This was the moment she had been waiting for. Her moment to confront him, and while it was nothing like she had envisioned, it was real and necessary. "I'm grateful you taught me how to defend myself. In an odd way you gave me purpose, something to focus on so that I could make it through each day. But you made me stop looking for my past. You exaggerated my love for you to the point where I became lost all over again. In you."

Rox could feel him digging around in her head. She snorted and turned back towards the office.

I gave you comfort when you needed it!

"Keeping me from my past isn't comfort."

I saved you from god only knows what at Mockingbird.

"But that never gave you the right to manipulate me. To *own* me."

Don't be so melodramatic. I never owned you, Rox. I taught you to fight. I prepared you for the world that we live in. Tell me my training didn't save your ass last night.

She turned on him. "You're missing the point!"

Then help me understand why you'd run away from me.

From our love and the family we had become.

"You took away my ability to choose for myself. I fought beside you, for you. *Nothing* was my choice. You, you guided me towards all my decisions. You took my vulnerable state and twisted it past gratitude to desire. I had feelings for you, yes. But I made love to you, Josh, and that should always be *my* choice and no one else's."

Rox wasn't sure if his silence meant he didn't know what to say or if he was formulating a rebuttal. She started back towards the main office again. She was beyond crying. She had spilled enough tears over what had happened. She didn't even hate him. All that did was consume too much energy. She just wanted to find her identity. Were those her children in the photo? Did she have a husband? An extended family who looked for her?

Knowing that she was once a prisoner at a place like Watership added a new complexity to her past. Did they take her because she was an EO or was she simply a normal human they experimented on and gave abilities to?

The photo was in the room where I found you. It was lying near your handbag. Everything had been dumped on the table. I grabbed it on instinct. They look a bit like you, I suppose. Maybe that's why I kept it.

Rox reached for the photo, but stopped when she remembered she didn't have it any longer. "I feel like they're mine. And for the life of me I can't figure out if it's instinctive or simply a desperate need to belong." Rox noticed all the lines running along the back of her hand that created the impressions in her skin. "I'm old enough. Let's face it, I'm definitely done with my twenties."

You don't look a day over twenty-five to me.

Rox snorted at first, but then she laughed. It was a good one. One that started in her throat but ended in her gut. She wiped the tears from her cheek before she spoke. "I feel … heavy. Like something's tethered to me."

Jay.

His son. Did she have a son of her own? And if so, how old would he be? How old was she? Thirty-five? Seventy?

Then you're in great shape. She caught him staring at her legs. *Not many senior citizens can sway like that.*

But how could a mom forget her children? Maybe they were her siblings. The girl looked like her. Maybe it was a picture of her and her sister when they were younger.

I'll help you find them.

Funny, a little over a year ago she would have jumped at his offer. But now?

Turn about

Rox walked into the main office and the familiar impulse from Sam greeted her as he came out of the restroom. She could tell by the look on his face that he had been worried about her, so she smiled.

Kamal and Walter were seated at the table having a cup of coffee and talking about their past to kill time. Kamal was not an EO. His brother had been. "He saw patterns in everything. I mean he tested off the charts gifted, but he began to connect dots that weren't meant to be. Like he'd draw the wrong conclusion because the traffic light turned red when he was driving home and had to go to the bathroom. It was weird, he was okay when like random bad stuff happened, but if he was having a bad day he'd see the barista forgetting to add cinnamon to his coffee as a part of a bigger pattern of bad events. Then he'd think he was the target of something to do with EOs."

"Conspiracy nut?" Walter asked.

"I prefer the term theorist," Kamal said. "But no, not really. I mean, I don't know. He just had trouble coping. Shot himself. Left a note explaining why that was the best way to end it."

"My wife's brother couldn't take his ability either," Walter said. "Empath. Or something a hell of a lot like it. I mean, I met him only a few times, but it's like he had this sense about the people he'd meet. She said he couldn't tell what they were feeling per se, but he'd get a vibe about someone he couldn't shake. He'd classified people as either fundamentally good, fundamentally bad or self-serving. Said he hated the self-serving folks the most because they were the least predictable."

"Yeah, glad I'm not a woman," Kamal said. "At least I'm out of the woods."

"It was my wife's brother, not my wife."

"Yeah I know. Oh wait, sorry. It's just that as a male, if my EO gene sequence doesn't kick in by the time I start or finish puberty, I'm safe. But if a woman's sequence doesn't activate when she starts or finishes puberty, there's still a chance for it to kick in around menopause. Learned that at Watership. They think it has to do with a woman's fluctuating hormone levels."

"No shit?"

Kamal nodded.

"Maybe that's what happened to me," Rox said, as she sat down and pulled her half-eaten plate closer. It made sense. Or at least it *could* make sense.

"That places you in your mid to late forties," Walter said. "Hell, you could be fifty!"

Rox winked at Walter as she took a bite of cold eggs.

Sam sat beside her and placed the sat phone on the table.

"Any update?" Walter asked, and he sat up a bit straighter like he was bracing himself for the worst.

"She's with Marissa now," Sam said.

Walter nodded and held that pose for a few moments before his shoulders relaxed and he seemed to fall into himself. Rox and the others respectfully looked away as he tried to maintain composure. His daughter was home. Rox wasn't sure what state Valence was in, but she supposed it didn't matter. One thing at a time. She was home, and that must have felt damn good to Walter and Sam.

Walter looked across the table at her and his eyes were filled with tears he wouldn't allow to fall. His mouth opened like he was going to say something, but then it closed so he could clear his throat. "Thank you."

"Josh!" Meita came running to the table. "Have you seen Josh?"

"He's taking a walk. Why?"

Meita looked at each of them. She was still clutching the sat phone that Abraham had brought over. Her hands were shaking and Rox was certain that her call hadn't gone as well.

"All you have to do is shout his name in your thoughts, and Josh will hear you," Rox said.

Meita shook her head. "Not with me. It doesn't work on me."

Rox shook her head, too. "No, trust me. I'm sure he's managed to touch you by now. And even without a touch, just shout—"

"No. None of your abilities work on me."

Josh! Rox wasn't sure what Meita meant, but she could tell from Meita's demeanor something bad had happened.

Oh, now you want me. Forgive me if I ignore you for a while.

Something's wrong. Meita's worried about something.

I'm on my way.

"He's coming. What happened?" Rox asked.

Meita had changed out of her nice clothes and into the pair of jeans and shirt they had been given, but she still wore her heels. It was a look she actually pulled off, though Rox had no idea how she'd run if she needed to.

"Jay – he was taken."

For a moment, Rox forgot how to breathe. "What do you mean, 'he was taken'?"

"I called the number Josh gave me, and Kevin said the building's fire alarm went off. In the middle of evacuating, Jay was taken."

"But, wait. What building? Where were they?"

"The New York penthouse."

But he would have security. Jay never went anywhere alone.

Meita continued, "Kevin said he received a text message a few hours later that said bring the healer if you want the boy back."

Rox's legs gave out and she fell back onto the bench. She might have toppled off if Walter had not steadied her.

"Who's Jay?" Sam asked.

"When was this?" Rox asked Meita.

"They contacted him about an hour ago, Kevin said."

Why are you panicking?

Rox didn't mean for him to find out this way, but her thoughts answered his question before she could stop them.

Searing pain echoed throughout her brain and she doubled over from it. When she opened her eyes, the room tilted. Sam grabbed her before she could fall, and the pain stopped.

"What's wrong?" Sam asked her.

"Josh."

The door to the main building banged opened. "Where is he?" His voice reached them before he did.

Meita shook her head. "I don't know. Kevin said that he'd pick you up himself."

Rox knew Josh was trying to probe Meita's thoughts from the intense look on his face. "Josh." But he couldn't hear her.

She let go of Sam. *Josh!*

He turned to Rox. *They took him.*

"We'll get him back."

They want you.

I know, and we'll figure something out.

"What's going on?" Walter asked.

"When did this happen?" Josh asked.

"They made contact about an hour ago, but he was taken earlier this morning," Meita explained.

"From where?" Josh asked.

Rox's mind answered him much faster than Meita could.

They're professionals. Josh told her. *Jay knows how to protect himself and he would never go with anyone he didn't know, even if the building was on fire.*

"I know," Rox said.

That means they've targeted him. Josh's thoughts were running faster than Rox could keep up. He was jumping from one possibility to the next before the thought was fully formed. *And they want you. Why? I need to go.*

"They won't take us to the drop site until it's time. You know that," Rox said.

"Fuck the rules!"

Rox saw Sam moving closer, but she shook her head, telling him to stay where he was.

"We've got just under twenty-four hours before we can be released from this place, so instead of rushing off, let's develop a plan," Rox said.

I cannot sit here!

"Look, they told you what they wanted, so they're not going to kill him. They're using him as leverage."

There's a lot worse things than death, Rox. You know that.

Sam put his hand on her shoulder and her connection with Josh ended. Warmth spread down her back, and she remembered that everyone else was only hearing one half of the conversation.

"Josh's son was taken. Early this morning."

"Shit!" Kamal said. "You think it's tied to you helping us break outta there?"

Josh looked at Meita. She shook her head. "The identity I gave you was secure. One hundred percent. There are only a handful of people who could've cracked the encryption code on your profile to back-trace it. And I'm talking a handful of people ... globally. And even then, they wouldn't be able to do it so quickly."

"What identity?" Rox asked.

Meita created a false identity to get me into Watership. We used what little we have about actual investors and clients. I had access to the main house and a few areas in the underground facility.

"What identity?" Sam asked.

Rox got the rest of them up to speed, but left out the part where the kidnappers wanted to exchange Jay for her. Josh was pacing. He was on edge, which meant it would be hard for them to block out his negative thoughts. He wasn't projecting them, but he was no longer concentrating on containing them either.

"How old's your boy?" Sam asked.

"Sixteen."

"You train him the way you trained Rox?"

Josh nodded.

"Aside from the fun-loving folks at Watership, who else wants to hurt you?" Walter asked.

Josh looked at Rox before his gaze settled on Sam.

"So who else is hating on you?" Walter asked again, as

he poured a cup of coffee.

"I've been told that my personality can be … a bit intrusive."

"No shit?" Walter said.

A bad kind of love

Everyone's thoughts were pouring in like he was a schoolboy. And his heartbeat wouldn't slow. No one ever really knew what a person thought. Josh had come to learn that everyone had evil thoughts, images that would shame them or could cast even the most saintly person in a bad light. But the vast majority of people never acted on them. So he had learned a long time ago never to judge a person based on their thoughts.

Erecting a barrier around his mind had been an excruciating process that involved many years of drug and alcohol abuse. But he got there. And when he finally broke free from the haze that had been clouding his life for years, he discovered that he had a son. He wanted so desperately to remember his feelings for Jay's mother, but the truth was he hadn't remembered her any more than he could recollect the sex they had to conceive him.

He had been introduced to Jay when the boy was nine months old, and it still tore through his heart to remember that terribly emaciated and disengaged child who looked up at him. But with Josh's love and attention, Jay came out of his shell and began to interact with the world around him. If he was honest, Jay had saved him, too. Josh had spent most of his life angry at pretty much everything. He hated his parents for dying when he was so young, and then when he grew up and realized it made no sense to hate them, he turned his hatred on everyone else. The only reason he got control of his addiction was because he hated how out of control he became. He considered it a weakness, and there was nothing Josh hated more than being weak.

But then he met Jay, and all that hate seemed trivial. Looking back, he couldn't say that his anger management problems were easy to resolve or that he became immediately less angry, but Jay helped him gain perspective, which was the first step to recovery.

Josh admitted what he had done to Rox and told his son it was a terrible mistake, but he was going to set it right. At no point had he actually thought of his actions as "stalking". His intention was only to find her, apologize, and tell her the truth about how he had found her. If he was lucky, maybe persuade her to come back home. But everything had gotten so complicated. It had been more difficult to track her down than he had expected.

All he had wanted was a second chance.

Walter placed a cup of coffee in front of him, but he just stared at it. Jay was a strong boy. He was much smarter than Josh had been at this age. If they wanted Rox, then they wouldn't hurt him, like she said. No, she said they wouldn't kill him. To take Jay meant someone got hurt. He wouldn't go easily. Josh had repeatedly told him his chances of survival significantly decreased if he was taken, and so he should make a stand and fight. His son would have done that.

A hand squeezed his shoulder, and some of his tension released. He loved her. As much as he didn't want to, he loved her. They had been so happy – even if it was a happiness he had created. She loved him and he loved her. Why wasn't that enough?

And yet, at this moment, he hated her. She hadn't even bothered to leave a note. He spent over a year looking for her.

"We'll get him back." *If they want me, they won't hurt him.*

He turned to her and pulled her hand to his chest. *They'll hurt him, babe. They may not kill him, but they've already hurt him.*

He felt her tense at his intimacy, and he wanted to crush their bodies together until he had his old life back, complete with his son and the woman he loved.

She gently released her hand from his and all of a sudden he found it too hard to breathe. The room was too small and he wasn't sure if he wanted to fight someone or curl into a ball and cry. His eyes filled with tears at the thought of what they were doing – had done – to his boy.

He lurched to his feet, and everyone took a step back except Rox. Her hair was pulled into one of those tight braids that ran down her back and stopped below her shoulders. You couldn't tell she had died at all.

You know those walls you keep up so that we don't hear your thoughts? Well, those aren't up right now. And I doubt that they can decipher exactly what you're thinking, but they know you're not in a happy place, Josh. And it's affecting them.

They. Took. Him. He looked for something to throw, something to break, someone to hit.

"Rox?" Sam's voice was soft, but it held a warning that only infuriated him.

But, thankfully, she ignored Sam and took a step towards him instead. He wasn't sure what to do with her. He wanted to hold her. He needed to feel her arms around him, but she belonged to another now.

That's the thing. I never belonged to anyone.

He lowered his head, and she pulled him into her embrace. Josh buried his face into her neck and inhaled.

There. Just beneath the clinical-smelling soap was her scent. He was losing everything. First the woman he loved and now his son. He fought against the urge to run his fingers through her hair and release it from the braid. She looked better when it was wild and free.

He lifted his head, and she stepped back. The release of her embrace was so unexpected it took him a moment to realize that he was still the only one holding on. His arms dropped and he hated himself for looking at Sam. He was standing just behind Rox, and the look on his face said that he was exercising his own restraint.

"Let us help you," she said. *You helped them. They're willing to repay the favor.*

And you? Why would you help me after all I've done?

Because I love him, too.

He held her gaze, and in that moment he let his thoughts remind her what it felt like when they were at their best together. When she was happy. He showed her what she tasted like when they made love. She inhaled and accidentally stepped back into Sam. Their connection was gone.

Josh turned and strode towards the entrance. Everyone was still staring at him, but he didn't care. His walls were back in place and his thoughts were silenced from all, except one. He didn't want a wall between them. First, he would get his son back. He would give the kidnappers Rox if he had to. His son was his priority. And then once Jay was safe, he would go back and get Rox. Because he was certain of two things: he was going to save his son, and that he loved the hell out of the woman he had named Rox.

CHAPTER TEN

Choices

The rays from the sun bounced off the sand, making the road look like it was carved through glass instead of the desert. The sky was a photographer's blue and the cacti interspersed along the empty interstate was a beautiful green, indicating that it received enough water.

Rox sat across from Sam with her head to the side. The steady rise of her chest meant she was asleep. Kamal was seated next to her, his head back and at an angle that meant he would be in pain when he woke. His father was on the other side of Kamal, which left Meita between him and Josh.

They were in a reinforced SUV. The lack of road noise gave it away. Sam was in the row of seats facing backwards, and even though the air conditioner was turned to max, sweat had broken out under his arms from where the sun cut through the tint in the windows.

The sun was still making its way across the eastern sky with an intensity that was hypnotic to a man caught in his own thoughts. He looked down at where her ankle rested against the back of his calf. He couldn't deny his attraction to her; he just couldn't figure out whether it had anything to do with her ability. He wanted to slow things down. Go back to when she first trespassed on Halo. Start over.

Sam could tell by the way his father cut a glance at her every now and again that he was intrigued. Sam would go as far as to say that his father probably even respected her now that Val was safely back at Halo. But Walter didn't trust her.

Sam needed more time with her. Away from … all this. He had questions, and even if she had no memory, he needed to see how she reacted to them. He wanted to help her, but everything had been so rushed since she arrived.

Sam had argued with her about the plan to rescue Jay. He was sure they could come up with something better, but neither Rox nor Josh wanted to discuss other options. Josh's reaction, he understood. Sam had been a father too, once, and so he understood the urgency that a parent felt when their child was in danger. But Rox? Surely she could see that giving herself over to secure Jay's release was a bad idea.

Finding out that Josh had a son brought back memories of his own daughter. Sam had been a father for two hours and eleven minutes. He and his wife had been trying for a few years and had all but given up. They had two miscarriages and one stillbirth. Each time, his wife died a little inside as the months went by and she wasn't able to conceive.

Their final pregnancy was an accident. Her eyes sparkled, and he remembered thinking it was impossible to love someone more. She did everything the doctor recommended. Ate nothing but protein and vegetables. Got reasonable amounts of exercise and walked away from stressful situations, which wasn't easy to do living as an EO. At seven months, she started spotting. There wasn't much to worry about, the doctor had reassured them. These things happened, he said, but he had put her on bedrest as a precaution given her history.

Jessica was born a few days later. One of her kidneys failed within twenty minutes of birth and her heart rate was erratic. Never before had he felt so torn between passing forward through time and wanting it to stop all together. He wanted to know if she was going to be okay, but feared he would miss something if he did. Her little hand was too small to circle his finger, but everything about her was beautiful. Sam thought it impossible to love anyone more than he had his own mother and then his wife, but Jessica changed all that. He knew instantly he would do anything to protect her. Lie. Steal. Kill. With her birth, all the bad shit he had seen, done, and helped to make happen, didn't matter anymore. He had been reborn.

But then, just like that she was gone. Most of her short life had been spent in surgery. He had gotten to touch her, so had his wife, but then she had disappeared from their lives leaving it much more empty. His wife was inconsolable and, if Sam was honest, he was incapable of offering any support anyway. Nothing had prepared him for this. Not his training. Not the missions he had led or the lies he had told and the lives he had ruined. This was a different kind of war he wasn't equipped to fight. He had been surrounded by sorrow and was drowning in grief.

A few days later, he found his wife in their bathtub, and all the pain he had been trying to sift through swallowed him whole.

Sam understood Josh's need to save his son in a way that he and his father could relate to. The parallels between asking Rox to accompany them to save Val and her trading herself for Jay were obvious. Everybody wanted something from her, but no one was willing to help her first.

He looked out the window and caught his own reflection. He had never thought much about how he looked. There seemed to be other things about him that were more important. But for the first time, he wondered how Rox looked upon him. Did she see a man who was desperately trying to do right even when he was surrounded by bad choices? Or did she see another version of Josh, a user and a manipulator?

Sam closed his eyes and allowed an image of Rox to fill his mind. A slow smile slid across his face. He bet when she let her hair free it framed her face in a way that drew men's attention. The memory of the knife sliding across her throat and the look of confusion on her face forced his eyes open. He looked at the steady rise and fall of her chest until he had convinced himself that she was indeed still alive.

Sam glanced over at Josh. *There's got to be a better way.*

Josh was staring at him with a cold anger behind his eyes, and Sam wasn't sure if it was directed at him or the man was simply trying to keep it together while they looked for his son.

Josh sighed and looked out his own window. *They have my son.*

She may have a son.

You don't think I've considered that?

She can heal herself, is that it? Doesn't matter what happens to her because she can always come back?

The rage rolling off Josh was almost palpable, but he remained silent.

Why her? Why do they want Rox? Sam asked.

There was a long moment of silence before Josh responded. *I found Rox at a facility like Watership. She was just lying there. Eyes open, but not seeing. I almost left her. But then I felt her heal me.*

And so you took her because she could heal you?

Josh snorted. *I wasn't exactly sure that she* could *heal me, but I saw her photo and ...*

And you thought of Jay.

Josh nodded. *And I thought of Jay. I hoped that if someone found me the way that I had found her, for my son's sake, they'd help me escape.*

Sam looked over at Rox. The thought of her being held in a place like the one they had just escaped from scared him. He and his father had been captured, Rox died, and the only reason any of them got away was because the man she was running from saved her, and them by default.

And you're okay with sending her back in there? Back to the people who did god-only-knows-what to her.

What would you do if it were Jessica?

Cariño

Rox woke when the window separating the front cab lowered and the driver told them they had fifteen minutes. They turned down an alley and drove into a carpark. They took the ramp up to the top floor and then followed the signs for the exit.

They were back out into traffic and circled the block twice before they joined a queue of cars funneling into the basement carpark of a shopping mall. The SUV pulled into a handicap space, the doors unlocked, and Josh was the first to open his door.

The SUV waited until everyone was out before it drove away.

For the first time Rox realized that they were all dressed in the same clothes, just different sizes. They looked like they were part of a cult. Or one of those families who felt the need to wear matching outfits.

"Now what?" Walter asked.

"Now, we find our people," Josh said, and they followed the arrows to the elevator that would take them into the mall.

The doors chimed open, and a teenage boy dressed in denim and cowboy boots stepped away from his girlfriend. They had clearly been making out, and Kamal smothered a laugh, but Rox looked up at Josh. She didn't need his ability to know what he was thinking.

Jay had been with his attackers now for over twenty-four hours. They could have him anywhere. Literally. If they had the money – and that was a strong probability – they could disappear using private aircrafts that flew out of places like Crossroads. But then whoever took him wanted her, and so they wouldn't disappear. They would just lay low until the exchange could be made.

"Is he showing signs of developing an ability?" Rox asked, as they stepped into the elevator. When she had left, Jay was just in the beginning stages of puberty. There was no way of determining – or at least no way that anyone had found – who would evolve. Puberty was the key, that was for sure, but at what stage during puberty was still a mystery.

"No."

They traveled as a group to the first floor.

"Information desk." Sam pointed as they exited.

Her breath caught when she saw Kevin step off the escalator nearby. He hadn't seen them yet, but he looked just as she remembered him, except more on edge. His eyes darted back and forth like he was processing data as a CPU might. Kevin was six-foot-two with limbs like tree trunks. He looked like he was someone's bodyguard, but he was Josh's best friend. Kevin belied all the stereotypes about a man of his size and ethnicity. He was smart and an incredibly good judge of character. Josh relied on his opinion more than anyone else's on his team, and it was with Kevin he entrusted Jay. Kevin would be killing himself with guilt and fear. He was like family to Jay, to all of them. Everybody would be hurting and looking for someone to blame.

It's not your fault. If anyone's to blame, it's me.

Rox looked over her shoulder at Josh.

I was out of line manipulating you like that. I should've just helped you. Let's find my son and then we'll figure out the rest from there.

Rox nodded.

"Kev!" he called out as he jogged over to his friend.

Kevin turned around and the two friends embraced.

"What the hell happened to you?" Kevin asked him as he lowered Josh back to the floor.

"Long story. What do we know?" Josh said.

The joy fell from his face, and he was all business. "I reviewed the surveillance footage and it looks like it was planned. He put up a damn good fight, Josh, but they had him beat on size and numbers."

Kevin was about to continue when he noticed her. He stepped around Josh and enveloped her in one of those embraces that showed her that not everything had been a fabrication. "¡Cariño mio!"

Tears blocked her vision, and she blinked them back. She wrapped her arms around the friend she abandoned when she had left Josh. In hindsight, she should have chosen a different way to leave, but when she finally realized what Josh had been doing, she wasn't sure who to trust.

"¡Que bueno verte! A bit flaquita, pero ..."

She laughed as the first of many tears escaped. He pulled her in again and kissed the top of her head. "Está bien."

Kevin stiffened, and she realized that he had caught sight of the others standing behind her.

"Kevin," Josh began. "This is Sam, his father, Walter, Dr Kamal—"

"Um, hi. But I'm not a doctor."

Josh rolled his eyes. "And this is Meita."

One of Kevin's eyebrows rose. "*The* Meita?"

Meita smiled and extended her hand.

"I heard you got some fine people-finding skills," Kevin said.

Meita shrugged as if she preferred to have the attention elsewhere.

"So, do we know anything about the boy's disappearance?" Walter said.

Kevin looked at Josh, who nodded it was okay to continue.

"Looks professional. Cameras were disabled, but we got visuals from the recessed ones. Partial, mind you, but shit man, that's better than nothing. They used rubber bullets, so I don't think they were out for blood."

"They make contact again? I mean after we spoke," Josh asked.

Kevin nodded. "Sí. Calling back tomorrow at 7am."

"Sam!" A man pushed his way through the crowd of people.

Curtis emerged and clasped hands with Sam before the two gave each other a brief, but strong pat on the back.

"I got her, man," Curtis said as they separated. "She's safe. Man, but you had us worried as hell."

"How is she?" Walter asked.

Curtis looked down at his feet before he met the old man's gaze again. "She's a fighter. Bethy looked her over, did a full scan and everything. Says she's fine. Just need to give her time to settle is all."

"We're starting to draw attention. Shall we take this somewhere else?" Sam said.

"A restaurant? Because I'm starving," Kamal said.

Meita nodded. "You bring my stuff?"

"Sí." Kevin reached inside his coat pocket and pulled out a tablet.

"I'll help you find out who took your son," Meita said to Josh.

"Add it to my bill," Josh said.

"This one's pro bono."

"You need a place with wifi?" Kamal asked.

Meita shook her head.

"All right, food while we discuss how we're going to get your son back," Sam said and turned to look at the map. He pressed a few buttons before he found a suitable place. "Down the escalator and hang a left at the split."

"It's good to see you, girl." Kevin fell in step beside her.

There was an awkward silence while she thought of a suitable response. She missed him, but she was struggling with the guilt at how she had left everyone.

"No one blames you, Cariño." Despite his size, Kevin had a soft touch. "When we realized that he was keeping you there, we understood."

Silent tears slipped down her cheeks. God, her life was a mess. She had no past and was looking at an even bleaker future. The only friends she had were the ones she had spent a year evading.

"You should know that I gave him a piece of my mind." Kevin's demeanor changed, and she knew he was telling the truth. "Had to show him that he was only alpha of this pack because I let him be."

She looked up at him, and the smile on his face spoke of the forgiveness and understanding she had desperately needed from him.

"You're one of us. And that's never going to change. I just want you to be happy."

Rox wrapped herself around his arm and squeezed. "I've missed you."

"Ay, amor. Yo también te extrañé."

Goodbye

They stepped off the chartered plane into sunlight reminiscent of Crossroads. The air here was different. It had a spice to it, a feeling of unpredictability that only ratcheted his nerves. This was a bad plan. Sam didn't need a lifetime of operational experience to know that meeting the "bad guys" on their turf never went well.

Rox paced in front of the nose of the aircraft with nervous energy that collided with his. She hadn't said a word and hardly looked at him, but he also noticed that she didn't look at Josh either. Although they could be sharing thoughts, he doubted it. Her forehead didn't have the crease that was normally there when she and Josh spoke privately.

She was scared, and he was surprised at how angry that made him. She wanted to get Jay back but she didn't like the plan anymore than he did. There just wasn't enough time to develop another one.

Sam looked over at Josh, but he was following Rox out of the corner of his eyes. In fact, they all were. Kevin was more blatant about it. Kamal was in the plane with Meita, who was doing something on her tablet. She hadn't spoken a word since Kevin handed it to her back at the shopping mall.

Walter was talking quietly with Curtis, trying to fill him in on what they knew and the plan at large, which mostly went like this: Rox would exchange herself for Jay. Josh would keep a mental connection with Rox, who would feed them directions so they could follow her, and the moment she felt like she could get the upper hand, she was to use her abilities to escape.

It was a shitty plan at best.

Calm down. I've got her.

That's part of the problem. She doesn't want you in her head anymore.

Silence. Sam had struck a nerve.

Rox continued pacing. She was mentally preparing for a fight while the rest of them were going to sit by and watch her walk into the lion's den.

"To hell with it." Sam walked over to her and scooped her into his arms. His mouth descended before he knew what he was doing. There was nothing about their interactions that led him to believe that she would be receptive, but he was driven by instinct, and her energy called to him.

The moment he touched her, the pulses stopped and the angst dissipated. He stopped worrying because nothing mattered more than this one moment. When her lips parted, his tongue slipped through for a taste, just a small one before he pulled back.

"Now," he cleared his throat. "No heroics. First chance you get, you take it." His kiss had surprised her, but the fact that she hadn't pushed him away meant it was a pleasant one.

She nodded and brought her hands up to cover her mouth, then quickly lowered them back to her sides. "Yep. Escape and evade until you guys arrive."

"Exactly."

They both looked up when Josh approached. "If you two love birds are finished." He pointed to the helicopter that had just breached the horizon. "Rox, I need a connection and I can't do that when you two are sticking your tongues down one another's throats."

Josh was jealous, and that made Sam smile. He gave Rox's fingers one last squeeze before he let go.

You ready? Josh asked him.

He nodded.

Just so you know, I hate you.

Sam winked at him.

The phone rang and Kevin answered it. He was quiet for a long time before he said "OK" and hung up.

"They want you to walk halfway. Lie face down on the ground, hands behind your head and your legs apart."

Josh swore under his breath.

"Jay will walk to you, then lay down. Once he's down, you get up and start walking towards the helicopter. Hands still behind your head."

"Got it." Rox said with a shaky voice.

Sam wanted to scream. He gauged the distance between the aircrafts was over a minute at a full sprint. Ever since he grew facial hair, he had made steady progress. First, it was just a twentieth of a second. Then in his early twenties, he made it a second and a half, and now at thirty-six, he was at three seconds.

It was time for Rox to go, but she turned to Walter. "I don't know if Val has something like I had. Have," she said, trying to keep control of her voice. "But, if she's having problems remembering, Josh is her best bet. Let him help her."

Rox turned to Kevin and he bundled her up in his embrace. "Cuídate. We will come for you."

When she turned to face him, Sam had to fight the urge to toss her over his shoulder and head back to the airplane. But the set of her jaw said she was ready. And Sam had been a father. It didn't matter for how long; the change that his daughter had made was instantaneous and permanent.

"I like horror movies," she said.

It took him a moment to understand where she was going with that comment, but as soon as he did, a smile spread across his face that belied the situation. "Horror it is."

Then she turned to Josh. They were staring at one another, but Sam knew they were communicating. She gave a sharp nod and started towards the helicopter. This was the second time he was torn between passing through time and wishing it would stop all together.

Complicated

Meita's fingers flew across the keyboard. <They're here.>

The response was not as quick. <Visibility?>

<No line of sight.>

<Probability of mission success?>

Meita looked over her shoulder from where she sat in the cockpit. Kamal was organizing the medical bag. He said he needed to keep busy, and she understood that. He didn't sign up for this lifestyle, but if Meita were honest, he had more than risen to the occasion. He was resourceful, and his medical knowledge, although limited, was enough for him to survive at Watership. He could have a future with GFO if he wanted. She would make sure to put that in her report. But ultimately it would be his choice. They had very little leverage over ordinary humans.

<PMS at 60–65%> Meita typed.

Meita bint Tariq al-Shaikh was a fourth generation citizen who had followed in the footsteps of her father, Tariq, who had followed in the footsteps of his father, and worked intelligence. Technically, she had no concrete evidence that either her father or grandfather actually worked espionage, but the rumors were there.

She had been on this assignment for nine months. Getting Josh to hire her was relatively easy. He was desperate and she had a reputation for helping people in impossible situations.

Kamal signaled to her that the helicopter had touched down, and Meita focused on the task at hand. Katherine told her that a new drone was en route as they were still unable to locate her regular one that had gone MIA when Meita was at Watership. This drone was commissioned for surveillance only. It didn't have any weapons, but could wirelessly transmit its coordinates back to a relay station that would then forward it on to Katherine's laptop. It was one of the older models and had a terrible battery life, requiring a recharge every forty-eight hours. But when it was eighty-five percent drained, it pinged local cell towers to alert the same relay station to launch another drone to take its place. It was an elaborate workaround and a relatively good backup plan, provided that the first drone wasn't too far from the handful of secondary drones spread across the country. Their best bet for tracking Rox still remained the trackers they had put in her clothes and the link between her and Josh.

<Contact when over. Update on terms> Katherine replied.

Neither Katherine nor Meita knew who had taken Jay. While Katherine might walk the line of legality and ethics, Meita couldn't imagine a scenario where Katherine would kidnap a child. What was most likely was that Josh hadn't kept as low a profile as he thought. A few of the wrong people could have learned about his ability, and subsequently about Rox. But luckily for Josh, Katherine had also found out about him. But the only way a man like Josh would work for the government (or government adjacent) was if they had leverage on him. And the only way to do that and maintain some level of trust was to help him get back the woman he loved.

But Sam and Halo had complicated the matter. It made sense that a man in Josh's circumstances would walk away once he recovered his son now that he had competition. Based on that kiss Meita and everyone else had witnessed, Rox may have already chosen. But one thing Meita had learned in the past nine months working with Josh was that he never quit; he simply changed the rules.

Meita was going to have to break cover if their plan didn't work, and Josh wouldn't handle that well. But he was a smart man and he would know that if he wanted help in rescuing Rox, he would have to cooperate. And Major Sam Watts? Most of the files she had on him and his father were heavily redacted and what wasn't was classified, and Meita hadn't the time to "un-classify" them. It was just too early to see which team he would support, but if she had to rely on instinct, she would bet that he would join them.

So that left Rox. All Meita had to do to get her onboard was find out who she was and then use that as leverage to work out some kind of arrangement.

Katherine's ability to manipulate a situation to her advantage was rubbing off.

～

Of mice and men

The sky was a brilliant blue with only the sun interrupting it. Rox felt the heat of the tarmac through her shirt as she laid down. The scent of tar and gasoline filled her lungs as bits of rubber dug into her palms and her arms.

If she said she wasn't afraid, she would be lying. The idea of handing herself over to the people who could be responsible for her memory loss made her stomach churn. She wanted to throw up, but she needed the energy. Josh had made her eat something earlier, and Sam had slipped two protein bars into her cargo pants for later.

The plan was simple. They slipped a tracking device in her sock and another in the hair tie of her ponytail. There was a high probability that both would be discovered, but that was okay because she was going to keep her mind open to Josh. Normally, Josh needed to be near his target, and it was a stronger connection if he touched them, but he was able to connect with her despite their distance. Perhaps it was because they had built a life together for three years.

Rox felt someone approaching and looked up. The sun was in her eyes, but she recognized his energy. It was stronger, but familiar. Jay. There was a bruise on his forehead and his cheekbone was swollen, but his chin was set in a way that reminded her of his father. Their eyes locked and he stopped. He hadn't known she would be here.

"Rox?"

"Hey, kiddo."

He looked back from where he came and then at the plane where his father waited.

"Wh-what are you doing here?"

Tell him to lie down.

"Jay, you gotta lie down."

He looked back at the helicopter once more as the

sound of a rifle shot silenced the helicopter blades.

"No, why are you here?" Jay lowered to his knees, but still hadn't put his chest on the pavement.

His words tore at her heart. Leaving him had been the hardest. He was just a boy transitioning into the early stages of manhood. He had needed her, but she chose a family that may be nothing more than illusion over a boy who was very much real. And here he was, alive and strong.

"I, um, I missed you," she said as tears blurred her vision.

"Wait. Did my dad trade you for me?"

She watched as the pieces fell into place in his mind and he stood up shaking his head. She pushed to her knees. "Jay! Lay down."

Tell him to lie down!

Jay shook his head and spun around. He started back towards the helicopter with Rox close on his heels. He had gotten faster in the year she'd been gone, or maybe she had just gotten slower. The sound of a second rifle shot echoed across the airstrip, and Jay rocked back with such force he spun around and fell into her arms.

"Jay!" Rox sent him energy without thought. She laid him on the tarmac just as blood began to seep out the exit wound at his back.

Rox heard Josh in her head, but she had to focus on Jay. She looked around for something to press against his shoulder, but she had nothing. Rox tugged the ends of her shirt free from her waist and up over her head. She bunched the t-shirt and pressed it over the exit wound.

Rox looked up and saw Sam racing towards her. A small smile crossed her face. So that was his ability. He was fast.

One second he was there and the next he was closer. Like he just—

"Rox?"

She looked down at Jay. He was coming to, but his body was still limp.

Rox felt the energy of someone approaching and looked over her shoulder as the butt of a rifle descended towards her. She ducked just in time, but still too late to avoid complete contact. It grazed the back of her head and sent stars dancing before her eyes. She rolled away from Jay and jumped to her feet.

"Get up!" she said as she sent more energy towards him.

The man facing her reached for his weapon and she drew his energy away from him with one strong tug. His eyes rolled back as his legs buckled and his head bounced off the ground.

Rox started towards Jay when something pinched between her shoulder blades. She used the energy from the man who attacked her to help heal what she assumed was a bullet wound in her back, but nothing happened. The normal tingle from healing was absent. Another pinch in her back and then another in her leg.

Rox! Goddammit answer me!

"Josh?" Her words were slurred.

Two pairs of hands grabbed her from behind. In her mind she struggled against them even though they dragged her back towards the helicopter. Her head rolled back and her eyes watered from the brightness of the sky.

Tranq …

Stay awake …

Jay! Her breathing was labored. *Thru and ...*
Rox!

A giggle started in her stomach and made its way up and out of her mouth. This was ironic, wasn't it? The first time she wanted their connection in over a year and she was about to lose it.

Don't think like ... Stay ... You're fading ...

She giggled again.

... Focus. What do you see?

Her head rolled to the side as she was lifted into the helicopter and the blue sky turned black. She was tossed next to the guy whose energy she had just drained.

Their faces ... Corazón ... their faces.

Rox's head bobbed twice before her eyes focused enough to make out his face.

Ugly. She giggled again and this time Josh did as well.

They can't all be as handsome as me.

Scar running ... what's that called?

I can see him. Can you look at the others?

Rox's head turned around as she tried to get her vision to focus on the others.

"How the hell is she still conscious?" Someone to the right of her spoke. His voice sounded funny over the sounds of the helicopter. She could feel them lifting off the runway and into the air. Another giggled escaped at how colossally bad the plan had gone. She was beginning to see a pattern of failed plans.

Oh shit! Josh, I can take their energy.

She started to siphon the one still holding her when her

vision focused on the man with the scar. He was holding a syringe that looked much too big for a normal human. The tip of the needle pierced her skin at the neck, and all too quickly everything faded black.

Delicate

Sam felt her slipping away. The last pulse was weak and they were due for another one that hadn't arrived. He held his breath and leapt. Things began to slow down and his muscles tightened as he pushed through the thick atmosphere surrounding him. He counted three and waited for the air to thin again, but it didn't. A force of habit wanted him to inhale, but something had always told him he shouldn't breathe when he passed through time. He watched the men drag Rox back to the helicopter in some kind of distorted slow motion, and despite their jerky movements, Sam knew he wouldn't reach her in time. He had finally surpassed three seconds and still it wasn't enough.

The air began to thin as he punched through to the other side. Jay was just a couple of feet in front of him, also trying to get to Rox. Sam grabbed him, and they all but fell into one another.

"It's all right, kid," Sam said. "I'm with your Dad."

"They took her." Jay tried to pull free, but there wasn't much strength to him.

"I know."

Sam watched the helicopter for a few more seconds before he carried Jay back towards their plane. He hated himself for turning his back on her, but if Jay died, she would have given up her freedom for nothing.

When they met Josh, what composure the boy had dissolved. His shoulders slumped as he started to cry.

"Sh, it's okay, mi hijo. Todo va a estar bien."

Kamal pushed passed him to help Jay, and Sam joined the others on the plane.

"We got a lock on her?" Sam asked as he stepped inside.

"Yes," Meita said.

Sam fell back into one of the seats. They weren't as comfortable as Josh's seats had been. These were made of the kind of leather that was easy to clean. He wasn't sure why he was thinking about the plane's interior and not devising a plan to rescue Rox, but he couldn't help but notice that the cabin smelled sickly sweet of air freshener.

His father sat down across from him and propped his feet up onto a table that was much too small to hold anything but a mobile phone. The silence between them stretched. The only noise was coming from Meita on her tablet. Her tapping was beginning to annoy him, as was his father's passive-aggressive posture.

"We knew she'd be taken." His father was the first to speak.

Yes, but it didn't make it any easier.

"She's resourceful. She was on the run for over a year. Nobody survives on the streets without knowing how to read a situation and turn it to their favor," Walter added.

Everything his father said made sense, but it did little to ease his frustration.

"Son, we're tracking her. We'll find her—"

"Just stop," Sam was on the verge of tearing the plane apart. He stood up to head back outside when his father stopped him.

"Son?"

"You don't even like her," Sam spat out.

"I didn't trust her," Walter corrected.

"Oh, now you do?"

Walter nodded. "A little."

Sam rested his forehead against the overhead compartment, all of a sudden too tired to argue with his father. "She needed help, and all any of us did was use her."

Walter nodded again. "Tis the way of the world, son. Yeah, sometimes we come across people who're good-natured, but far more likely we encounter people who need something and are willing to barter for it."

"We 'bartered' with her life."

"No, *she* bartered with her life. That's not on us."

"The hell it isn't," Sam shouted.

"I get it. You like this one. Honestly, I'm happy for you, but sitting here feeling guilty because your new love interest is more altruistic than intelligent ain't gonna help anyone right now."

Sam cast a look at his father that explained how he felt about his comment.

"We're tracking her," Walter said. "We'll get her back. She might be a bit worse for wear, but I'll tell you one thing, I don't think I've ever met a woman as resilient or able to make her own bit of luck as that one."

Sam sat back down in a seat adjacent to his father and looked up at the overhead lights until it hurt his eyes. He liked Rox and it wasn't just the connection of their energy. He liked her tenacity. "She damn near killed herself with that shock grenade," Sam said, reminiscing about her arrival at Halo.

His father chuckled. "Shaira took a nice chunk out of her shoulder, too."

Sam shook his head in amazement. "What was she thinking coming to Halo in the dead of night like that?"

"She was tired of running," Walter said. "And just a wee bit bat-shit crazy."

CHAPTER ELEVEN

~

Pain

A white-hot pain pulled Rox from the effects of the tranquilizers.

"I can tell by your breathing and the heart-rate monitor that you're awake, my dear."

Rox opened her mouth to speak, but it was too dry to form sound, and she coughed instead. She was lying on her side, and whatever was stuck into the back of her neck was quickly pulled out.

"Tsk, tsk. You must stay still." The voice behind her sighed. "Now, we're just going to have to start over again."

Panic seized her. "Wait!"

The needle pierced her skin and continue to probe deeper until it pushed against bone.

"Now, this is the part that's really going to hurt, but I'll need you to remain absolutely still. I know you can heal, but let's not test that against spinal nerve damage just yet."

Rox bit down and moaned. Tears squeezed from her eyes, and she hadn't realized she needed the bathroom until her bladder surrendered to the pain.

"That's it. Just breathe through it."

She immediately hated his voice. She tried to grab on to his energy and pull, but the pain made it impossible to distinguish between organic and artificial energy.

"Another 30 seconds. Just hang in there. You don't want to have to start this all over again."

Rox held the bile in her throat and started to count backwards from thirty. She lost count somewhere around nineteen as stars formed behind her closed eyelids.

"Pleeeaaseee!" She hated herself for begging, but she had never experienced anything like this.

A few seconds later, the needle slowly retracted and her entire body relaxed into a steady ache. She caught the first scents of her own urine, and embarrassment washed over her.

"That's it, my dear. It's over for now. I need you fully rested before we begin again. I'll have someone clean you up."

"Nancy, increase her dosage. It seems she's developed somewhat of a tolerance to the sedative." He patted Rox's shoulder like she had been a willing participant. "Which is simply remarkable, isn't it? I posit that her white blood cells adapt at an astonishing speed. But I won't know until I run more tests."

His voice started to fade as Nancy pushed more of the sedative into her IV. Rox's eyes closed without her knowledge and just before she tumbled into unconsciousness, she heard her name. *Rox.*

Trying to form a response felt like lifting weights. "Josh?"
Rox, tell me where you are?
Help me.

Betrayal

"What do you mean you lost her?" Sam shouted at Josh. The two would have come to blows if Walter hadn't broken them up. Testosterone was too high in the other room, and it was all directed at one woman.

Meita was hardly jealous. She felt sorry for Rox. No memories, betrayed and manipulated by a man who had been the only family she could remember. She had spent over a year on the run, searching for her "real" family with no idea where to start looking. To be wanted by so many, but for all the wrong reasons.

There was an obvious attraction between her and Sam. But where could that go? Rox might have a family searching for her, mourning her even. Or she might just be no one. Someone whose past had been permanently erased.

Meita wouldn't trade her memories for all the attention in the world. When things got bad, she thought of her father or the sound of her mother's voice on a message she couldn't bring herself to delete. Meita had a happy place, a mental escape hatch that led to a place where the horrors of reality could be left behind. Happy places were built on memories. But Rox had none.

Meita used the suite's hairdryer to blow her loose curls straight. She had just got the "go-ahead" to tell Josh and Sam about her assignment. She knew that Josh would hit the roof. But Sam? He was more calm. He was a thinker, and that made him dangerous because he was less predictable.

But she was counting on him to see the big picture. If he wanted Rox back, then they were going to have to play by her rules.

Meita wasn't *trying* to be manipulative, but it was obvious that the bad guys were winning. Right now, evolved humans were disappearing at an alarming rate. Like Rox, they were being scooped up by literal mad scientists trying to evolve everyone. But not everyone should evolve. Evolution, by nature, was selective for a reason. It favored those with a strategic short- and long-term advantage. Giving everyone an ability was irresponsible. Besides, she doubted that it would work. Chances are most people wouldn't make the next leap in evolution if they weren't ready.

Meita's job was to convince them that joining Katherine and her team was the right choice, for them and for their people. Sure, GFO had its flaws, but they were the best chance evolved ones had at living in relative peace.

Meita finished her hair and put on fresh clothes. She didn't have a new bra, but this wasn't a romantic encounter. The drone tasked with following Rox had stopped transmitting, the way hers had stopped when she was at Watership. All they had of Rox's locations were the coordinates from its last cell-tower ping. To Meita, this was good news because chances were the drone malfunctioned because it was near a jamming device situated around the facility that had Rox, but this was also bad news.

Meita brushed a stray strand of hair off her shoulder and decided to put her hair in a bun. A bun was much harder to grab, and she was certain that Josh was going to lunge for her when she told him who she was.

Meita opened the door to Sam pacing and Josh staring out the balcony doors. The city below was too bright for them to see any stars, but it was a beautiful view nonetheless. Josh had rented them the "superior" suite, which meant that everyone had their own private bedroom with an en suite bath. In the center was the living room, kitchen, and entertainment area.

Walter had poured himself a drink and was sipping it by the bar while he watched his son. She understood him. He had used Rox to get his daughter back, and he wasn't ever going to be apologetic about it. Kevin and Curtis were not interested in fighting one another simply because their compatriots had designs on the same woman. Instead, they appeared genuinely interested in discussing how best to go about protecting evolved ones from anti-EO groups.

Kamal was checking Jay's bandages. The boy reminded Meita so much of Josh. Fearless and stubborn. After they left the airfield where the men took Rox, he let his father have it. He shouted at Josh for letting Rox put herself in that position. He asked his father how long had he known where she was and why he hadn't told the others? And then he blamed Josh for her running away. By the time he finished, his breathing was labored and Kamal had to forcibly make him sit. It became obvious to everyone that Rox had been a surrogate mother to him.

"What're you having?" Walter asked.

"What've you got?"

"Whisky."

"Yes, please."

"On the rocks?"

"Neat."

Walter poured her a double and she knocked it back like this wasn't her first time. Meita inhaled deeply as she positioned herself next to Walter. Chances were they would hesitate to attack her if she were standing near him. He was old enough to be all their fathers, and that meant just by his age he garnered a certain amount of subconscious respect. She would need all the leverage she could find if she were to make it out of this.

"Another," she said to Walter, and then, "Josh, Sam. We need to talk."

Her voice was loud and strong. She felt the whisky make its way down her chest and settle in her stomach. She could handle more, but she was taking it slow. She was in a room of men whose trust she was about to shatter with wits as her only weapon.

"You found something?" Sam asked as he came over to the bar.

Meita waited until Josh joined them. "My name is Meita bint Tariq al-Shaikh and I work for the Global Frontier Organization."

"What?" Josh looked confused.

"I've been on assignment to determine whether you presented a threat against national – and international – security."

The room fell silent, and Meita let it linger. Silence meant they were thinking, and thinking was good.

"Have you known where Rox was the entire time?" Josh attempted to get up from his seat, but Sam placed his hand on his shoulder to keep him still.

Kevin and Curtis stood and made their way to the bar, but maintained their distance.

"No, I was genuinely searching for Rox, but my mission was to get enough information about you," she paused before she continued, "and persuade you to come work with us."

There was another long moment of awkward silence, then Josh threw back his head and laughed. It was the kind that precipitated an outburst, and that she was prepared for, but instinct told her to keep her attention on Sam. He was the wildcard and he was the one she hadn't figured out yet.

"Is that where she is?" Sam asked. "Is she with your people?"

"No, we don't have her. I had a drone over her last known location two hours ago. That drone has since moved on, but I can give you her last coordinates."

"Oh, I'm going to have fun with you, sweetheart." Josh tried to launch himself over the bar, but Sam pulled him back. For a moment, the room stilled as everyone waited to see if Josh would turn on Sam, but things settled into a tense silence.

"And what do you want in return for her location?" Walter asked.

Meita took another deep breath. She'd rehearsed this part of her speech while she was in the shower. "While we are responsible for the day-to-day operations of Project EO, the congressional Intelligence Subcommittee has budgetary oversight."

"She's not a project!" Josh spat.

Meita nodded. "I understand that, but our aim is to ascertain the domestic *and* international threat level that your kind poses."

"Kind?" Sam asked.

"Josh's ability to manipulate the mind is astounding. Imagine what would happen if he fell into the wrong hands? Or what would happen if he decided that he wanted to rule? He has the power *to control people.*" Surely they could see that was a power that needed to be checked.

"He didn't ask for that," Sam said. "None of us *asked* to be evolved."

"What does any of this have to do with Rox? Where is she?" Josh demanded.

"I've been given the authority to release her last location as of two hours ago if you agree to work on retainer for Project EO."

"Oh, you can so go fuck your—"

"Elaborate," Sam interrupted.

"There are occasions when we could use someone with your … unique abilities on certain assignments."

"Would we get to select the assignments we work on?" Sam asked.

Meita shook her head. For what it was worth, she had tried to give them that flexibility, but Katherine wouldn't hear of it.

"And if we say no?" It was Kevin who asked the question, and it was the silence that answered him.

"How many other governments have our kind working with them?" Walter asked.

Meita was surprised by his question. She told him she

didn't know the exact number, but there were at least six of their ally nations with EOs on assignments and twice as many non-ally nations.

"If you say no, then they will not send me the coordinates and therefore you'll have to find her without our assistance."

"And why should we trust you? You lied to him," Walter nodded towards Josh. "And to the rest of us."

"I just outed myself. I have no weapons and I'm literally standing here at your mercy. I told my superior that you were men of honor—"

"Save the sweet talk," Sam said. "I want to talk to whoever is in charge."

Meita shook her head.

"Either I speak with the person in charge or I'm letting go of my newfound friend here and I don't give a shit what he does to you."

Meita believed him. She sensed that Sam wasn't needlessly violent, but he wasn't afraid to use it as a means to an end. She was due to receive a call on her tablet in just over an hour. Kathrine wouldn't have a problem speaking with them, it's just that Katherine didn't care about them the way that she did. She had worked with Josh for some time, and while she had only recently met Sam and the others, it was obvious they were just trying to make the world work a bit better, perhaps more equitably for EOs.

"I have a call scheduled in an hour and twenty minutes."

"Now," Josh said. "I want to talk to her now."

Meita shook her head. "It doesn't work that way, Josh. She calls me. Not the other way around."

"Surely you have a fail-safe. A number to call if your cover is blown."

That was what the drone was for. "There is no one coming for me, Josh. If this doesn't work out, then that's it. Project EO will continue and someone else steps in to replace me."

"And Rox?" Kevin asked. "What about her?"

"This was always about Rox," Josh said. "Sure, I can listen to thoughts and even influence them, but a healer? Someone with the ability to heal *and* take life? No one is passing that up."

"It was a twofer," Sam said. "Rox was simply your honeytrap. They're going for her regardless of what we do here."

Meita hadn't thought of that, but it definitely sounded like a contingency plan that Katherine would have in play. Rox had no ties to anyone. No past. No family to prance in front of the media. No best friend who would look for her the way Kamal had done for his friend. All she had were the people in this room, and they were already in GFO's pocket whether they realized it or not.

"He's right," Meita said. "I don't know the details and I have no confirmation that is the plan. But it's what I'd do if I were in charge."

It was Jay who broke the silence. "If your guys find her first, will they return her to us or will they wipe her memories again?"

Josh banged his fist on the bar and the glasses jumped dangerously toward the edge. He stood up and kicked the barstool into the far wall.

Meita wasn't sure how to answer the boy. Everyone thought of her as the bad guy now. She was used to that. She had spent almost twenty years in this line of work. She knew the importance of perspective, but if the next generation of EOs considered their governments to be the enemy, couldn't they see that they would all be screwed?

"We don't have the technology to wipe her mind." It was half an answer.

"So you'll return her back to us?" There were dark circles under his eyes, but the hope was still there.

Meita cleared her throat. "That's above my pay grade."

The silence in the room resettled as they waited for her tablet to ring.

The box

Rox slipped into consciousness and was surprised by her ability to move. She attempted to sit up and banged her head against the roof. She looked around and realized she was in a box made of reinforced glass.

"Hello, my dear." His voice was muffled, but she recognized it anyway. "I'm afraid for this next one, we're going to need you conscious."

Rox was trapped in a container that resembled a coffin just a little too much for her liking. There were others in the room. She counted four, five if she included the doctor. She reached out with her energy, but the box created a barrier she struggled to penetrate.

Rox saw his face for the first time and she was surprised

by how ordinary he looked. There was nothing to suggest that he was the type to hold a woman against her will.

"Who are you?" Rox asked him, her voice bouncing back off the walls.

"Dr Clifford Tusk." He introduced himself with all the casualness of a coffeeshop encounter.

"Why are you doing this to me? I don't want to be here."

Dr Tusk nodded. "I suppose you don't. Humans are innately selfish. It's hardwired into our genes. Did you know that?"

He walked over to her box. "Now, I know that it will be impossible for you not to worry, but try to find some comfort in the fact that I've a team of the world's best doctors, scientists, epidemiologists and geneticists at this very facility." There was an audible grinding as an invisible valve opened. Then an intense cold hit the soles of her bare feet, and the realization of what was happening hit her: they were filling her box with water.

Rox banged against the walls. "Stop. No, please. Let me out."

"Relax, we will not let you remain dead for long."

Rox tried to sit up twice, but both times she hit her head. She was panicking and she knew it. She scooted down and kicked at the end where the water entered. It was rising fast and she was forced up onto her elbows to keep her head above it.

"What do you want from me?" she screamed.

"It'll be over soon, I promise."

The adrenaline rush made her numb to the frigid temperatures. *Josh!*

In or out

Meita's tablet rang and the room stilled. She slid her finger across the screen. "Hello."

"Is the line secure?"

"No, ma'am."

There was a pause. "Are they listening?"

"Yes, ma'am. They want to speak with you."

"And you are?" Sam said, as Josh came out of the bathroom.

"I am Director Katherine Cheung, Head of Global Frontier Organization and Project EO. To whom am I speaking?"

Shit. A bureaucrat. Just what they needed. She would have no problems talking in circles until she got what she wanted. And in the meantime, Rox was being tortured, possibly having medical experiments conducted on her in an undisclosed location and only Katherine had the coordinates.

"This is Sam."

"Ah, yes, Major Watts. Your jacket is impressive."

"What is it going to take to get Rox's location?"

"A man about business. I can respect that. Well, I'm putting together a special team. A unique team, with unique abilities. And we'd like you to head field operations."

Sam ran his hand through his hair. As much as he wanted to save Rox, he had to take the emotion out of his decision-making for all their benefits. "What's Project EO?"

There was a long pause before she answered. "That's classified."

"Then I'm afraid our answer is no."

Josh looked like he was about to protest, but Walter stopped him.

"I was told that all you wanted were the coordinates of your healer friend."

"Well, I guess you were misinformed."

There were a few tapping of keys and the rustle of paper. "Project EO is the assessment of known and suspected evolved human beings."

"Is Rox currently being held and assessed by you, your people or anyone you know?" Sam asked.

"That's a very specific question."

"I'm looking for very specific answers," Sam replied.

There was an awkward silence before she responded. "I'm afraid I don't know the answer to that." Katherine sighed and it sounded like she had picked up the receiver and taken them off speaker. "Look, the people who used to run Project EO had a very different definition of assessment. I'm not going to lie to you, Project EO has more than likely hurt a lot of people. But I'm trying to stop that."

"Because you're just so naturally altruistic," Sam bit out.

Katherine snorted. "No, son. Because I know you don't gain loyalty through threats. Your people are going to be forced to do some very bad things so that other people can get what they want."

"And what is it that you want, Katherine?"

Katherine took her time replying, as if she were giving it genuine thought. "I want to win. I want to show the entire world that this is the place to be if you're an EO. I want EOs loyal to my flag so that if the time ever came, they'd fight for us and not against us."

"And you're willing to let an innocent woman suffer to get what you want?"

"Oh, make no mistake Major Watts. I'm getting her out of there. The question is do you want to be a part of our operation."

"What will you do with her once you have her?" Walter asked.

"I'm afraid that's a private matter between Rox and I."

"Not everyone's cut out for this lifestyle," Sam said. "She doesn't strike me as the kind who is."

"Then let's hope whoever takes over field operations will take her training seriously."

Meita stood up. "I know it seems like we're the bad guys, but this is much bigger than any of you realize. Evolved humans are literally being kidnapped out of their own homes. And in the cases when the kidnappers discover that they've taken an ordinary human, what do you think happens to them? What we're proposing is that we take the good work you've done through Halo, Sam, and what you've accomplished, Josh, and we combine our resources and work together."

"You know no one in this room is ever going to work with you, right?" Josh said to Meita.

"Whoever took Rox was able to take your son despite having him under twenty-four-hour security," Meita countered. "What's to stop them from coming back when they're done with Rox?"

The tension escalated, and Sam knew by the squint in

Josh's eye he was trying to control Meita.

"Meita?" Katherine's voice cut through the silence.

"Yes, ma'am?"

"Are you prepared to lead the mission to extract the healer?"

Meita looked at Sam before she replied. "Yes, ma'am."

"Good, I'm assuming there's a lot of valuable information onsite. Your priority will be to recover that intel. I'll assign two others who'll locate and recover the healer."

Sam swore under his breath. Katherine was making it very obvious that if they wanted to ensure Rox remained a priority on this mission, they needed to join her.

"Meita, I have your coordinates and will send transport to your location in forty minutes. Gentlemen, you have until then to decide whether you're in or out."

Bat-shit crazy

Rox was sitting in the middle of a movie theatre. She had popcorn in her lap and a latte in her seat's cupholder. Seated on her left were the two kids from the photograph. They were excited, talking to one another about the movie they were about to see.

"Excuse me. Is this seat taken?"

"No, please."

In her happy place, Sam and her met at the movie theatre. Her kids were there because in the happy place, they were her children and not some anonymous faces in a photo. She knew a husband had to figure into the mix, but because she didn't have an image of him in her mind, she would let Sam play his role. She hadn't worked out all the kinks in her happy place yet, but it kept her focused when the pain was at its worst. It kept her from screaming like she had promised herself.

Rox had lost track of the cuts and the wounds, the blood and skin samples taken before she healed, as she healed, and after. After she woke from drowning, Dr Tusk had set part of her arms on fire and watched under a microscope as her cells rehydrated themselves, then made new copies until her skin looked new and unblemished. As she writhed and screamed in pain, he only seemed capable of remarking on how extraordinary her ability was.

She wasn't sure if that was a few days ago or only a few hours, but she did notice that they had stopped restraining her. They preferred to keep her unconscious on sedatives and had worked out her rate of adaptation to the medicine. They realized that pain broke through the sedation, regardless of the dose, and for some reason Rox felt it was important that she remember that bit of information.

Josh had stayed connected with her through most of it. She asked him about Sam, and he reluctantly answered. He told her about Meita, and Rox had to admit she wasn't surprised. Nothing seemed real anymore. Josh told her that Walter missed her, and she laughed out loud because she couldn't imagine a reality where he would miss her.

At night, when he was alone, Josh would sometimes speak to her in Spanish, confessing his love and sorrow for all he had done. He told her that it had been three days since she was taken, and they were getting close to her location, but she had to hold on and not give up hope.

In the moments when everything hurt, she had found true forgiveness for him. Her anger served no purpose, and it was in letting go of that anger that she realized the only way to be truly free was to let go of her past. That included him. She knew it would hurt him, but she had told him goodbye. She couldn't take the pain and his feelings of helplessness as he listened to her cry out. Besides, Jay needed him. So, she broke their connection.

The door slid open some time later, but Rox was too tired to turn her head to see who entered.

"Oh, are you awake?" It sounded like the nurse who wore that horrible shade of pink lipstick. "That's about forty minutes earlier than predicted. We'll have to adjust your meds."

The nurse hesitated in the doorway as if unsure what to do. Rox continued to lie there, disconnected and disinterested in whatever vitals she had come to check or from which arm she was going to need to draw blood.

"Honey, you awake?" Rox heard the nurse step closer, but the latch on the door did not catch, which meant it was still open.

Rox had been kept so heavily sedated that it took her a few moments to realize that she could feel the nurse's energy. Her body reacted on instinct and drank. The nurse managed one step before crumbling to the floor.

The energy Rox took was enough to counter the sedatives in her system, but she sat up too quickly from spending so much time lying down. She fell face first onto the floor as the lock on the door reengaged. When she opened her eyes, she was staring at cotton-candy-colored pink lips.

CHAPTER TWELVE

Alliances

Katherine had the same helicopter waiting for them on the roof of the building two blocks from their hotel. Its rotors were shaped like wings, and Sam had learned that helped to reduce their sound. There were also the same two black duffle bags of weapons and the same sets of armor for each of them. Looking new and untouched.

This was their third straight day looking for Rox. The drone went down just on the outskirts of the city, which meant they had a lot of area to cover. All the locations they checked before came up empty. Despite crossing places off their list, they were still no closer to finding her. Their morale was dropping, and if they didn't find her soon, they wouldn't recover. Experience taught him that.

Josh had asked Katherine if Rox would be forced to join their team when they last spoke. Katherine reiterated that that was a private conversation, but added she couldn't *force* anyone to join. Sam agreed. Katherine probably had a team looking into Rox's background. She would hold that carrot in front of Rox and let her decide. He hated that he knew what she would choose, but he couldn't deny that he was excited about seeing her again. Working with her could complicate their relationship, but they were going to take things slow. Have that date. He was going to find out her favorite flavor of ice cream.

Strawberry.

Josh held up his hands in mock surrender. *Sorry, but your face gave it away.*

Gave what away?

That you were thinking about her.

What am I thinking now?

"You first," Josh said.

Meita reached above them to connect her tablet to the monitor mounted on the ceiling. She swiveled it down so everyone could see. "Gentlemen, we are headed to this location."

"And what's there?" Sam asked.

"Nothing. But according to old zoning maps, this used to be a fairly large retreat facility. Corporate execs would go there to relax and team build, wealthy couples would host their wedding receptions there. Stuff like that."

"And just how likely do you think this is the place we're looking for?" Sam asked. He was starting to feel like they were chasing their tail.

"Given that I'm struggling to get any type of surveillance over the location, I'd say pretty likely."

"Could these be the same people who took Rox the first time?" Josh asked. "I mean, it's a different location, but they could've just relocated."

"There's no way to tell. You found her at Mockingbird – that was the first facility we discovered when Katherine took over. We've since closed it down, but we always knew there were more."

"And what's your plan for this one?" Sam asked.

"That's what I need to talk to you about. We have two goals: recover as much information about the facility and its types of research as safely as possible, and to get Rox out without being detected. So that means no unnecessary kills. I know it's a tall order, but let's try to get in and out without being detected."

"You don't think they'll notice when Rox's gone?" Walter asked.

Meita nodded. "Sure, but we don't think that'll immediately lead to a facility closure. We're hoping that someone will rely on the chain of command to figure out what to do next."

"And you want to see who's in that chain," Sam said.

"Exactly. See if there's any financial exchanges occurring as well."

"So we're just going to leave the people in there to continue to be experimented on?" Sam asked.

"Nothing in life is clear cut, Major. You, of all people, know that."

I never properly thanked you and your father for helping me get my boy.

If you hadn't shown up when you did, not sure we would've made it out of Watership.

There was an awkward moment of silence between them.

Sorry about your daughter.

Sam coughed to clear his throat. It was better when they stayed annoyed with each other.

I need to know if you're good enough for her.

Sam ripped off his headset and leaned closer to Josh. *Well, I won't manipulate her into thinking she loves me, if that's what you mean.*

She does love me. The thought was confident and succinct. *But yeah, I fucked up.*

Sam expected the connection between them to end, but when it remained open, he reached out tentatively to explore the thread.

Josh was ashamed about what he did to Rox. He was still in love with her, but had accepted that she needed space, and he was willing to give it to her. Meita had struck a nerve when she mentioned his inability to protect his son. And that was the real reason he joined. He had no disillusions about how much control he was giving up, but he believed that he had a better chance of protecting Jay this way.

Sam understood the need to protect his family.

Can you reach out to her? Sam asked.

Josh sighed. *They've been pumping her with sedatives. So it comes and goes. When she's unconscious, her mind is blank, so when she wakes up, that's my best bet of reaching her before she shuts me out.*

You ever establish a link with three people?

A few times, but I'll have to touch you. And it won't be for long. There was a moment of silence before he continued.

When she wakes, let her know we're coming.

You think this is the right location?

It had better be.

One to go

Wonderland was located about one hundred miles west of the airport, which was at least ninety minutes outside of the city. The road up to the facility was a single lane that curved through a moderately dense wood. A creek ran about half a mile through the property from the main building along the back end. According to old satellite images, it looked like the ideal location for those who valued privacy.

Meita could feel the vitriol in Josh's gaze, but she had a job to do. It was easy enough to understand his position, but she wouldn't be good at her job if she allowed her feelings to hurt every time she had an assignment. Her line of work was messy. It got complicated. Sometimes lies were the only way to get at the truth.

The helicopter dropped them off at the private helipad located on the edge of the airport. She waited until the pilot gave her the signal to alight, and she made her way over to the two black SUVs waiting for them. She didn't bother to look over her shoulder because she was certain that the others were following.

The doors to the SUVs opened, and for the first time since breaking her cover, Meita relaxed. She had worked with Danny and his team on a brief assignment a few years ago. He and his men were sent to "deal" with a situation and extract any survivors. Luckily, she was one of them. These men were composed, ready, and armed.

"Nice to see you again, Eagle Eyes." Danny said when she stopped in front of him. For a moment, she thought maybe he was going to hug her, but then the absurdity of it registered.

"Danny," she said and returned his nod. "Team One has search and rescue responsibility."

"Then they're with me." He turned to the others. "Name's Danny. You can call me Danny. I heard that you guys still haven't found what you're looking for."

Meita nodded, but kept on task. "Team Two is looking for any intel they can grab."

"Then they're with BS."

"Let me guess, I can call him BS?" Josh said.

"No, you can call him Boggs. Can call him Stein if you survive this mission without getting him or one of us killed, Pretty Boy."

Josh walked into that, and Meita couldn't deny she had derived a large amount of satisfaction from it. Boggs was short for Bogstein and only those who had served with him had the right to call him BS. It was an inside joke – one she didn't even know the details of. But she had earned his respect, which meant he was BS to her, though she rarely used it.

"You Major Watts?" Danny asked Sam.

The two quickly sized each other up, both quietly nodding at their assessments. Katherine must have forwarded Danny copies of Sam's and Walter's files. She would have left out most of the redacted content, but included just enough details to let Danny know that Sam would be an asset.

"Then that makes you First Lieutenant Watts," Danny said. "Normally don't get father and son on the same mission."

"'Fraid this ain't a 'normal' mission."

"None of them ever are, Pops."

Walter nodded his agreement.

Team One followed Meita into one SUV with Danny, while Team Two followed Boggs into another. Danny passed them a pocket-sized map of the property as they drove. "This map is old and probably no longer accurate. We're on radio silence unless absolutely necessary."

"We have until sunrise to pull this off. That gives us just under eight hours," Meita said.

They rode the rest of the way in silence as everyone familiarized themselves with the map. Meita glanced over at Sam and could see from the look on his face that he didn't like his father heading off with men neither of them knew, but Walter knew how to handle himself. Despite his age, the man was fit. Fitter than most men half his age. What he might have lost in speed, she knew he would make up in experience.

While Meita was trained in physical combat, her skills were subterfuge. She could blend anywhere. Most of the world had a brown-skinned population somewhere. Even in the fjords there was a small contingent of people who stood out amongst the fair. She had learned to let people's stereotypes work to her advantage. In Europe, she was moderate Muslim; in the Americas, she was mixed-race; and in the Middle East and East Asia, she was what she was. Her fast thinking and innocent smile got her out of most situations, but this one would require a more physical approach.

"Our target from here on in will be referred to as Paladin," Danny said. "If we need to break radio silence, I am Team Lead. The rest of you are numbers." He looked at Sam. "You are Two. Meita, One. And I'll make an exception for you," he turned to Josh. "You're PB."

Surprisingly, Josh just nodded, and Meita realized that he was busy trying to connect with Rox.

Meita put in her earpiece and confirmed it was working. Then she slid the balaclava over her head and face. For a brief moment, she thought of her mother before she pushed the thought away. She was her father's daughter, and the ability to be many things at once was her inheritance. A woman who had spent the past year of her life looking for her identity was being held against her will. Even if she didn't know who had taken Rox, she could tell by the look on Josh's face that they were hurting her. He was trying to keep it to himself, to hide it from Sam, but they all knew.

To be an evolved one wasn't like the movies. Everyone was in an arms race to find EOs that could be weaponized, which left far too many of their kind dying for nothing. And as much as Meita hated manipulating people who were just trying to get by, she knew what was coming. Everyone would have to pick a side. Most would choose to put their heads in the sand and protect their self-interests. She couldn't blame them. Not everyone could stand for something. The world needed its sheep. But Meita had made her choice a long time ago. She had picked her side, and she was going to die playing for it. Those EOs with passive abilities deserved to live in peace. But the Sam's, the Josh's, and especially the Rox's didn't get that choice. They had a responsibility to the next generation of EOs with active abilities. They would fight and die so that the ones who came later wouldn't have to. She understood that, and it was her job to convince, manipulate, or blackmail anyone who could help further that cause.

Two down. One to go.

Wonderland

The sedatives were still coursing through her body, but taking the nurse's energy was helping to counteract it. Rox's movements were clumsy as she got to her feet, but she was steady enough to search for the nurse's access card.

¿Qué tal todo? You okay?

Rox jumped and almost fell back down, but quickly realized it was Josh.

I just stole the energy from a nurse. I've decided I don't want to die here.

Good. Because I'm not risking my life to save a dead woman.

Where are you?

The perimeter. We've got two teams coming in. What can you tell us?

Joy filled her. *How'd you find me? How long have I been here?*

Long story. Over thirty-six hours. Now your turn. What can you tell us about this place?

Rox used the card to open her door and entered the empty hallway.

Not much. This is my first time outside of my room without being sedated or dead.

Each door she passed had a narrow window that reminded her of a hospital. There was a keypad by each handle and she wondered if Nancy's card would work, but she didn't have time for exploration. She needed to get to the perimeter. The nurse would wake eventually and sound the alarm.

The growl from Rox's stomach reverberated down the hallway.

When was the last time you ate?

I don't know. Having trouble accounting for time.

You alright?

No, she felt lightheaded all of a sudden. The hallway seemed to be getting narrower, and lying down on the cool tiles felt like a very good idea.

Rox! I need you to keep moving. Don't stop. Find someplace to hide and stay connected to me.

Josh was right. She was very low on energy. She couldn't remember the last time she had eaten, and that nurse wasn't enough to counteract the sedatives *and* keep her adrenaline pumping.

She pressed the keycard against the pad and a soft beep sounded. The light turned green and the name Nancy Flagstaff appeared across the screen. Rox opened the door and entered the next hallway. She waited until the door was almost closed before she caught it to make sure it didn't slam. A room was just ahead of her on the right. She could hear voices and someone was screaming. Fear stopped her and she placed her back against the wall. She grabbed the back of her neck where the memory of pain still radiated. She wasn't sure she could do this again.

Yes you can. You rescued Sam's sister from Watership. This is no different.

This was very different. She had been the patient. She now knew the pain. She had experienced the cause of the man's screams. His voice was raw, and she wondered if hers had sounded the same. Her hands started to shake. The confidence she had at Watership was born of ignorance. She had been in her share of fights: she had been shot, stabbed, had her throat slit, and spent over a year on the run all alone. But, she had never experienced the defenselessness or the vulnerability of being at the mercy of someone else's evil desires. Being strapped to a bed, drowned and set on fire just so others could catalogue her body's reaction illustrated just how vulnerable EOs truly were. It was naive to think that she could have ever done this on her own. Her real name was meaningless if there was no one there to say it. Life was about creating authentic relationships. It was about people, and sometimes those people shared your DNA, and other times family were the people you met along the way.

Rox leaned against the wall to catch her breath. It wasn't just the sedatives that syphoned her energy, it was the fear. The fear of getting captured. The fear of having to live through that pain again. The fear of not being able to give either Josh or Sam what they wanted.

In that moment, when all her thoughts should be

centered on escaping, the truth was shining as brightly as the fluorescent lights overhead. She couldn't be anything to anyone because she had no idea who she was. Discovering her past would only tell her who she used to be. She had spent too much time looking for memories that weren't there and had missed the entire point of living: creating new ones. She didn't have to stop looking for her past or the family she knew existed even if she had no reason to believe so. It just couldn't become all-encompassing. It was time to value the relationships she had, no matter how messed up they were.

Can we do this psychoanalysis shit later? I'm about two secs from making Sam stab himself. And if this GI Joe wannabe calls me Pretty Boy one more time, I'm going to make him shit in his hand and eat it.

A bubble of laughter burst free, and Rox jumped to cover her mouth. It was like she had a revelation of sorts and all she could think about was who she wanted to be. It felt ... freeing.

Rox pushed off the wall and continued forward. She was going to make it out of there. There were so many things that she wanted to discover about herself.

Your favorite color is green, but do you think you can keep moving forward or should I ask your kidnappers to pause for a moment while you continue with this existential train of bullshit thought!

The hall silenced as a sharp pain originated at the base of her neck where they had used the needle to extract something from her. Probably her DNA. Bone marrow. She had a feeling they took everything they could and would come back for more. She was a woman. They would eventually want to examine her reproductive system if they hadn't already.

She peered through the small window and saw another doctor sticking a long needle into the back of a man's neck. He was strapped to the bed just like she had been. She wanted to—

Don't. We can come back for him ...

How could she leave him? It was like walking away from herself. She remembered the unconscious man she stole energy from after she had been attacked and died at Watership. She left him and countless others in that facility. And then there was Connor. She had killed him. She hadn't wanted to, but he was dead nonetheless. She had to stop making decisions that were guided by some past ideal of who she was. It was all about who she wanted to be.

No. You can't help him!

Sometimes, the only way out was through, and the only thing left was hope.

One doctor and one nurse.

Rox!

She could take them.

Déjà vu

"Shut him the hell up or I'm going to put a bullet in him now."

Sam had never seen Josh that agitated. He had been distracted as they made their way through the woods and out to the perimeter of the facility. For the most part, he kept quiet, but every now and again he would hear Josh muttering something aloud. It sounded like words of encouragement, and people didn't need motivation unless they were contemplating giving up. He hadn't known her long, but the Rox he had grown to admire wasn't a quitter. He had watched her die, and then get back up. He watched her willingness to sacrifice herself to go back and help Josh, and then knowingly walk into a trap to save Jay's life.

"Rox!"

Sam clamped his hand over Josh's mouth and placed him in a chokehold. He wasn't trying to put Josh to sleep, he just needed to get him to quiet.

The moment he grabbed Josh, the night became awash in shimmering black and whites, and Rox was there. Inside his head. He tripped over her thoughts as they collided with his.

"Rox?"

He felt her awareness of him. She was scared and determined. Her mind was frenetic, and he was struggling to grasp a coherent thought. Who was Connor and why did she feel responsible for his death?

It took every ounce of his training to not use his ability to sprint across the field to the main building. He had no idea if Rox was even in there, but progressing at this pace was heart wrenching. He felt her wavering resolve. Her preference to death over restraint. She hated herself for her fear, but at the same time she felt relief at finally having a purpose. And he couldn't deny the joy that burst into his heart when he realized that she felt the same about him as he did about her. It was there. Buried behind all the shit that they were going through. But just behind her attraction was a sadness that brought tears to his eyes. Why would being attracted to him make her sad?

Josh elbowed him in the ribs, and he tightened his hold. Sam's connection wavered, and he squeezed Josh harder as if that would help him stay closer to Rox. He watched as she pushed into the room. The nurse gave a small scream and someone took Rox by surprise from behind the door. He grabbed her, but she twisted free from his grip and pulled at his energy. The guard slumped to the floor at her feet, blocking the door.

Sam felt fresh adrenaline pour through her.

"Stop!" Rox shouted at the doctor, and he lowered the syringe from the IV bag. She looked at the man on the bed, and Sam had to squint through her dilated pupils to get a better look. It was a boy. Older than Josh's boy, but too young to be anyone's test subject.

The nurse! Josh's mind screamed.

Rox turned her attention to the nurse. She took another small step towards the counter at her back. She was going for the red button on the wall that would sound the alarm. The nurse saw the moment Rox realized her intention and lunged for the button, but instead crashed into the rolling tray that held the medical instruments. Her stumble gave Rox the time she needed. She grabbed the nurse by her arm as it flailed out in an attempt to regain her balance. She pushed the nurse onto the floor and reached up for the first thing her fingers closed around on the tray. The nurse broke free just as Rox plunged a scalpel into her shoulder, just between her collarbone and shoulder. She fell forward as the nurse's energy called out to hers, threatening to take what Rox didn't want to give.

Sam felt like someone was sucking the breath out of his lungs. "What's happening to her?" Sam asked. "Why's she healing the nurse?"

"Finish her!" Josh shouted.

Sam was yanked away from Josh, and his connection with Rox ended before he could see what happened.

Awareness returned to Sam just as Danny released him and stepped back out of his reach.

"Will you two shut the fuck up?" Danny whispered as loudly as he dared. "We don't have time for this shit."

Sam squeezed his eyes shut and tried to reacquaint himself with their surroundings. Danny was right, they needed to stay focused, but he couldn't stop thinking about Rox. Why would she heal the nurse?

You grab me like that again and I will literally make you put an eye out, Josh said to Sam.

"We need to move." Danny's voice held a sense of urgency that helped focus Sam's thoughts. He nodded, not trusting his voice, and Danny helped Josh to his feet. "The patrol is gone, but we've about half the time now to make it across this opening before the next group comes along." He raised his weapon and started at a crouched sprint across the open yard.

Sam waited until Danny was halfway before he sent Josh afterwards. "Get down and crawl if you sense someone coming."

Josh nodded and followed behind Danny in the same fashion.

By the time Sam made it to the building, Danny had secured the entrance and the front door was open. Two guards were down in the foyer. Dead. He hated that taking out those two might jeopardize finding other facilities like this, but he remembered the look on Rox's face as she bled out from the throat.

Danny used one of the keycards he had taken from the guards on the door and it opened with a quiet swoosh. Steps led down into a small office. There was a door just ahead of them, opposite the one they had just come through. A filing cabinet was pushed against the wall to his left and on his right sat a desk with three monitors, a keyboard, but no discernible computer. A clip-light was attached to the bottom of the center screen that shone down on the desk. Whoever sat there was assembling something.

Sam couldn't make out what it was supposed to be based on the parts, but he spotted a box in the trash. "Battery-powered robot," he whispered to himself. Someone was sitting here doing their hobby while Rox was being tortured.

There was a soft beep from the other door where it had rejected the keycard that Danny had used. *Access Denied* ran across the keypad in bold, red letters. He pulled out the second one, and they all breathed a sigh of relief when the lock disengaged.

Sam clicked the safety off his weapon and took a few calming breaths. He focused on the door as Danny opened it. Another hallway, thankfully empty.

Sam took point. *Can you feel her?* he asked Josh.

There was a moment of silence before Josh responded. "She's shut me out."

Sam was worried about her. The nurse had been pulling on her energy. Was that what Josh meant by "finish her"? Either Rox killed her or inadvertently heal her?

He searched his memories and realized that for the moments he was joined with Rox and Josh, his thoughts didn't exactly belong to him. It reminded him of being in a dream where he was able to slip between characters. She had been scared, but most of all he felt her resolve. She was resigned that her fate lay in that room.

"Josh?" Sam spoke without looking over his shoulder.

What?

"Why'd she go in there?"

Danny snorted. "Can't wait to meet this woman."

Sam turned back and watched Josh look at Danny. *He has no idea that I could make him do things to himself that would make him question his sexuality.*

Sam swallowed back his smile. *The room. Why'd she go in it?*

There was a man in a room she passed.

And?

She went to help him.

OK. That'll slow her up, sure. But escaping with someone can only help her if they're discovered.

They reached the end of the corridor and Sam peeked his head around. Nothing. He signaled for Danny to resume the lead.

Cornered

Josh's voice echoed inside her head as she yanked out the scalpel and the nurse fell to the floor, hitting her head on the edge of the counter, a half-dozen rapid heartbeats away from death.

Another energy source was calling to hers and she realized it was the boy on the table. A needle that was much larger than anything she had seen was dangling from the base of his neck, like the inside of his head was the only thing keeping it from falling to the floor. His eyelids twitched and she felt his energy pulsating. He was in pain, but not all of it was physical. He was fading into a place that instinct told her was bad. She slowly pulled the needle out of him and then placed her hands on his head. She didn't need to touch him to heal him, but something about him called out to her.

"Tara, where's Nancy?"

The doctor's back was pressed against the wall, and Rox ignored him as she reached for the nurse's remaining energy and pulled. She pushed as much of death's energy towards the boy as she could. She kept a little for herself, but without food and proper rest, her chances of staying upright were quickly fading.

The boy started to pull against his restraints, but Rox turned her attention on the doctor.

"What are you doing?" he asked her.

Rox assumed that he hadn't made a run for it because

the guard was essentially blocking the door, and she would be able to attack him before he could move the body out of the way. And she would definitely attack him.

"Why would you do this to him?" Her voice caught when she saw the needle marks and bruises along the back of the boy's neck and spine.

"When Dr Tusk returns, Tara, he's—"

Then Rox looked up. Did the doctor know her? "Why did you call me Tara?"

The only look she recognized on his face was confusion.

"Where's Nancy? What have you done with Nancy?" he asked her.

"Why did you call me Tara? Do you know who I am?"

He took a step towards her, and Rox reached for the scalpel she had placed on the bed when she began to unbuckle the boy. The doctor stopped and then studied her. "Same height. Same face. Your hair is different, but then that's to be expected."

"You know me?"

There was an awkward moment of silence when he realized he had the upper hand.

"Don't think I won't use this on you." Goosepimples ran down her back and along her arm. He knew who she was. Josh had rescued her all those years ago from the very people who knew her identity. They were the ones who probably took her. "What do you want from me?"

"I see your memory has still not returned."

So he knew! "What did you do to me? Why can't I remember anything?"

"We have no idea why you lost your memories."

Rox looked down again at at the boy on the bed. "What are you doing to him? Are you trying to steal his abilities?"

"Not 'steal', sweetheart. Replicate. We want to replicate them in the un-evolved."

She reached for his energy and pulled a little of it to her. The doctor looked like he was about to take a step towards her, but she shook her head. He was very familiar with her, calling her "sweetheart" and speaking to her as if they had shared more than just a laboratory relationship of test rat and scientist.

"I can see you haven't thought this through. I'm guessing you were able to incapacitate Nancy the same way you did the guard there. An ability that I must admit is new to me. But once you got in here, then what? Even if you manage to kill me, how are you going to get out of here?"

He was stalling. He thought her escape was luck, which it had been, but he didn't know that others were coming for her. Did they really think Josh would leave her here after spending well over a year looking for her? Maybe they thought he wouldn't have a choice. How would he possibly find her?

"Cat got your tongue, dear?"

"Stop calling me that. I'm not your 'sweetheart'. Either tell me what I want to know or I'm going to lay you down by the guard there."

He laughed, but it lacked sincerity. He held up his hands and backed up against the wall again. "What do you want to know?"

"Who I am?"

"I'm afraid you'll have to be a bit more specific."

He was toying with her, and she knew it. If she were smart, she'd incapacitate him, but he had answers she'd been searching for.

"What's my name?"

"Well, when you were in our care, you were simply called Tara."

"Is that my real name?"

"I have no reason to believe otherwise."

"Help me." The boy on the table looked at her. She'd forgotten to release his hands.

"Go on. Take him. I'm genuinely interested to see how far you get."

Rox kept the scalpel in her hand as she unbuckled the remaining straps. She should have just pulled the doctor's energy and let him fall to the floor, but she was hoping he would say something more. Perhaps let a small detail slip that could help her find out who she really was. It was selfish, not to mention stupidly dangerous, but she had just learned more about herself in three minutes than over the past four years.

"But know this," the doctor said. "I will have him killed when we recapture you both."

The boy sat up with surprising ease, and Rox remembered the energy she gave him. He looked straight at the doctor when he spoke. "I still want to go." His voice was hoarse and was only a whisper, but it held a finality that shouldn't have been there in one so young.

"It'll be quick, and something *you* can't heal."

The boy had started to pull the guard away from the door while the doctor just stood there with his arms crossed, looking like he had all the answers. And who knew, maybe he did, but he talked about taking this boy's life like it had no meaning.

Rox felt shame when she realized she almost hadn't come in to help him. Maybe that would have been for the best. Maybe if she had kept going, he wouldn't be facing a possible execution.

No. He'd be stuck on that fucking table wishing over and over that someone would just kill him.

Rox looked at the doctor one last time before she took his energy with the same determination that the boy had shown when he said he would take his chances. The doctor's eyes rolled back as his legs collapsed. He fell onto the side of the bed, and there was no way that the impact had hurt him, but she took solace in the headache he would have.

His energy filled her and the adrenaline counteracted the utter fatigue she was feeling, but she pushed some to the boy. She had no idea what his ability was, but she hoped it was something aggressive. Something really aggressive like melting people's faces off.

Josh?

Babe?

Stop calling me that. She had enough of sarcastic terms of endearment.

Really? You want to have that discussion now?

I need your help.

No shit.

Where are you?

Basement. Making our way to you.

Voices sounded on the other sound of the door.

Is that you?

Not yet, ba—

"Shit," she said.

Can you get out?

No. She didn't think it wise to stick her head out to have a look.

Barricade.

"Have a seat," she told the boy.

"What? Why? I don't want to stay."

"We're not, but the guards have just arrived and we need to hold them off until my friends get here."

"You have help?"

Behind the pain in his eyes, hope shone like love did when first awakened. It brought out an intense protective instinct in her. "Yes." She was getting him out of there.

Rox pulled the guard back in front of the door and then unlocked the wheels on the bed and pushed it so that he was wedged in between. He would be bruised when he came to, and she hoped a little more than sore. She looked through the drawers while the footsteps drew closer. She doubted she would find a weapon, but perhaps she would find something that could give them an advantage if they had to fight.

"Someone's really coming to get us out of here?"

"Keep an eye on him." Rox nodded to the doctor. "Yes. But I think the guards have arrived first."

There was a knock on the door. "Doctor?" It was one of the guards. He knocked again, before someone else told him to step back. The keycard beeped and the lock released. The door opened a small crack, but no more.

"What do we do?" the boy asked.

The drawers had come up empty except for medical equipment, and they couldn't do much with a box of bandages and sealed syringes. Rox wanted to scream in frustration. She didn't want this boy's life to end in some cold laboratory where mad scientists performed experiments on people as if they were nothing more than a means to an end. He was too young.

The first pulse of energy washed over her. *Sam!*

And me! I'm here, too, you know. How many in the room?

Three. Two unconscious and one dead.

OK, there's three or four outside in the hall. Get down and stay down.

"What's your name?" Rox asked the boy.

"Miles."

"My friends are here, Miles, but we have to stay down."

The commotion outside the door announced that they had made contact. Men screamed while others were silenced. The door burst open as someone threw their full weight into it. It was just enough for two men to fall inside, one on top of the other. Miles shrank back and slipped in the nurse's blood. She heard him go down, but she didn't take her eyes off the two guards clambering to their feet.

Without any shoes on, this was going to hurt, but she kicked the one nearest her. He blocked her second attempt and raised his weapon. She sucked all his energy with one rapid pull, but then felt giddy from too much adrenaline. He passed out, but the other guard had already taken aim at her. She dove to the side just as white hot fire erupted at a single point in her arm and then spread down the entire side of her body.

Rox tried to push the bed into him, but she had relocked the wheels and she couldn't get enough leverage. He had fired two more shots, both of them wide, but dangerously close. She scampered under the bed away from him when a sickening crack echoed throughout the room. She glanced over her shoulder and saw Miles wielding a fire extinguisher. She wasn't sure where he had found it, but she was grateful. The guard fell unconscious on top of his colleague, but Miles struck again.

Death's energy filled the room and Rox's gunshot wound healed around the bullet. The second wave of energy collided with her, and she found herself struggling for control. On one hand, she needed the energy, but she hadn't eaten and rested since … since Crossroads.

"We need to move them." Miles' voice cut through her thoughts.

The guard that Miles had killed was still wedged between the door. She grabbed the back of his shirt and began to pull him in when the ringing started. The door's alarm was going off, probably because it had remained open too long.

More guards were coming.

CHAPTER THIRTEEN

Fear and loyalty

It took Rox and Miles a lot longer than she had anticipated to get the guards' bodies in, past the other guard and the bed. When they finally closed the door, the alarm stopped, but Rox felt the rush of too much energy. She could open the door and take the guards by surprise.

Bad idea. Just stay put.

She didn't need their help. While Sam and Josh distracted the guards, she could attack. They wouldn't see it coming.

Do some jumping jacks.

What? Are you saying I can't handle them?

"Why are you doing squats?" Miles asked her.

She was beginning to feel lightheaded. Something was wrong. She wasn't sure how much longer she was going to be able to hold out. The sedatives, the lack of food, and the emotion and physical fatigue of the last few days had finally caught up with her. Death's energy was keeping her upright, but she was burning through it much too fast.

Sam. It was just a thought as the room tilted. Rox wasn't sure if it was in her head or if reality had somehow become distorted. She wanted to get Miles out of there, but she was having enough problems saving herself at the moment.

"Rox!" Sam's voice cut through the commotion, and the first sign of peace swept through her.

"Is that your friend?" Miles had dark circles under his eyes that made them look small and ineffective. His lips were cracked and she heard the dryness in his throat.

How could anyone do this to another human being? Did being evolved mean so much that people were willing to lose their humanity to gain abilities? Tears slipped down her cheeks as exhaustion seeped back into her bones.

Babe? You're scaring the shit out of me.

She was so very tired. Ever since she left Josh, all she'd been doing was running. Her limbs felt leadened and her mind was a maze of wool. She couldn't reconcile the fact that Miles was just a child. Did she have children this age? Were they an experiment in another facility like this one? Did they have a father and if so, was he protecting them?

Rox!

There was a lot of shouting going on and if she simply let go, it would all disappear. Sam's pulse was like a promise of paradise she no longer had the will to strive for.

The door pushed open a fraction. "Rox?" It was Sam.

Miles was the first to react. He dropped the extinguisher and began to move the bed.

Each of Rox's blinks were lasting longer than the previous one. It was strange to be this close and still feel so distant. Then Sam enveloped her in his arms and it was like waking from a deep sleep. Energy poured back into her.

Calm settled in her mind as fresh tears fell. His hands on the back of her neck were peace. He guided her head into his chest and she let out a sob. His lips brushed her hair as he whispered something she couldn't make out over the hiccuping sounds of her release.

"More are on their way." It was a voice she didn't recognize coming from just outside the door.

Sam stepped back, but didn't let go. "Are you hurt?"

She hurt everywhere. Her teeth were sore, and she had no idea that was even possible. Her neck and shoulders felt like they belonged to an action figure with limited movement. She didn't want to think about her back and arms. The wounds had healed, but she didn't think her muscles and nerve endings would ever forget the pain.

"Can you get us out of here?"

Rox looked over at Miles. There was bright hope in his eyes.

It took Sam a moment before he spoke, and Rox wondered if he too had noticed how young Miles was. "Stay behind me," he finally said.

A man whose girth gave her hope that they had a chance to make it out stood outside the door, his weapon raised with his back to them. All his attention was focused on the corridor. Rox chanced a look and saw a guard seated, his back against the wall, his chin on his chest. A trail of blood led down the wall and disappeared behind his back. She might have seen a pair of boots peeping around the corner, but she didn't care. This place was evil.

She followed Sam away from the bodies and around the corner were Josh crouched. Creases lined his forehead. He was attempting to control someone, someone he couldn't see.

Sam put his hand on Josh's shoulder when the man with a broad everything joined them. "Our fastest option is to head back the way we came, but you can bet your ass we'll have company."

Josh shook his head as his vision slowly refocused on her. A genuine smiled crossed his face.

Can I have a hug?

She launched into his arms and inhaled his scent. *"Thank you."*

He drew back and kissed her neck. *Siempre.*

She felt Sam tug on her arm and they all started moving down the hall as a unit. The large man took point. It wasn't too complicated, but there were a few twists and turns, and Rox knew if she had to lead Miles out of here on her own, they would never have made it. They went up some steps, over a few guards that had been taken out, and through a door with one of the fallen guard's keycard.

"There's two about fifty meters outside this door," Josh said, when they were at the last door leading outside.

Rox closed her eyes and tried to let her energy reach out, but her stomach turned at the effort. The room tilted and Josh was the first one to reach her. "Let me look."

"I'm all right," she said, but her voice was weak.

A crash sounded behind them and they spun around to see Miles leaning over the desk. He had knocked one of the computer screens to the floor. Rox reached out to him and again felt a shiver down her back at his energy.

What's his ability? Josh asked.

Didn't have time to ask.

"What's wrong?" Sam asked as he put himself between her and Miles.

Miles looked up as if he were seeing them for the first time, then he shook his head and his eyes lost some of their fear. "You guys are … it's … complicated. I think it'd be best if I follow him."

Miles pointed to the big guy, who looked at the kid for a moment. "Name's Danny. You stay fifty paces behind me. I'm running point, and so it's my job to scout ahead. If you fall behind, he'll help you." Danny nodded towards Sam.

Miles looked at Sam and then at Josh. "I'll keep up."

"BS?" Danny was talking into his earpiece.

Sam told her to sit down in one of the chairs. "We're almost outta here. Hang in there for me, okay?"

"We're going to have to make a run for it," Danny said. "BS and his team made it out about fifteen minutes ago. They are making it to our side of the perimeter and will provide assistance. But we've got to make a sprint for the woods."

"That's like five hundred meters out in the open," Josh said.

"You got a better plan, PB?"

Wrinkles formed in Josh's forehead, and Rox ran her hand along his arm. *Stop. We need all the help we can get.*

"You get them to turn on one another just like the other two back there, and I'll open the door and tap 'em both." Danny stepped back and looked over Rox and Miles. "But PB is right. It's more than a five-hundred-yard sprint, and you two look like you all but died in there."

That's because they did "all but died in there". In fact, one of them *had* died in there.

"She can keep up," Josh said and turned to her. "Take what you need." He was offering her his energy.

She took a deep breath and shook her head. "I'm fine."

"When was the last time you ate?"

She looked away in shame, but then anger flared in her empty stomach and she turned back to him. "When have you ever known me not to keep up?"

He smiled. *That's my girl.* Josh closed his eyes as a soft whisper sounded in her mind, and Rox knew that everyone else had heard the same thing. Miles started scratching just behind his ears, and moved closer to Danny. The whisper faded and then one of the guards outside shouted. And then a gunshot.

Danny yanked the door open and put a bullet into the other guard. Then he took off, running at an awkward sprint with his weapon raised, locked against his shoulder and every few strides turning to the left and the right.

"Go!" Josh said to Miles.

A short burst erupted ahead. Danny had taken down two patrols. Miles was trying his best to keep up, but had stumbled when Danny shot the guards. She reached out to him, but he wasn't injured. At least not physically.

Rox and Sam went next, with Josh on their six. Sam wasn't letting go of her hand and she had to admit she was grateful. She was on the precipice of unconsciousness and he was the only thing keeping her from the edge.

She stumbled and Sam yanked her back to her feet. A

wave of excited energy assaulted her and she looked to the left. A guard had spotted them and was taking aim. She curled her arm around her head and waited for the pain of the bullet to explode in the left side of her body, but it never came. She lowered her arm and looked as his head jerked to the side and he fell. Rox looked in the opposite direction of his fall and saw that Danny had dropped to his knee and fired.

The energy from the dead guard slammed into her, and she felt her body go rigid from the force. Her muscles locked and Sam pulled her after him, but her legs refused to move. She fell at an awkward angle as she absorbed his energy and her adrenaline spiked. She would be able to keep a much faster pace now, but she knew the moment that his energy was gone, she was done.

They made it to the first bank of trees when she felt the last of the energy she had absorbed dissipate. She reached out to steady herself against the tree trunk and the bark bit into her palm. The hum was dimmer out here, but the pain along her back returned with an intensity that caused her to see double. The brittle grass and dried cones felt like needles stabbing at her feet with each step.

Rox pulled away from Sam and dry heaved into the roots of the tree. Her body was moments from shutting down.

"She needs food," Josh said.

A part of Rox hated him for knowing her so intimately, but she couldn't deny that another part of her, the part that desperately wanted to belong and to feel connected rejoiced that he had come for her. He had been with her during her darkest hour.

"How much farther?" Josh asked.

"Danny and Miles are about two hundred meters that way," Sam said. "We need to keep moving."

Sam squeezed her hand and she took a little of his energy to help with her next step.

So close

Sam had never felt this vulnerable during an assignment, or this desperate for one to be over. His heart was beating so fast it felt like there wasn't enough oxygen in the air.

Emotions always ran deep and fast in life-threatening situations. But the moment he pulled Rox into his arms he wasn't sure he would ever be able to let her go. It was different with her. He wanted to talk to her. OK, and kiss her, but mostly he wanted to do *normal* things with her. Maybe he also wanted to make love to her a little. Slowly. In the rain. But none of that would happen if they didn't get out of there.

Sam glanced over his shoulders and saw Josh running backwards behind them. For a man with no formal training, he was impressive. Something in Josh's past had taught him the importance of preparation. Sam hated to admit it, but he had grown to respect Josh. The man had made some pretty bad mistakes when it came to Rox, but he was trying like hell to atone for them. It was obvious that Josh loved her, and Sam knew a love like that didn't just go away. He had been inside of Josh's head, and Josh was filled with the kind of regret that no amount of beautiful women or an open bar could fill. Time was his only hope.

Rox stumbled again, and Sam held her hand a little tighter. Her feet were probably bloodied, but there was nothing either of them could do about it. He wasn't sure of all that had happened to her, but he knew it was bad.

A volley of shots were traded up ahead and he pulled her down behind a tree. Josh took cover about ten meters behind them. Bullets whizzed by and a few embedded in the trunk of a tree just to the left of them. He cradled her head against his chest.

A ringing sounded in his ears, and for a moment Sam thought he had been shot. But then he realized it was Josh creating a link.

We're taking fire, Josh said.

The fuck? Danny's voice was loud in Sam's head.

When Josh spoke, his voice was even. *Don't panic. It's just faster to communicate this way, but I can't hold it for long, so focus.*

Danny's mind jumped from one thought to the next. Sam felt like he was on a roller coaster. *Danny! It's Sam. Focus on my voice. We're pinned down about a hundred meters behind you.*

There was a long pause before Danny replied. He told Miles to keep straight and head down the hill until he ran into a black SUV.

On my—

The link broke as Josh cried out. Sam felt the bullet tear through him as if it were his chest and knew Rox did as well. She screamed his name and would have run straight into the line of fire if he hadn't wrestled her back to the ground. They were pinned, and from the sounds of it, the guards were getting closer.

"Josh?" Rox cried out. She pushed at him, trying to lift his body off hers.

"Danny is coming," Sam said. "We have to stay down."

"Get off me," she shouted. "Josh?"

Sam grabbed both her wrists and slammed them down above her head. He hated doing it, but she was going to get them both shot if she didn't calm down. "When they stop firing, I'll go get him. You keep heading towards Danny."

She held his gaze for a moment before she nodded.

She closed her eyes, and if he hadn't been laying on top of her, he would have missed the wrinkle forming on her forehead. She was trying to reach Josh.

"Anything?" he asked.

Her eyes flew open and she breathed out an audible cry. "He's alive."

Rox broke out into convulsions beneath him. He eased off her just as he heard a twig snap. Sam sucked in a deep breath and was about to use his ability when a hand snaked around the guard's neck, bowing out his torso and lifting him to his toes. Danny pulled the knife from the guard's back and made his way to them. "Let's go," he whispered.

"Get PB," Sam said as he went to Rox. She was lying on her back with her eyes opened wide. He went to lift her, but her body was too rigid and wouldn't bend at the joints. Then all of a sudden she relaxed and blinked. "Where is he?"

"Danny's got him. Can you walk?" She nodded, and he helped her to her feet. He grabbed her hand and pulled her behind him.

"We're coming in hot," Sam said into his earpiece. "One down. Taking fire."

"I got you in my scope." It was Meita. "No sudden lunges and keep her as steady as you can." The sound of rifle fire echoed throughout the night.

Relief washed over Sam. Meita was providing cover. He ran as fast as Rox would allow him, which was beginning to slow. She kept looking over her shoulder, and he suspected what energy she had left she was feeding to Josh. He had never known a healer and had no idea if it were possible for them to kill themselves, but he was going to have a word with her about her choices when they got out of this.

Another crackle blasted through the night as his shin collided with a tree root. He stumbled and Rox fell hard. "Sorry." He pushed to his feet, but pain lanced up his lower leg. Almost immediately he felt a warm sensation around the injury and he knew she was healing him. "Stop it!" Was she *trying* to die? "You're barely conscious."

When he looked at her, he noticed that her eyes were half open. Her head was rolling to the side and she was two steps from collapsing. "I can't."

He caught her as she lost consciousness. He picked her up and slung her over his shoulder like she were dry cleaning. Each step hurt, but it was infinitely better than a few moments ago. He saw the flare from a muzzle on the ground to his left and thanked all the gods that it was Meita.

"Keep moving," she shouted.

He reached the end of the woods and the hill sloped down. Sam pulled Rox from over his shoulder so that she was cradled in his arms as he slid down the embankment. He got to the bottom and laid her in the back seat of the SUV as carefully as his speed would allow and turned back to Danny, who was a few paces behind him. Danny was just heading down the embankment. He was coming down at an awkward angle and would have toppled over if Sam hadn't reached out to catch him.

Boggs was standing on the steps on the far side of the SUV, his weapon resting on the roof. Danny laid Josh into the seat next to Rox as Sam sprinted back up the hill to provide cover for Meita, who was just beginning to make her retreat.

By the time they made it back down, Boggs was firing at an approaching vehicle. Sam and Meita jumped in as the SUV pulled off. The door slammed close with Boggs still hanging from the side. He let loose on the car that was tailing them, and there were the sounds of a crash followed by a loud explosion.

Sam reached out for Rox, but she remained unconscious. He slapped her face gently, but she didn't respond. They took a curve at high speed and his shoulder slammed into the door. He felt her breath against his face and knew she still lived.

"She all right?" Meita asked.

Sam shook his head. "I don't know."

Meita handed a flashlight to Danny and ripped open Josh's shirt. His chest was covered in blood, so she opened a bottle of water and poured it on him. Meita exhaled and took a swig from the bottle. "She healed him."

"What?"

Sam looked down at Rox and then over at Josh's chest. No blood pumped out. No gaping wound. Just a smooth, blood-stained chest.

"The bullet's still in there, so I'm sure his internals are all fucked."

"But what about her?" Miles asked. He was strapped in the front, middle seat and had turned around.

Meita searched through a medical kit before she pulled out an IV bag. "Hold her as steady as you can," she said as she searched for a vein.

Tara

Pain pulled Rox into consciousness. The room was dark and she must have been caught in an earthquake it shook so much. Another sharp pain ran up her right arm and she tried to yank it free, but was unable. The fear was paralyzing. They had captured her. She was back in the labs, strapped to a bed.

"No!" Her voice was barely above a whisper as she pulled against her restraints. They hadn't tied her legs yet, so she used those.

"Keep her still!" The voice was familiar, but she couldn't place it.

Rox wrenched her arm free and struck out. She knew it connected because she felt their retreat. Someone bigger was leaning over her. She felt his breath against her ear and she paused. It was too dark to see, so she let her energy reach out.

"Sam?"

"Shh. I need you to relax."

His lips were so close to her ears that she could feel them against her skin. Her fear fled as she relaxed back into his lap. She was beyond exhausted and had lost track of the last time she ate. She was so tired of running, of being chased, and of the gnawing hunger.

"Please don't cry." Sam's fingers brushed the hair out of her face.

It was that single act of kindness that broke her. She buried her face in the crux of his arms and sobbed. How many sleepless nights? How many shelters in god knows how many cities? How long can a person live in fear before they're forced to just let it go?

They went over a speed bump at top speed, and for a second she was airborne. She came down hard, and Sam repositioned her so that her head rested on his shoulder. Her next breath was full of him. He smelled of sweat. It was a musky scent that should have turned her off but had the opposite effect. He rocked her and whispered softly. She didn't need to understand his words, she just needed him there. Holding her. Reminding her that she wasn't alone.

"I think my name's Tara." It came out in between hiccups.

Sam's lips brushed her nose. "It's beautiful."

She had hoped that if she ever learned her name it

would trigger a memory and the wall of dominoes that surrounded her past would fall. "I want to remember." But that hadn't happened.

His arms tightened, and she knew that he wanted to share in her pain. It felt nice having someone who wasn't trying to make things all better, but who was willing to just sit with her and let her figure it out for herself.

Josh moaned, and she remembered they weren't alone. She reached over and put her hand on his shoulder. Meita and Danny were watching her now that she had slipped out of Sam's lap. She had healed Josh's gunshot, but the bullet was still in there, just like the one in her arm. Luckily, his tissue was healing over it, but chances were if they didn't get it out soon, it would get infected. She could help him fight the infection, but that would take more energy than she had.

"I need to eat something."

Danny rummaged through his backpack and passed her a protein bar that tasted like cardboard, but she gratefully ate it nonetheless.

"Thank you." She extended her hand to him.

"Name's Danny." His grip was firm but not harsh. "Pleasure to make your acquaintance."

CHAPTER FOURTEEN

Vulnerabilities

"How long are we going to keep her there?"

Katherine stared out onto the busy street below. It was lunch time and people were walking with a purpose. The majority of them had their heads down, staring into some device to combat the monotony of walking from one place to the next, while the rest were engaged in conversations, a mixture of virtual and corporeal. Maybe they were discussing the fact that evolved humans existed. Surely somebody was excited, imagining super beings who could fly, shoot fire from their eyes or freeze with a touch. But reality was less sexy and a lot more messy. Those who could do the next generation of mathematics and quantum were in the highest demand. The one or two with actual physical active abilities – if they made it through puberty – typically died shortly after, because they were nothing more than an ordinal prototype in the next step of evolution. But a few of them made it past adolescence, and apparently an even smaller few into their second hormonal shift.

Rox was an anomaly among anomalies. Not only had her abilities remained dormant past puberty, but they hadn't become active until much later. Maybe there was something special about her. Or maybe, the scientists only knew a fraction of what there was to know. This was uncharted territory, the next frontier of humanity.

"Have you brought up the idea of testing with her?" Katherine asked.

"I hardly think this is the time," Meita said.

Katherine sensed that Meita had lost a bit of her objectivity on this mission. It was the first time she worked so closely with evolved ones, and in her own way, Meita too was evolved. Like Rox, Meita was one of the extremely rare ones. She could sense other EOs and was immune to their abilities, yet had no active one of her own.

Katherine liked Meita, liked her more than any other operative in her care. She liked her because she was a woman, and a woman didn't survive in this kind of world by being half-assed. No, a woman in this line of work had to be exceptionally quick on her feet and know how to play poker when the stakes were often her career and her life. So by the time Meita got on Katherine's radar, she knew the woman would be twice as good as any of her male counterparts. And she was.

It was inevitable that Meita would develop a weak spot for her own kind. There was a war on even if most of the world lived in complete oblivion to it. Most of the evolved population just wanted to live in peace. Too few of them had any real abilities to warrant a government round-up and forced registrations. But living with your head in the sand was a privilege that they didn't have. While they wanted to live in peace, there were enough organized groups wanting to exploit their abilities, which meant they became a threat to national interests because these groups were willing to do anything to get their hands on them.

"No, I suppose you're right," Katherine said. Now wasn't the time to discuss Rox's willingness to play guinea pig for the betterment of all humankind. "Did you find her identity?"

Meita nodded towards Katherine's desk. "I'm about as sure as I'm going to get without DNA confirmation."

Katherine walked silently across the Egyptian silk rug that had been a gift to one of her predecessors who died while still in office. She picked up the file. It was surprisingly light, but then again, the most salient points in a person's life could be edited down to five hundred words or less.

Tara Alexandra Harding. "Date of birth puts her at forty-two when she went missing. Married. Three kids."

Katherine exhaled and sat down. This complicated things. She had to admit she was hoping that Rox's fixation with her family was nothing more than some sort of pipe dream. Something cooked up when she woke up and was forced to accept that she had no memory and no idea where she came from. It wouldn't be unheard of. Most kids who never knew their family concocted sensational stories that helped them cope with the fact they were orphans. But Rox – Tara – had a family. Living and breathing.

Katherine skimmed the rest of the report. "They're in Singapore?"

Meita nodded. "Seems they were living there when she disappeared."

"Is her husband Asian?"

"No. They immigrated a while back. I need to do more research, but someone went through a painstakingly tedious amount of trouble to erase her from the net."

Katherine looked up. "That's impossible."

Meita nodded. "Yeah, but if you have the patience and the resources, you can get about ninety percent."

"So how did you find the ten percent?"

Meita laid her head back on the chair. Katherine could see that it hadn't been easy. "I had some help. Having Rox's real name—"

"But it was just her first name."

"More than we had when I first started this. And her race, which was complicated because it's obvious she's a mix of something. But we added that into the search parameters, along with at least two children and was older than thirty."

"I guess there weren't a lot of those?"

"Tons. It's absolutely terrifying the number of mix-raced Taras over the age of thirty with a family who go missing."

Katherine looked down at the photo Meita had printed out. The eldest girl resembled Rox the most. It was in the eyes. The set of her mouth.

It made Katherine hate what she had to do next. Her breath caught, and she stood and went back to the window. Some things never left you. Some experiences had to be had if they were to be understood. Motherhood was for life, no matter how long or short your children lived. Once a mother …

Katherine cleared her throat and turned back to Meita. "I think it's time that she and I met."

Meita looked surprised.

"The kind of conversation I'm about to have isn't one you do over the phone."

"What are you going to say?"

Katherine grabbed her handbag from the bottom drawer. She checked that the pistol was loaded before she let the magnet pull the bag close again. "Just going to remind her that there are worst things than living without memories."

∼

Gratitude

Rox stepped off the treadmill and grabbed a towel to wipe the sweat she left behind. She took a long drink from the bottle of water she let warm to room temperature before she laid on the mat to start on her core. Josh had instilled in her the importance of remaining physically fit, and even when she was on the run she did what she could. Most of the rooms she stayed in lacked a window, let alone a treadmill or an onsite gym, but she would go for a run, always varying the times.

Twenty minutes later, Rox was debating a shower versus a plate of scrambled eggs on toast. She didn't much care for eggs as a main meal, but she was short on options. While Meita had told her that she was in an undisclosed safe house, Rox knew a holding cell when she was in one. It was the lack of outside communication that gave it away. No landline, no computer, and no mobile phone. There was a single lock from the inside, but the locks that sounded whenever Meita arrived or left told Rox she wasn't free to come and go as she pleased. There was cable, and Rox supposed she should be grateful for that. At least it had voices to break up the silence that followed her throughout the day.

She had been there for seven days. One solid week. The only information she got about Sam and Josh came from Meita. Apparently, Sam and Walter returned to care for Val, who was showing slow signs of improvement, but she was still far from mentally stable. 203, whose name was Su Chen, had refused to leave her side. Her parents had come down from Vancouver to see her.

Meita said that Josh was getting Jay settled in some new location that she wasn't allowed to share. But Rox knew that to be a lie. She had reached out to Josh a few times, and his reply was always brief, like he was either asleep or somehow incapacitated. He had to be rushed into surgery after they escaped the facility that Meita had told her was called Wonderland. She had managed to stop the internal bleeding, but the bullet had to be removed as infection had set in and was beginning to spread rapidly. Chances were Josh was still in a hospital somewhere. But why lie about it?

Rox gave herself about a sixty-forty chance of overpowering Meita, but then what? She didn't have the code to open the additional locks that ensured she didn't leave without permission. And even if she made it out, where would she go? Back on the run? Make her way back to Halo, and to Sam? As much as the idea appealed to her, she now knew she had been marked by some very dangerous people who were willing to kidnap innocent children to get at her. And those people had performed one method of torture and disfigurement after the next to study how her skin cells regenerated. A shiver went down her back and she looked at her hands as they shook. She still woke in the middle of the night, her mind remembering the feel of the flames as it spread across her skin, the sweet poignancy of the knife as it slipped between two ribs with precision, the aches that kept her awake as her bones calcified, and the itch that was its own form of torture while her skin stitched itself back together. For all that she wanted to remember, those were things she would never forget.

Maybe it was best that she spent her days alone. It gave her time to think. Reflect. Let go. She wasn't sure if she had a family or if it had been a necessary fabrication her mind created to give her life purpose. Either way, as long as Dr Tusk was still out there, still looking for her, it was best she didn't form any sort of attachments.

No man is an island.

She smiled. *How you feeling?*

Ever try morphine?

Rox laughed.

Best. High. Ever.

I've been worried about you.

Same. Where are you?

Safe house. You?

Hospital. You hear anything from Sam or the others?

Tears flooded her eyes, but she swallowed them and stirred her eggs over the fire. *Just Meita.*

There was a moment of silence where Rox could only

feel Josh's thoughts. *I saw her yesterday. She paid me a visit in between my meds.*

What'd she say?

That Jay was safe. Sam had taken him and would keep him until I recover.

You believe her?

She used his safe word. She wouldn't know it if he hadn't given it to her.

Rox let her eggs fall onto the toast. She wasn't sure how hungry she was at the moment, but she knew she needed to eat. *She told me about the deal you guys made.*

Josh swore. *That wasn't her place.*

A tear fell down Rox's face as she stuffed her mouth full of eggs. *I want to be able to tell you that I wish you hadn't ...* but the truth was, she was grateful. And she hated herself for it. She wanted to be strong enough. But the memories ...

Don't. You would've done the same. Hell, you gave yourself over to save Jay.

I love him.

And I love you. We love you.

Rox swallowed the lump in her throat and knew that her breakfast was going to give her indigestion. She tried to hold back the tears, but her feelings demanded release. Embarrassment. Gratitude. Confusion. Desire. Hope. And fear. Always fear. A never-ending chasm of fear.

Anyone ever tell you you're too hard on yourself? And don't you dare throw those eggs out!

She chuckled. And then it spread to a laugh that encompassed her entire body. She shook as the last year and a half caught up with her. She put the plate on the counter and just sunk down to the floor and laughed until the sobs subsided.

Thank you. And she knew she didn't have to say more.

All or nothing

The intercom buzzing pulled Rox from the first real sleep she'd had since ... well, since she couldn't remember. She sat up and looked around in confusion. Her hip had gone stiff from sleeping in a ball on the kitchen floor. Memories came rushing back as she slowly pulled herself to her feet. The buzzer sounded again.

She hobbled to the door and looked into the screen. It was Meita. She was sure the buzzing wasn't necessary, but she was grateful for the pretense. "Come up."

Rox sat on the arm of the sofa facing the door and waited. A few moments later the locks slid back and Meita stepped in, followed by a woman Rox had never seen before.

"Rox," Meita greeted.

"Meita."

"This is Katherine, head of the Global Frontier Organization and Project EO."

Katherine stepped from behind Meita and extended her hand. "I've heard a lot about you. Nice to finally meet you."

Rox stared at her hand for longer than what was considered customary. She wasn't sure what she had expected, but a short, insanely fit, older Asian woman was not it. Her accent held no trace of her obvious ancestry, which made her even more of a mystery.

"Oh, I don't have any abilities," Katherine said.

"Why am I here and why can't I leave?" Rox said. There was no point in formalities. She was too tired. Too little sleep. Too much running and a lot of searching had left her on the brink of a mental meltdown, and now she feared that Wonderland had pushed her over the edge.

"Ah," Katherine finally lowered her hand, then turned to close the door. She took off her coat and tossed it on the back of one of the two kitchen chairs. "I can respect your need for answers. You are here, Tara, because on one hand, we do wish to protect you from the psychopaths we rescued you from."

"And on the other hand?"

Katherine stepped closer and locked gazes with her. "Because, whether you realize it or not, you present a danger to our national security as well as our national interests."

The air left her lungs. The small one-bedroom seemed instantly smaller in a way Rox hadn't known was possible. So this was it. They had rescued her from one prison only to put her in one of their own making. And to make matters worse, Sam and Josh were equally imprisoned.

Rox looked at Meita and couldn't hide the disgust she had for the woman.

"It's not her fault." Katherine moved to stand in between them. "Actually, it's because of her that I'm able to offer you a proposition of sorts."

"Let me guess. I get to come and work for you. Same

sort of one-sided arrangement that Sam and Josh got?"

Katherine smiled. "Yes, I suppose that bit was fairly obvious."

"So what do I get in return?"

Katherine released the magnet on her handbag and took out a folder that had the words *Confidential* in thick, black letters. "Your life back."

Rox stared at the folder like she was expecting it to burn a hole in Katherine's hand. "What do you mean, my life back?"

"Just what I said." Katherine put the envelope back in her bag, and Rox had a feeling that Katherine had done that for some psychological purpose she couldn't figure out at the moment. "Meita has spent the greater part of this last week, with the help of a few others, looking for your original identity. And I believe she's found it."

Rox turned her back on them. This was too much. A strand of hair fell from her ponytail and she reached up to tuck it back in. She inhaled her scent and remembered that she hadn't taken a shower after her workout. How long had she slept?

"And if I refuse?"

"I withdraw the protection that I've placed around your family."

Rox felt as if she'd been struck by a blow she hadn't seen coming. It sucked the air from her lungs and the room tilted. She reached out to steady herself against the treadmill. She had a family. Her legs were shaking so badly she had to sit down.

"It is an expensive endeavor to provide 24-by-7

protection for a family on foreign soil."

Her family needed protection, and if she didn't agree to whatever terms that Katherine was about to propose, Katherine would remove their protection. Maybe she could protect them? She *was* a healer. She knew how to take care of herself. She would train harder. She could ... wait. "Foreign soil?"

Katherine reached over and flicked the switch for the lights. Rox hadn't noticed that the sun was setting and they were basically talking in the dark. "You and your family weren't living in this country when you went missing. That would be one of the main reasons it took us so long to locate your true identity."

Rox nodded like she understood, but her mind was reeling from *knowing* she had a family. "Do they remember me?"

It surprised her when Meita answered. "There's no reason to suspect that anything has happened to their memories. If I am correct, and we have located your family, then I suspect that you are ... well, I mean to say that ..."

"You're dead to them," Katherine finished.

Rox rose to her feet and began to pace. It made sense. She had been gone for over four years. Of course they would think she's dead. And if Katherine was right and there were people after her, then they could target her family. If Meita found them, how long before Dr Tusk?

"If I don't want to work for you?" Rox asked.

"You don't have a choice," Katherine said softly.

"You always have a choice," Rox said. Josh had told her that and for the first time she believed him.

Katherine closed the distance between them and shook her head. "You've spent over a year searching for a family you can't even remember. Why? Because of a feeling? You're a mother. You don't get to forget. You don't get to walk away and figure out the next step. You decide in the moment. And your moment is now. You either accept this offer or I remove the protection I've placed on your family."

Rox's body tensed as every instinct in her body wanted to attack, yet a small part of her knew that it would be pointless. She could suck away Katherine's energy, but she'd still have to face Meita. And with Katherine's energy, she could win. But how did she know that the information about her was actually in the folder. She had to decide.

"I want a year." A year to reconnect with them. Create new memories. "I want a year with them before I come with you."

"Three months," Katherine said.

"A year." Rox circled the head of Global Frontiers without noticing the change in her own actions.

"Nine months." The energy around Katherine increased, like she was preparing for a fight. Good, because Rox was itching to release the frustration that had accumulated while she was stuck in this "safe house".

"I get one year with my family or so help me god I'm drawing all your energy and I will sit here and watch you die."

Meita moved towards them, but Katherine held up her hand. "One year and after the first six months if I need you for an assignment, you will come. No questions asked."

"And I get time in lieu." If a mission took two weeks during that year, she wanted her time with her family to be extended by two weeks. "And the protection remains."

"All right."

"Forever."

Katherine raised an eyebrow.

"Until my children draw their last breath, you will protect them from harm. Whether that harm be from Tusk, another government or our own."

Katherine hesitated, and that's when Rox drew. She took enough to bring the woman to her knees. Meita advanced and Rox used the extra energy to feed her adrenaline and punched Meita in the face. The woman flew back into the sofa and over its back.

"Decide?" Rox stood over Katherine, ignoring the pain in her wrist.

It took Katherine a moment, but she finally nodded.

"And this deal extends beyond my death. *Your* death." Rox turned her back to both of them as she grabbed Katherine's bag and took the folder. She slammed the door to the bathroom and turned on the water. Her intentions were to shower first, get cleaned so that she could look at her family fresh. But she opened the folder without thought. A picture was the first thing she saw. And she laughed. Fresh tears streamed down her face as she found herself back on the floor wracked with sobs. She was a mother of three ... two girls and a boy. Ruby, Emma, and MJ, Michael Junior. And standing behind them was their father. Her husband.

EPILOGUE

Sam

The door banged open, and Sam grabbed his head. "Oi!" Light flooded his retina and he squeezed his eyes shut at the sudden invasion to his senses. "What?" he shouted.

"Really, son? Really? I get the darkness. I can even turn an eye to the blatant disrespect you've been giving to my vintage bottles of whisky. But I draw the line at smooth jazz."

The music switched off. Walter grabbed a glass and picked up the almost empty bottle at Sam's feet. He read the label. "Shit son, this is for contemplation, not for drowning your sorrows. Any idea how much this cost?"

No, he did not know how much that bottle of whisky cost, nor did he know the value of any of the other bottles. And he didn't care.

"Man, all this from a single kiss." Walter poured a glass and sat down next to him. "Maybe healing ain't her only talent."

"Dad, go away."

"Starting to understand PB a bit better," Walter chuckled.

Sam hadn't seen Rox since Wonderland. She and Josh were taken away by a team of medics when they got back to the private helipad at the edge of the airport. In fact, he hadn't seen anyone since that night. Jay was with them at Halo, and so was Miles. Miles refused to contact his parents, and Bethany was trying to convince him that he should, even if he had run away from them. Sam didn't have much interaction with either of the boys, mostly because he had spent all his time in this office, drinking.

Meita had called to give him an update. In a few days, he was to report to a soon-to-be-disclosed location for training and briefing. She had told him that Josh was on the mend, but still heavily sedated. When he had asked for the hospital, she reiterated that he was safe and not taking visitors at the time. Sam knew that the drugs were to keep him out of everyone's head, and the isolation was so that no one could come and get him out. They were all prisoners of some sort.

Technically speaking, they didn't have to join Global Frontiers. They had signed no paperwork, and they had clearly agreed under duress, but that's not how the government (or "government adjacent", as Meita liked to call it) operated. They wouldn't make you work for them; they'd just make you wish you had.

"Spoke to Meita today," Walter said.

That surprised Sam. "I thought we agreed that you weren't joining."

"And I'm not. Just wanted an update."

"Oh."

"She told me about Rox. Sorry, Tara. They found her

family."

Sam nodded. He'd heard. He was happy for her. He was *trying* to be happy for her.

"Living in Singapore. Can you believe that? She would've searched her whole life and would've never thought to look there, I reckon."

"Yep." That was all there was to say.

"Son, the last time you were sitting in this room like this was, well, let's just say things had gotten pretty bad."

"Yep."

"Do you love her?"

"I barely know her!" There was no reason for him to shout, but he couldn't help it. He reached for the bottle, but his father placed his hand on his arm. Sam leaned back in the chair and thought about throwing the glass across the room, but didn't because of the clean-up. "I want her …" His voice caught and he swallowed hard. He wanted to say that he wanted her to be happy, but the truth was, he simply wanted her.

"I know, son. She'll reach out."

Sam shook his head. It was probably best she didn't. He didn't need to know her husband to know that he wouldn't appreciate his wife going out on a date with another guy to see a horror movie. No, she was where she belonged, and Sam told his father as much.

"You think?"

Sam nodded. "Why not? Meita said they had a family, two girls and a boy. He hadn't remarried, so he obviously still loves her."

"You might be right. He could still love her."

Sam rolled his eyes. "Thanks."

"Feel bad for him though if he does."

Only his father would feel bad for the man who was getting the woman that he loved – liked. "Why? Why would you feel bad for him?"

"Those kids are expecting to get their mom back. He's expecting to get his wife back. They're all expecting for this woman they know as Tara to walk through the door." Walter looked at him like he was *expecting* Sam to go "oh I get it", but Sam didn't get it.

"Yeah, and?"

"Son, one thing I know for certain is the woman on her way to reunite with that family will never be Tara again any more than you can be the man you were before you lost your family. Yes, she may look like their mom, she may even smell like her, but Rox has seen and been through too many things to ever be Tara again, with or without her memories."

Sam hated himself for the spark of hope that flared inside.

His father pushed himself to his feet and grabbed the bottle on his way out. "She just needs some time to figure that out."

Hugs and chokeholds

MJ was the most exuberant to see her. He was all smiles and talked incessantly. And he was funny. Rox couldn't remember the last time she had laughed so much. Emma was in a state of shock, and Rox could tell she was afraid to accept that her mother was back for fear that it would be a dream or some kind of misunderstanding and she would have to grieve all over again. Ruby was ... well, there was always one. She was cold and reserved. A handshake instead of a hug. Murderous stares instead of eyes lit with wonder. And Michael, her husband – it still felt weird to think of herself as married – sat in one of the chairs in her hotel suite and simply stared at her. Because she didn't know him, she wasn't sure how to interpret his glances and she didn't have much time to ponder them because MJ was impatient with questions about where she had been for six years. That was how long she had been gone. Six years. Two of them she had no recollection of.

"Can I call you mom?" MJ asked.

"MJ!" Emma said.

"But she *is* our mom."

"Why don't we give her a chance to adjust," said Michael. "Don't forget that she's lost some of her memories."

"That's convenient." Ruby sat at the desk near the door, drawing on a piece of hotel paper.

"I'm hungry. Can we order room service?" asked MJ.

"I have an idea. How about we go to the hotel restaurant and eat. We've not had a meal here for a long time."

"Not hungry."

Michael turned to Ruby and gave her a look that made her lower her head. "Take MJ and Emma downstairs. Get a table for five. Your mo—we'll be along shortly."

Rox wasn't sure what to make of it all. Nothing had gone the way she had thought it would. But if she was honest, she had no idea what to expect. Perhaps this was normal.

When the door closed, she turned to Michael to see him staring at her. He looked like he had been caught in a trance before he shook his head and smiled. "I'm sorry, but as you can imagine, this has been a huge shock for us."

Rox nodded. This man was her husband, technically speaking, but she had no idea who he was.

"Even though we were told you'd lost your memories, I guess we'd been secretly hoping that seeing the kids would've ... you know, helped you remember something."

So they were disappointed. Rox swallowed back tears and turned to the window. She was at the top of a very impressive hotel, overlooking the river and a skyline that rivaled any city's. It was a breathtaking view, yet she wasn't sure how to let go and just enjoy it. "I ... I suppose, I'm sorry."

"No! That wasn't said to make you feel bad. It's just that, MJ is nine and so the return of his deceased mother is like something out of the comic books he reads."

"My memories only go back four years. I mean, I have this photo, or I should say I *had* this photo. It was just of Ruby and Emma. But I lost it."

She turned back to him and he was staring at her in that awestruck way again.

"I'm sorry. It's just that, you look like her but then again, there's something different."

Rox didn't know what to say, so she waited.

"My wife, Tara, she had this birthmark. Do you mind if I ..."

Rox hesitated.

"No, it's not anywhere inappropriate. It's just there, beneath your hairline at the back of your neck. No, on the right side."

She turned around and lifted her hair so that Michael could inspect. His fingers brushed her hair out of the way and she felt him suck in his breath. Instinct told her that he had found what he was looking for, yet she wasn't sure whether to be relieved or not.

"I can't fathom why anyone would create such an elaborate hoax. Especially one that would involve children."

Rox turned around, but Michael had taken a few steps back.

"I promise you this is no hoax. I have nothing to gain from this. I want nothing from you or your family." She took a deep breath and slowly let it out. "I guess, I just needed to know I belonged somewhere. That I hadn't just been handed over to some research facility, that I had someone missing me."

He was about to say something, but Rox stopped him.

"If this is too much for you or for your children, then I'll turn around and go back to where I came from. No questions asked, no strings attached."

It took him a while to speak, and Rox wondered if he was going to send her away. "You were loved and sorely missed."

Rox laughed even as a few tears escaped. "I'm so sorry that I couldn't come back sooner. And that I come back … in pieces."

When she looked up, there were tears in his eyes as well. He crossed the room and pulled her in his arms. "I'm just glad you're back."

He placed his lips briefly on hers. It felt nothing like Sam's.

"That was awkward, I'm sorry. Why don't we start over." Michael stepped back and extended his hand. "Hi. My name is Michael Harding. Pleasure to meet you."

She took his hand and matched his shake. "My name is Rox."

He looked confused for a moment, but then he smiled. "You look a lot like my former wife. Her name was Tara."

"Nice name."

"Would you like to have lunch with me and my family? My youngest will undoubtedly talk nonstop, but it'll give us a chance to get to know one another."

"I'd like that, Michael."

She grabbed her room's keycard off the desk as Michael opened the door and waited for her to go through first. "I should warn you, while MJ will talk your ear off, my eldest might put you in a chokehold."

Rox threw back her head and laughed. Chokeholds, she could handle.

Author's Note

Acceptance is about motherhood at its core. The idea was born during one of the many nights when my youngest wouldn't sleep, and I was up pacing, feeling linked to all the mothers who had taken that very same journey of postnatal insomnia and had made it to the other side.

I struggled with my identity after becoming a mother. I wasn't sure how to get back to the woman I used to be. She was accomplished and flawed, but I liked her and missed her terribly. Then one day (probably after a few good nights' sleep), I realized that the woman I had been had been irrevocably lost. She was never coming back because motherhood had fundamentally changed me. Sure, there were large parts of who I was that remained the same, but having children was a detour of no return.

This revelation, in short, blew my mind! One thought led to another and slowly, over several years, Rox was born.

I do hope that you've enjoyed reading the first book in this series. Rox's story doesn't end here, it continues in the next novel, *The Evolved Ones: Sacrifice.*

From the second book in this trilogy:

The Evolved Ones: Sacrifice
(Book 2)

"We've located the boy," the caller said.

"Did your guys get him?" Dr Clifford Tusk asked.

"No. We think he might have left the country."

"What? Then he knew we were after him?" Tusk heard papers shuffling. "Harry?"

"Yeah, I'm still here. Listen, we think he used his brother's passport and booked a flight to Singapore."

"Singapore?" Why would he go there?

"I had his records checked, and he's not from Singapore. At first I thought he was running to his family overseas or something, but he's an American of Taiwanese descent. I'm thinking family friend perhaps."

Tusk's main interest in Miles was the link he had to Tara. She had walked into Miles' room with a purpose, which meant she must have known him. The kid had to be the key to finding her.

"One of my guys got picked up in Seattle at the brother's house," Harry said.

"What?"

"Yeah, we've been watching the empath's family, just seeing what surfaced. And then Major Watts and Josh Mendez showed up. I haven't been able to access any satellite footage over that area yet – probably Katherine's doing – but when I do, I'm hoping it'll show me what their abilities are. My guy was good, so it stands to reason they might have active abilities."

"Will he talk?" Tusk asked.

"Did Nancy talk?" There was a moment of silence before Harry continued. "Sam showing up means that Halo's still in operation."

"Halo? That group you said your old military friend started? That's a Mickey Mouse operation hardly worth our time—"

"Let's not forget that it was that same Mickey Mouse operation that infiltrated your Dominican facility despite me giving you the head's up that they were coming."

"They had the healer, Tara."

"Being able to heal yourself is impressive, but benign to what we're trying to achieve here, Cliff," Harry said.

"Yes, but I'm certain she's able to ... I don't know, harm other people as well." Tusk couldn't exactly explain it, but somehow her ability enabled her to incapacitate people. The man at the helicopter when they were exchanging Josh's son, the guard inside Miles' room, and Nancy. No one ever got the drop on Nancy.

"You really think she's that powerful?"

"Harry, look, we pumped her full of sedatives, and I'm not talking horse tranquilizers, I'm talking enough to fucking knock out a goddamn elephant. And she kept waking up. That's ... that's ..."

"Extraordinary," Harry finished. "And you think this kid, Miles, is the key to finding her?"

Tusk nodded. "Why else risk your escape? She had Nancy's access card, which gave her *carte blanche* to the entire facility."

Harry Carter and Dr Clifford Tusk had been roommates at university and had developed a friendship that lasted long after graduation. Harry went into the family business of politics while Tusk went into biology. He had accepted a long time ago that he would never have money like Harry, but it had never been about the money. They were both pretty much after the same thing: legacy.

"Alright. Then Tara is the new priority. Hell, Cliff, if you're right, then she is priceless," Harry said. "How's the new girl?"

Tusk chanced a quick glance at Leona who was sitting just out of earshot with her laptop. "Fine. I guess."

"Yeah, I did some digging. She's got deep pockets, and the money's legit."

"You say that like being legit is a bad thing?"

"It is," Harry said, "so tread carefully. She's got property all over the world, literally. And she pays her taxes."

Tusk hesitated. "How's that relevant?"

"It's relevant because she's got enough money that paying taxes is the equivalent of a charity donation to her. And secondly, it means she's smart enough to avoid tax evasion. That's how most of her kind go down."

Tusk began to take on a new respect for the wealthy who paid their taxes.

"Anyone not motivated by money is someone you definitely shouldn't trust," Harry said.

"You're not."

"Yeah, but I don't pay taxes."

The final book in this trilogy:

The Evolved Ones: Acceptance
(Book 3)

Acknowledgements

There are so many people to thank who have been instrumental in helping me bring Rox to the world. Firstly, I'd like to thank my village, the women who supported me through those rough, sleepless nights, who celebrated my accomplishments and picked me up after my failings. And of course, to my family, who have believed in me and kept me striving. A special thanks to my hubby for allowing me to quit my job to become a writer in 2004, and then encouraging me to go back to work when it didn't pan out like in the movies.

To a very special lady, Anita, for believing in Rox and for guiding me through this process. It's your experienced, gentle touch that has made this journey a dream instead of one fraught with anxiety. I look forward to working with you on many more projects.

And finally, to you, my reader. With so many options and genres, I feel beyond grateful that you have chosen to read about Rox's journey. I hope that you continue to follow her as she explores her new life as a mother with responsibilities that will impact the world.

If you're interested to know more about me – wife, mother, and writer – please follow my personal blog, www.peaceandcenter.com. I share the challenges I've faced and the lessons I've learned. It's the best window into me as a human being. I am also on Instagram as Natasha_Oliver_Author, Facebook as @NatashaOliverAuthor, and occasionally on Twitter as @natashaoliver. I hope to see you there.

About the Author

Natasha Oliver earned a Master of Fine Arts in Creative Writing at Goddard College and a Bachelor of Science in Marketing at Lehigh University. Born in South Carolina, USA, she has lived and worked in Japan, Singapore and throughout Southeast Asia. Natasha has published several short stories and articles, and is also a professional ghostwriter and editor. In creative writing, Natasha's focus is on adult science fiction and fantasy.